THE ROMULUS CHRONICLES

THE ROMULUS CHRONICLES
Mary's Tale

Alexander Mescavage
& Eunice Beauchman

The Romulus Chronicles

Copyright © 2021 by Alexander Mescavage & Eunice Beauchman.
All rights reserved.

No part of this publication may be reproduced, stored in a retrieval system or transmitted in any way by any means, electronic, mechanical, photocopy, recording or otherwise without the prior permission of the author except as provided by USA copyright law.

The opinions expressed by the author are not necessarily those of URLink Print and Media.

1603 Capitol Ave., Suite 310 Cheyenne, Wyoming USA 82001
1-888-980-6523 | admin@urlinkpublishing.com

URLink Print and Media is committed to excellence in the publishing industry.

Book design copyright © 2021 by URLink Print and Media. All rights reserved.

Published in the United States of America
Library of Congress Control Number: 2021904252
ISBN 978-1-64753-720-3 (Paperback)
ISBN 978-1-64753-721-0 (Digital)

22.02.21

Contents

Introduction vii

Chapter 1:   I Am Weary 1

Chapter 2:   Asylum 9

Chapter 3:   What Passes for Treatment 18

Chapter 4:   Blood Moon 31

Chapter 5:   A Big Bowl of Beef Chow Mein 41

Chapter 6:   Free in the Woods 50

Chapter 7:   Ghosts in the Darkness 53

Chapter 8:   All Hell Breaks Loose 59

Chapter 9:   Refuge 69

Chapter 10: Two Dreams 75

Chapter 11: Meat is Murder 79

Chapter 12: Questions and Answers 86

Chapter 13: All Roads Lead to Rome 93

Chapter 14: The Rape of Sabine Women 101

Chapter 15: The Feast of Neptune 108

Chapter 16: The Fullness of Life 121

Chapter 17: The Invasion 127

Chapter 18: The Field of Mars` 133

Chapter 19: A Tale's End..140

Chapter 20: Beautiful Dreamers...145

Chapter 21: Dark Rider 159

Chapter 22: Off to See the Wizard......................................172

Chapter 23: On the Way Home..184

Chapter 24: A Meeting of the Minds 190

Chapter 25: Disguises 197

Chapter 26: The Way of the Hand and Blade 210

Chapter 27: The Gathering Storm 216

Chapter 28: Hunter's Moon..224

Chapter 29: The Hare Shem Tov 231

Chapter 30: The Waning Moon..239

Epilogue: Entering the Borough of Brooklyn
 Fugheddaboutit 245

Introduction

Daily, the walking undead eat brains, vampiric mouths drip gore, there is full frontal nudity, simulated sex and the explicit depiction of torture and murder on cable TV. All caught on DVR so that they can be enjoyed endlessly.

So much more used to be left to the imagination. All was conveyed with shadows, gestures and innuendo. The first kiss in silent films caused a scandal. Older relatives tell us stories of seeing Bela Lugosi's "Dracula" in 1931 and women's fainting when they realized the Count wasn't simply kissing his victim's necks.

There was a time when showing violence on the silver screen was strictly censored. Deaths always occurred off scene. Sex scenes used to consist of a man taking a woman's hand and then cuts to trains going into tunnels and fireworks to dramatic music.

TV cowboys would "wing 'em'" or if they were really good like Hop a Long Cassidy, shoot the guns out of the black hat's hands. Hugh O'Brian's Wyatt Earp never shot to kill. Enemies in war movies would be machine gunned or hand grenaded and either simply clutched their chests and dropped or flew up in the air propelled by trampolines.

Special effects were simple but effective in those naive days; Claymation King Kong and actors in garish costumes walking through miniature models of Tokyo. Things that are by today's standards just strange were terrifying to older generations. Little children in the early 1960s were horrified and would hide if someone even hummed the theme from the Twilight Zone.

We remember page turning Peter Beatty's "The Exorcist" at three o'clock in the morning and being unable to sleep for several nights. We knew we should never see the movie. Of course, when it came out in 1973, we found ourselves sitting in the front row almost catatonic at the supernatural doings on the screen. We woke up sweating from nightmares for months and Regan's demonic face intruded on us and prevented us from falling asleep.

The Amityville Horror obsessed and haunted us at the same time.

Of course, now these things have become the amusing cultural icons and we hear about "Dracula…blah..blah…blah", "Linda Blair pea soup" and Norman Bates shower curtains. When the hippies were kids, on Halloween they dressed as flappers. Now their grandchildren trick or treated as hippies. What scared and shocked the bejeebers out of our grandparents, have become our children's cartoons.

Entertainment has had to become darker and more graphic.

We find ourselves in the era of IT, The Game of Thrones, The Walking Dead, Supernatural, Spartacus, Outlander and The Boys. HBO had a documentary about a cat house and the Russian rock group, "Pussy Riot" is talked about in the news. "Oral sex" is freely spoken about during the news coverage of the impeachment of one president, and another president was recorded talking about "grabbing pussies".

In Prime time, people say "ass", "suck", "getting laid" "bow job" and other graphic things without a second thought. A recent study found that most children learn "the facts of life" from TV.

A book about sexual bondage has become so mainstream that a movie was made of it. Former child actresses flaunt their bodies on public TV, "twerk", and touch men in naughty places with large foam fingers. Two Broke Girls and Game of Thrones leave nothing to the imagination.

Tweens face hundreds of lurid monsters each week and graphically slay them in video games. Heads explode and guts spill. It has become the cultural norm…only common place.

Prime time police dramas have mutilated, and dissected cadavers displayed in vivid, anatomically correct 'and torture movies are among the most popular.

Through advanced technologies people like Zak Baggins, Jason Hawes, and Katrina Weidman treat us to videos and voices of things that we were told as children are "just make believe."

We are no longer sheltered from the disturbing parts of life. Everyone carries a video camera, and we see vivid recordings of violent and other worldly happenings on the evening news. Perhaps this is not polite or genteel, but it is as it is. We make no judgments about the state of our culture. We know that society's tolerance and acceptance of explicit sex and gory violence waxes and wanes. We are in a phase of tolerance and we do not understand all its implications.

As long as there have been people there has been sex, murder, rape, torture and all manner of human depravity. There are monsters among us, even demons. The earth is populated with bad people and evil intent. It always has been and always will be.

There are also the heroes but mostly unseen.

Now we watch and love the TV series we mentioned because they give the characters humanity and reveal things which we have been hidden; even evidence of unseen dimensions that are very real.

Under these circumstances, how can two humble authors entertain and amuse?

"Shock and awe!"

We try to make our books like train wrecks that are too horrible and raw to look away from. And at the same time tongue in cheek. We have pushed some boundaries of reality and thought. Our aims are to entertain, titillate and educate. We hope to shock, scare and challenge the reader.

We present a new "origins" yarn and account of the experience one woman's development as a werewolf.

The retelling of this genre ties it to Western mythology, explains and moves it forward. We also offer insight into the nature of humanity. It is through these characters that we see how the will lets the soul carry on through vast stretches of time; how nothing really changes between loved ones; how we take only to give to others.

We offer shocking characters and subplots. We have included new archeological information and views of authentic and mythical events. Most of the ancient back story is taken from actual descriptions of historical events. Appealing to theoretical physics, we raise questions about the nature of reality and question deeply held beliefs.

Isn't the nature of good fiction to advance possibilities and point to the future? But fiction is above all entertainment and should be relaxing and fun. We hope it allows the reader to escape into our exciting world of heroes and villains. If we offend, we offer again that this is fiction; imagination, "make believe", "let's pretend".

In homage to the fiction we have enjoyed we have included "Easter eggs" as they do in video games. Some of them are obvious, while others are obscure. We hope finding them is engaging and fun.

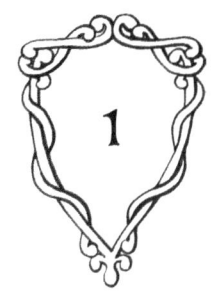

1 Am Weary

*O God, O God, how weary, stale, flat, and
unprofitable seem to me all the uses of this world!*
~ William Shakespeare

Death is a delightful hiding place for weary men.
~ Herodotus

At first glance he did not seem especially impressive. He worked hard to keep up that appearance. He tried to look like an everyday dull and uninteresting businessman, banker or professional man; no one to be concerned about.

Nothing to see here.

He stood just under than six feet tall and as a physical type he favored the British actor, Jason Statham. However, he could not conceal his stealthy prime predator gait.

He was said to be "handsome". He had olive skin and a shaven head. Unlike many men he seldom showed stubble on his face and head. His eyes were dark brown, and he had a Roman nose. His expressive eyes seemed to reflect ancient wisdom and the pain that he had seen too much.

His hands were scarred as was much of his body. His dress was always neat, non-wrinkled shirts and sharply pressed pleats. He had a penchant for Jerry Garcia ties and cowboy boots.

He tried to seem prim, even effete. However, his rugged presence often somehow seemed regal.

He considered himself a soldier on a mission.

Tonight, he was pensive and introspective. His mind wandered as thoughts from his past broke the surface and then dived deeper. One disconnected thought gave rise to another in a stream of consciousness.

He had searched constantly before, and today was the same as every day. There was no sanctuary in death for him. His was an eternity of watching humanity until the end of time. He could only remember the names he took during his more memorable "incarnations". He lived his life like he was a character in a play. He had to be consistent with his role.

He had homes and secret refuges all over the earth.

Unfortunately, his gift of eternal life came with dire curses. During the full moon, he transformed into a ravenous beast, retaining full consciousness of who he is and memory of every savage thing it did. The beast was his ultimate weapon against evil.

However, it cursed him with an insatiable hunger for the most forbidden of foods…human flesh. From the beginning, he only took contemptible criminals who eluded human authority. He tasted only upon the flesh of the most iniquitous; and he pillaged their ill-gotten fortunes.

He found his early years contemptible, full of arbitrary slaughter and lessons learned hard and fast. He had crawled out of too many shallow graves to remember. Reality was an unforgiving teacher. Anger and despair turned to loneliness. He had watched too many friends and lovers wither and disappear before his ageless eyes. Isolation was crushing until he remembered he had the power of creation as well as destruction.

He had been reluctant to burden another with his fate but, his forlornness had become crushing. He thought that, out of mercy he had impulsively made his first companion. With all her imperfections, she became a partner and lover. Someone to breach time with, until she wearied of the mission and became disillusioned with mankind. After four hundred years, she turned her heart off and her mind wandered far away.

Only after she was gone, he understood that he had turned her to sooth his loneliness.

Each of the others he created and lost became like time stacking the unrelenting weight of stones on his chest.

During those days, he hated himself. He had come to think of himself as only the monster. The three-day spree of death and destruction was laced with the thrill of killing, hunting and vengeance. He was at once sickened and plagued by his actions but compelled in a relentless spiral.

But deep inside, he knew he liked the power of the arcane wolf.

He was lucky in his confusion and rage to have found rare refuge with "Daedalus", an immortal of similar fate. Daedalus was of even more ancient origins, a scholar, engineer and scientist, and yes, a wizard. This immortal became his mentor.

Daedalus nurtured the man in him and gave him a model for one who survives at all costs and still finds ways to serve humanity. Daedalus showed him that he was more than just the beast. Daedalus touched his soul and set him on a course of higher learning and humanism.

Under this wise tutelage he became an apprentice. His early lessons had to do with the soul, how the soul needs to understand itself and exorcise its own demons. As he became nothing, he could do anything.

He had lived for more years than he cared to count, changed names and locations always searching.

In most lifetimes he made his living as a merchant. But at the times he was a mercenary, pirate and a raider. There were many wars. They provided plunder. As a result, he created secret caches of wealth.

Wealth became a weapon; riches gave him freedom.

Each time "The Cabal" as he called them was behind him, lying in wait to eliminate him. They are the minions of corruption personified. Their aim was absolute, and their intentions are evil; to do the will of a primordial demon of death and decay. Over the millennia they hid in secret, illegitimate cadres in powerful societies such as the Mysteries, the Ancient Order of the Hierophants or the Rose Croix, Freemasons or Opus Dei.

Ages ago, they had hideously murdered his wife.

He missed her with a longing that he could not reconcile with sense or reason. She was gone because of his failure. He would have to find her, lose her, wait and find her; over and over.

He had grown weary and restless with the world, feeling as if his very soul would break

The same curse that afflicted him caused her to reincarnate in every generation and for him to be compelled to find her. He had lived for more years than he cared to count, changed names and locations always searching. She became one of two of his primary missions.

The fiends had unsuccessfully tried to ensnare him for years.

Powerful magic kept the Cabal from uncovering him, so they tracked and watched for her instead. Unless he attacked them, they could not detect him. Elusive as a wraith, he baffled their leader and his many tendrils. His wolf was created to terminate this demon and to negate its plans. So, he stalked them as well.

From ancient days their strategy was to cause dissent by pitting people against each other. Whenever one nation persecuted and enslaved another, he knew the Cabal was behind it. Their merciless, infernal leader delighted in setting men against women and fostering brutality.

Where the worst abuses were, he could find their nefarious lord. He had many scores to settle with that infernal shade.

Moving his eyes over the books and papers in his vast library, he remembered having saved the scrolls. Some were spoils of wars long forgotten. Some saved in the flood that destroyed the Library in Alexandria.

His eyes lingered on his personal copy of 'Cotton Vitellius'. This famous manuscript contains an epic poem based on his adventures in the Eighth Century. He had been a sacred warrior by the Norsemen. He had taken a Viking woman as his companion and owned land in Geatland.

Eyeing this manuscript, he is taken back some 1200 years, to the wild hills of what is now England. The horror and alienation had caused his Geat companion's mind to abandon her. A cold winter hard on cattle and women had kept him in the Nordic great hall for many months. Until he saw the shimmering curtain of dancing lights and heard the calling of ethereal music summoning him to the shores of East Anglia.

This pulling left him with strange feelings of despair and the heights of passionate love. He could feel a drawing from the rocky shores of Lochlanach. He followed the call and abandoned all to find her.

He had searched, but found only her body wrapped in white linen, wildflowers in her hair. She had died in childbirth along with the tiny infant at her side. His grieving wail was heard almost throughout the British Isles.

Each time he came closer and closer to finding her, but he always came up short.

He retreated from the world after that. He turned to the mystic arts. In subterranean chambers, he learned to separate body and soul and set out on journeys for extended periods. He slowly learned some of the arts of controlling elements, space and time. With his newfound skills, he wandered around Europe, finally settling with a community of Spanish Jewish mystics.

At that time, he took the name "Melchizedek" and joined an early community of mystics. They knew he was not a Jew but welcomed his intellect. His association with them lasted almost 120 years. He plumbed the depths and breadth of these teachings, finding secret codes within early Hebrew texts, leaving his impressions on the movement from the beginning.

The community whispered that, with each full moon, he summoned the golem.

He delved into the play of the light and the dark. He mystically wandered paths of light and saw how it all balances. Even evil was a part of the plan and was an exercise in free will. He investigated the dark to find the divine sparks within.

His greatest lessons were that he received only to share with others and that mercy and justice had to temper each other.

The wolf had to take, but only to serve the greater good. He was fighting a just war. Sometimes acts of loving kindness and charity had to take the savage form of annihilating those who exploit the powerless. George could only become a saint by slaying the rapacious dragon. The defender meting out justice to oppressors above human laws was equal to any saint.

After the age of Enlightenment, he adapted to modernity by becoming a scientist and engineer. Science and medicine gave him hope that perhaps humanity could change from bewildered children to rational adults. He had been a physician in many of his identities and found freeing the sick from the slavery of illness nourished his soul and made amends.

Over the centuries, he worked behind the scenes advancing causes of human freedom and dignity. He was active in many of the events that changed history for the advancement of humanity.

He was at the signing of the Magna Carta; a witness to the signing of Brother Aymeric, Master Knight Templar. He attended the signing of the Declaration of Independence and paid the massive bar tab after the deliberations. In France he financed the Revolution, arming the just citizens and organizing groups setting up community kitchens and work programs.

He pleaded for mercy for Louis and Antoinette. But the mob had made its murderous decision,

He had been part of the Underground Railroad; ushering escaped slaves to the north and financing many of their home-based businesses. He had advocated against the genocide of the indigenous people. When the Nazis moved their vile hands across most of Europe; he secreted thousands of Jews, Gypsies and Armenians out of Nazi dominated countries.

He was in Selma, Alabama facing the dogs, hoses and nightsticks.

In his current sojourn, he became a Doctor of Clinical and Neurological Psychology. He needed more freedom and being a modern physician was too all consuming.

He knew that many of the people the Cabal persecuted they labeled "mentally ill" and locked away in hospitals that became their prisons and torture chambers. They were always under treatment by corrupt men, who only served the Cabal, in private sections of reputable institutions.

He had seen over the past hundreds of years that the mentally ill were the least understood of the afflicted. They were misjudged, feared, and isolated in asylums; treated worse than cattle.

In ancient times, it was easy to call them "witches" or say that they were "possessed". Later they had been the subjects of scorn and entertainment or hidden away from wealthy families who knew nothing about mental illness. In the early twentieth century, in many of the large state-run hospitals of they were treated like servants by the staff.

Their situation had gotten better over the past sixty years, but most societies still shun the psychiatrically impaired. They are stripped of their independence and ability to make decisions governing their own lives.

He had to act alone. His situation was so incredible that to reveal what he is and the corruption he fought was likely to label him as psychotic. He could only trust his instincts and flashes of insight to lead him to the Cabal's victims.

But enough introspection and gloom. He had a mission to fulfill.

He scoured the news media for suspicious items. He knew that when he found where groups of subjugated women were mysteriously disappearing, he would find the demon; and where he was, she might also be.

News articles and professional journals alerted him to the surprising resurgence of prefrontal lobotomies among schizophrenic patients at Creedmoor Hospital in the rural Mt. Summit. This is an old and extreme procedure rarely used today because it destroys brain tissue. Significantly, no male patients were treated.

The results seemed impressive, but many questions remained. There were concerns about data collection and the criteria for surgical selection. The professional journals indicated the need for psychological evaluations to determine the efficacy of expanding treatment. His instincts and the auguries screamed that evil was behind this.

Soon, he had secured a professorship in the Psychology Department of nearby State University as a clinical researcher. The position came with an appointment to the professional staff at Creedmoor Hospital tasking him with pre- and post-evaluations of surgery candidates.

However, this put him in indirect opposition to the physician in charge.

He soon found that this surgeon was blocking the flow of information and statistics thorough piles of paperwork. He was taking advantage of the bureaucratic system to conceal his actions.

He hid that many of the candidates died pre-treatment. These deaths were falsely documented. The psychologist came upon convenient and ludicrous explanations. But these were medical procedures, and he was not a licensed physician, so his opinions were excluded from consideration.

Bringing these crimes to the attention of the authorities would contradict his prime goal.

Therefore, he began his own investigation. The skills he had acquired over the millennia allowed him to easily gain access into secret areas of patients designated for surgery. He found that the women were always vulnerable wives of rich men who all belonged to a particular extreme religious congregation.

There were terrible signs of physical abuse on their bodies. He found the terrified eyes of women who had been brutalized. Most would not speak to him, but he could feel and smell the fear emanating from them. There was an unusually high rate of pre-surgery suicides. Their bodies were promptly cremated and could not be examined. No autopsies meant there was no physical evidence.

But then, he heard the empyreal music and saw the mystical curtain of dancing lights.

The psychologist was the outsider. He found his hands tied.

However, when the time was ripe, the wolf could not be denied.

Asylum

*Yeah, a storm is threatening
My very life today
If I don't get some shelter
Lord, I'm gonna fade away Rolling
Stones–Gimme Shelter 1971*

It may have only been a dream, the sensation of someone desperately searching for me as I slept. I could hear the echo of a whisper calling my name. Glimpses of a beautiful man flitted through my dreams. It seemed he was gently shaking me.

I woke with a start feeling as if someone was in the room. I leaned over and switched on the light and pulled the white down comforter up around my breasts.

I scanned the room, everything was in its place, the window was open and the crème-colored sheers that framed the windows fluttered with the warm breeze. I could hear the chorus of tree frogs outside in the grass and ponds.

I switched the light back off and turned over. I tossed and turned thinking about what was to happen tomorrow. Insisting that I was not right in the head, tomorrow he was sending me to hospital. Demanding that I must sleep the xanax he had given me made me drop off.

Morning came faster than I thought it would. The breaking of night into day was not soft or pleasant it came with a ringing in my head and eyes that felt dry. He knocked hard three times on the door, I could sense how his knuckles must have felt hitting the painted wood so hard.

I sat up and said a sleepy "Yeah".

My bag had already been packed; all I needed to do was change clothes and head downstairs. There would be three men that would take me; two orderlies and a physician, all of whom were my acquaintances from our church.

My husband would be already gone, so there would be no goodbyes. I dressed–a prim white dress and a light sweater over my shoulders, white shoes and then pinned my hair up and grabbed my case.

The men were waiting for me; one of the orderlies took my case and put it in the side of the ambulance. I was approached by an immaculately dressed man I knew as Dr. Sterling who was a church elder.

He explained that for us to have a nice ride to the hospital I would be required to have an injection; something that would calm me down. I felt calm already I told them, he smiled and shook his head as the orderlies grabbed both my arms. The doctor administered the shot.

It took a few moments, but I wasn't asleep as much as I was extraordinarily sedate. My eyes wanted to close, and my body went limp. The orderlies lifted me and placed me on a gurney, strapped me down, and placed me into the back of the ambulance. The doctor would ride in the front seat with the driver the two orderlies sat in the back with me.

Because I was so sedated, and my body felt heavy, thick and weak, I could only make out fragments of what the orderlies were saying to each other. They chuckled about the way my breasts would jiggle as the ambulance moved over the road.

This made me terribly worried and frightened. I looked at their hands as they sat alongside of me, broad work worn hands with thick calluses. Their uniforms were crisp white, shoes polished to a high sheen black.

I could feel someone's hand on my stocking moving up my inner thigh. Their words were warbled in my mind; all I could do was let the warm gritty feel of hands move up my thighs, pausing along the top of my stockings where my flesh was not covered.

Both hands lingered there and moved closer towards my underwear. They had pulled my dress up, they lingered along the edge of my panties…I was frightened to my core. Even under the best of circumstances, there was nothing I could do.

I was so sedated all I could do was just lie there. I also knew that if I acted up, then the chances of me leaving the place I was being sent to would vanish forever.

I felt helpless. It was an old familiar feeling

As the car went over what must have familiar bumps on the causeway, the orderlies abruptly stopped what they were doing and put my dress back down.

The institution was far from the fenced-in shoreline, I could see from my view at the window the road glisten from new rain. The island is where I was now, behind bricks and mortar, a door without a key.

I could only see shades of grey. The building was long and big, I could not imagine all the rooms inside of it. There was another structure with two pyramid shaped roofs. In my mind that one burned sepia tones. It made me sick to think of what had happened in that building. I closed my eyes and waited.

The faces of the people were a blur, they moved too fast, talked too fast. They gave me medicine and poked me with needles at first; laid me on white starched linens, in sterile` white rooms, with checkerboard linoleum floors. Everything was frigid. I thought that they must have done this on purpose, kept in a thin cotton gown, no real blankets, kept the temperature down, an island that was a meat locker.

I could hear the shuffling of medicated feet pass the metal door, see the shadows cast by the staff as they hurried past the door. They were only shadows, light and dark, the bend of light and object. There were mesh screens that ran along the tops of the doors; sometimes they would close these if the person in the room became too loud. They would shut him in with his screaming, rambling diatribe, accusations, hatred, vengeance, and wrath.

Patients were wheeled around on gurneys, strapped down while looking at the passing ceiling. The buzz of the electric lamps; each one emitting its own noise, its own little tune. I would see the concrete dips of the ceiling, how they looked like garden rows. If the world were upside down, they could be filled with water.

I laid there thinking about all the different types of ceilings in this place. I wondered if the builder had done the same and looked up and decided to give us something to look at. I wondered at this small act of kindness that no one would see but the patients strapped to beds or gurneys.

The baths were large and made of stone set in some sort of box, blue drapes on metal rings hung from metal poles. The curtains were for show, there was no privacy. The only private place was in one's mind. The baths were longer than a person could be in them comfortably. This was the only time I was warm. I could feel their eyes moving over me.

They used large canvas toppers for the tubs to secure patients. The same used as ships sails, with metal grommets sewn into place and canvas tie downs along the edge of the tub. They would place patients inside, and then unceremoniously move canvas up to the neck. They would wrap patients' foreheads in gauze a few times to catch the sweat.

They circled like vultures, dark creatures in their scrubs. They did not speak directly to me or me to them. I considered the yellowish tiles on the walls, and how they connected to the floor. If I looked long and closely enough, I could see the slight difference in yellow on each of the tiles. One day I counted them, they had left me to lie in the tub.

When let outside, the sun be would blinding, moving from inside the stone womb onto the green soft lawn. The building was so very big. Now that I think about the large stones on the outside, and the pressure that they would exert on the minds of those inside. The stones were impossibly big, and the windows were black. Dark like the eyes on the wood and lacquered Jesus on my mother's wall; eyes that seemed to follow you around the room.

I looked at all the sterile furniture, the cabinets, metal upon metal, the trays, the plates, the doors, the fixtures. The beds, metal upon metal, steel tubing holding onto electricity that ran along the walls and into the floors. The desks of the staff were heavy great metal battleships of bureaucracy.

The sea outside would swell, and eat away at the shoreline, the constant lapping of the waves; the sea encroaching on the land; the wind whipping across the sand. The wind would become angry and throw sloppy punches against the walls of my prison. I could hear the wind outside the walls, pushing and shoving at the land, the trees, pulling at the roof top to get inside. I was afraid of the wind as I had been afraid of a mad father home from an all-night drunk.

Since his recovery, father had become extremely religious. We had become members of a small, nonsectarian church that preached letter of the law. Recently, with a new minister, there had been a huge influx of new members who were more extreme. They were all aloof and very clannish.

A month after admission I was transferred to a treatment ward.

I found myself in the portion of hospital with the pyramid rooves. I was introduced to several nurses, and the therapists with whom I would be having sessions. My eyes were blurry, and it was hard to focus.

I noticed that a well-dressed, shaven-headed man wearing a geometric patterned tie seemed to startle when he saw me. He looked almost like he was spellbound. He took several almost trance-like steps towards me, but then seemed to catch himself and quickly walked away.

He stopped at a discrete distance away and appeared to be perusing a medical file. I could see him discretely peeking over the file and I somehow felt drawn to him; like two magnets being compelled together by invisible forces.

They escorted me to my room. I sat on the bed, and the charge nurse gave me a fresh set of hospital gowns and a robe. She told me to change and put my soiled robes in the hamper, and that she would be back with the doctor in a few minutes.

I wearily looked around the room, everything was metal. The room was small, and halfway up the wall there were small white tiles in an irregular pattern. I changed as I looked out the warbled glass of the windows and tried to see past the black bars. I folded my gown and underclothes and placed them in the hamper and put on a fresh thin gown.

Within minutes Dr. Sterling entered the room with his clip board. "I am going to have to recommend full restraints Mary. Since you have been uncooperative, I will start you off on 75 milligram injection of Thorazine," he said. I was shocked "What, I was just sitting here…when was I uncooperative with you?" I asked him.

He began taking notes on the clip board, and muttered to himself, "Patient is a twenty-five-year-old, white female; uncooperative, questioning therapeutic dose of sedatives, will not discuss course of therapy, or possible resolution, patient was combative" …I looked at him, with abject fear in my eyes, my stomach a tangle of fear.

He walked over to the door and called in two orderlies to apply the bed restraints. "What are you doing" I said, "I didn't do anything, I was just sitting here" …the orderlies rushed in and pushed me onto the bed. They attached the ankle and wrist restraints and pulled the white sheet up to my waist and left the room.

"Now Mary, I hope you understand that you will be in restraints until you learn to be a good girl. You are only to speak when spoken to. And you will NOT discuss what goes on in this room, that is my business" he said with a sneer.

Dr. Sterling called in the nurse for the syringe, dismissed her and walked over to the bed. He pulled my hips side wards, jabbing me several times. I gasped in shock.

He smacked my behind as he pulled the sheet up.

"You will sleep now, no supper for you, tomorrow another doctor will come and do an interview with you. I suggest you be a good girl. Watch your tongue, or I will do worse to you. Answer as if you have a knife held to your throat.

I cherish the old ways. I love to take guidance from the good book. 'If a man loveth his children he will punish them'." Dr. Sterling said with a self-satisfied grin. He moved away from the bed looked at me and then turned and left the room.

I pulled against the leg and arm restraints; they were padded leather attached to small chains that were fastened to the underside of the bed. The more I wiggled around the more the sheet moved down my body. I resolved to lay still. I could feel a black cloak of sleep coming over me.

It was still dark when the orderlies came in to place the bed pan underneath me as I pee'd. They had on white latex gloves; they talked amongst themselves as they hoisted my hips up, put the cold hard bed pan under me, and then used coarse paper to wipe me with. They then washed my face and removed the hair pins from my hair; one of them started stroking my hair when it tumbled down from the pins being removed.

I asked, "Shouldn't you be women?"

"She is a pretty one" – one of them said… said as he wiped the outside of my vagina. He chuckled to himself and pulled the sheet up towards my chest and then they left the room.

Soon after they left, a duo of female orderlies entered the room. I watched them remove the restraints from my wrists which I rubbed and itched at and moved my arms around to get the sensation back in my shoulders. The red head was unbuckling the leg restraints.

The black woman removed my robe, and donned gloves and began washing my neck and arms. The water was warm and soapy; she seemed to hum a little as she rubbed my arms and shoulders with the warm washcloth. The red-haired orderly started washing my toes and feet, moving up towards my legs. I closed my legs out of modesty.

"What is your problem?" The red head declared. She seemed annoyed. "Just do it, or we will get Dr. Sterling in here".

I moved my legs apart, and she started to intensely wash my inner thighs, and then she took a hot rag to my privates and buttocks. As she did this, I squirmed a little. The black aide was washing my breasts, moving the washcloth in circles as she went her washing me and the rough rubbing was exciting and repugnant to me at the same time. I felt guilty for becoming stimulated by it, for being exposed to other women.

"Hold still bitch" the black female said as she began to put the restraints back on my wrists. "But the doctor said I didn't have to have them on" I said now confused.

"We say they need to go on" she said with a smug smile as she finished latching them into place. "We don't need your squirming and fighting us. We are in a hurry. We have a tight schedule. You are not the only patient we have." She roughly pushed me back onto the bed.

"Get off of me" I said as I squirmed in the bed, trying to move away from the heavy red headed woman, but the medications made it hard to think and move. I kicked and unintentionally hit her in the shoulder. "Fucking bitch keep still!" she said as she grabbed the other leg restraint. "Please, you are hurting me" I cried.

The black woman put her hand over my mouth. "Now you're going to be still, and you're going to be quiet, or we will get Dr. Sterling in here. And he will punish you, and trust us, you don't want his punishment; she said with a satisfied grin. I tried to pull my knees together, and pull against the restraints, but it was no use.

She pushed my knees open and began you roughly rub me with a coarse brown towel. It felt like sandpaper. My screams were muffled. With one hand on my mouth, she socked me across the eyebrow with her right hand dazing me for a moment. I pulled harder on the restraints and tried to scream for help, wiggling my hips away from the woman who was vigorously abrading the skin off my thighs with what felt like shop towels.

"Shut up bitch! Angie switch positions with me, you're stronger. Hold this bitch down while I check her mouth to see if she 'tongued' any medicines". They quickly switched positions. The black woman put two fingers on my lips. "If you bite me, I'll make you pay. Be a good girl and let us finish" the nurse said to me.

She pushed into my cheeks with her middle knuckles from each fist at the same time and forced me to open my mouth. She took her index and middle fingers and roughly scraped under my tongue and between my back teeth and gums. I felt the insides of my cheeks burn and tasted blood in my teeth.

I wondered what the point of this was. It seemed like it was just to hurt and belittle me.

I spit out blood and screamed, "Damn you, you hurt me!"

They laughed and the red head said harshly, "We are already damned".

The black aide picked up a fresh gown and roughly undid my left arm restraint. She grabbed my forearm with her left hand than and punched my bicep with her right. The pain was like an electric shock and I screamed out. My arm became too weak to move. She then did the same to my other arm. She spit out "That will take the fight out of you".

Afterwards, each twisted my arms sharply back and began putting the gown on me. "Next time stay fucking still and be a good girl, or we will get you when you sleep" the red head said. She covered my mouth again, knocking me in the head with her knuckles, the pain shot through my skull.

They finished wiping me down, closed my gown, securing it at the neck, put the covers back up over me. They gathered their things. "By the way dear, your combative nature is going in your file, and we are telling Dr. Sterling that you lashed out at us, good luck getting out of here", the red-haired nurse cackled, and they left the room. My eyes looked at the tiles as tears streamed down my face.

In the night, I heard boot heels clomping on the hard linoleum. For an instant I saw the outline of a black figure peering through the wire mesh covered window in the door. I heard a sound like a dog sniffing under the door. I could swear I saw yellow balls of light appear where the eyes should be. I saw the door lock jiggling and move harshly to the side as if someone were trying to force it open. The hinges were beginning to come loose.

I tried to scream, but I was too enervated, and a squeak emitted from my lips. At this, the door began to shake and buckle outwards as if someone with great strength was trying to pull it off the hinges. I could hear the hinges and lock groaning and the wood moaning under the strain. It bowed and seemed like it was about to crack.

As suddenly as it began, the door stopped moving and snapped back to its original position. I heard a "Haruumph" sound like a frustrated dog might make.

A nightmare or hallucination?

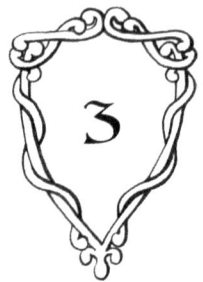

What Passes for Treatment

*The world is a dangerous place to live; not because
of the people who are evil, but because of the people
who don't do anything about it. Albert Einstein*

It was early in the morning when he came in the room; he had pulled the chair from under the small desk and sat next to my bed. He sat very quietly watching me as I slowly became aware that someone was with me.

I shook myself awake and started to back up in the bed, the restraints made this difficult. Although I knew I had never seen him before I had an impression that I knew him intimately. I somehow knew his face well. It was like I had seen him in dreams.

"It is O.K Mary, I am your evaluator and psychotherapist, Dr. Gentlesse, and we will have our therapy sessions several times a week" he said as he watched me. I blinked my eyes, and I couldn't shake a feeling of familiarity. However, I could not place him; the haze of drugs made it hard to think.

I did not speak to him, my mouth and gums itched and burned from the previous night's abuse. I examined the wall. "We have to do an interview to evaluate your ability to make decisions concerning your own treatment; and to get your side of the story." he said.

I moved my eyes from the tile wall to his eyes and stared at him for a while. It was not a look of hate or mistrust. I was just waiting, pausing to see what he would do or would not do.

I shook my head…no.

He sighed heavily, made a quick note on his clipboard stood up, and started walking towards the door. "If there is anything you want to say to me Mary, you know that you can." He said with his back to me.

I bit my lip wanting help but was unsure of this man.

Then Dr. Sterling and some orderlies entered the room

Dr. Gentlesse walked up the corridor leading to the secure room. It took all his control to contain his excitement.

It was her! In this generation she was the one. His heart beat harder when she was near. She was identical to his wife. There was the unmistakable aura he always saw when he found the one! He wanted to grab her and carry her out in his arms. But he had to be cautious not to scare her further or ruin his chance to save her.

It was the day before the full moon, and he had to be careful. He had slipped and become impulsive at the door to her room last night.

Already, he could feel his senses sharpening. The almost imperceptible clicking of his high heeled boots on the ceramic floor sounded like small explosions to him. The figures in the pictures on the walls seemed to jump out at him.

His body felt good, almost too good. He wanted to run outside and howl. He had to be cautious, especially now. The creaking of the seclusion room door assailed his ears. He had to not wince; to be careful to seem normal. He could not let his heightened senses distract him. He had to bring all his focus on to the task at hand. This was familiar; he had done it hundreds of times.

Later that day he entered Mrs. Young's room and the smells assailed his nostrils. He noted the crack the thick door he had made the night before and shook his head. Most people would have noticed only the smell of antiseptics and cleaners.

They were as plain as day to his heightened olfactory sense. There were the smells of three women's angry sweat and odors of her blood and fear. Two were Caucasian and one had a different genetic dynamic. It was ever more slightly distinct.

He could feel his wolf bristle.

On the bed was his patient, tightly bound to the bed but with a longer hospital gown and her hair combed. "What the heck", slipped out of the professional man. "I cannot conduct an interview with you bound like this! What happened?"

Gentlesse heard steps in the hall and the door pushed open. "We are not yet ready for you yet, Van" announced Dr. Sterling. At either side of him, stood two large orderlies dressed in white clothes and polished black shoes. "It would appear that Mrs. Young is still in an agitated state".

The psychologist motioned with his hand towards the woman in the bed who had purposefully turned her face away from them. It was as if she was trying to disappear from the room. "She looks the opposite of agitated, Hayward; her history is incomplete.

There are statements from her husband that she has been acting uncharacteristically, confused and aggressive. But there are no statements from her. That is a medical records requirement. It is almost a month since her admission; we are noncompliant with governmental regulations".

The psychiatrist looked down his nose at the therapist and announced in an inflated tone, "She is selectively mute and will not give accurate information. I am afraid I must dismiss you due to medical emergency."

"I will examine her and let you know when you can see her." Sterling announced.

"We are going to do this dance again?" the therapist retorted. "This time it will not be so easy for you. I am going to take a special interest in this case. By our hospital by-laws, I will exercise my rights to visit her whenever I deem it necessary.

Something is not right here. Or shall we take this to the medical board?

I am obligated to contact the federal authorities issuing the grant to report these procedural irregularities. It could invalidate the whole study and end funding".

"Oh Van" the psychiatrist sputtered. "You can be such a crusader. Is it because she is a beautiful woman? The orderlies guffawed. "Even with those boots, he ain't big as no 'van'. He isn't even a sedan" the 6-foot-8-inch orderly quipped. The doctor's party snickered.

Gentlesse gave him a knowing smile.

Dr. Sterling replied dismissively. "Mike, his whole name is a mouthful.

Please leave us to our medical procedure, Ravenwulf. It is beyond your area of expertise." Then he pointed to the door.

Was that a growl they heard as Gentlesse left the room?

The three men moved with practiced precision once the door was locked. One of the orderlies forced a gag in my mouth and they undid my 4 points restrains and used the belts to tie my hands behind my back and my legs together. They placed me roughly on the floor and adjusted the bed. They folded it at the middle making a large hump in the middle and pulled out two leg extensions.

They placed me face down on the bed with my buttocks up in the air. My hands were tied at my sides next to my hips and my chest and ankles were secured; my chin rested on the edge of the bed. I felt empty and lost; nothing was going to save me.

The doctor walked up to me and raised my chin. "Open your eyes Mary. It would be a shame to have to cut off your eyelids so that you cannot close them". I complied.

"Now, you have been especially naughty towards your husband, and you have resisted our best attempts to help you. Further, I shall have to contend with the good Dr. Gentlesse.

We must break your defiance. You have been, in the colloquial, 'a pain in the ass'; and now you must be punished. The punishment must fit the crime; "I am an 'Old Testament' kind of guy: 'an eye for an eye and all that. If thou lovest thy child, thou wilt discipline him.'"

Sterling dramatically pulled out the thick belt from his pants. Then walked behind me and pulled up my gown and ripped off the hospital cotton panties I was wearing. "Not that these will offer much protection, but I do like the view", my tormentor explained. Now, there will be ten strokes and then you will make a gesture of compliance.

If you do not, there will be ten more strokes."

Now, this will not 'be uncomfortable, or 'sting' or 'feel like pressure'. This is going to hurt, and you will be bruised for days."

Dr. Sterling then pulled back the belt and slapped it against that perfect target with all his force. The belt made a cracking noise as it hit my butt.

With that stroke of the belt, I was jolted back looking at the frame of the bed. I wanted to throw up but the gag in my mouth barely made it possible for me to breathe.

I was shaking with humiliation and rage. The pain seared up my hips and into my back, and the tears blinded me. I shook my head no and tried to scream with the gag in my mouth. I made a muffled sound and bucked.

The doctor admired the deepening, angry red welt that was raised across the cheeks of my behind. Tears began to form in my eyes.

"I'll bet that was...bracing... dumb bitch", Sterling sneered. And that was only one". He then methodically and slowly completed the nine other strokes.

As belt snapped across my behind, I started to cry out to his extreme pleasure. My head and hair rocked back with each lash he gave me; I tightened my thighs and butt in anticipation of each harsh blow. I pulled against my restraints. He kept hitting me and my mind would reel.

I retreated in my mind to a room, locked on the inside. I tried to run to the wheatfields with golden tones and trees in the distance that I had created in my mind when my father was drunk.

I was sobbing uncontrollably. One of the orderlies held my head, while the other washed my face with a cool washcloth. Once I had regained some of my composure, I noticed that there were huge bulges in the front of their white trousers.

"Now, for your act of contrition; 'Slaves in every way obeth thy earthly masters'", the doctor said.

Of course, all of this has made me excited, and I will then relieve myself in you.

If you do not comply, I will deliver ten more blows and you will be given another chance to comply; and so on".

I continued to cry and relaxed my body. "Good decision the doctor suggested.

The doctor stood behind me, dropped his pants and entered me. Each probe felt like a hot branding iron. I cried out in pain; my muffled noises were meaningless. I lay my head down wanting to die. Mercifully, he finished in a matter of moments

The doctor pulled up his pants and re inserted his belt. "Umm, that was nice. Call in the others when you are done. Oh, and afterwards, clean her up, make sure she has her medications and make her look presentable. Attend to her bruises and ice her bottom.

I must intercept Ravenwulf!"

I swallowed hard, and he removed the gag from my mouth. I was relieved that I could finally breathe. I screamed and cried uncontrollably.

Two of the men in the room left to get something, closing the door behind them. The third orderly removed his pants, exposing a massive erection. Which he showed me, I bit my lip, and gulped hard. "Please mister, please..." was all I could utter as he moved around to the bottom of the bed.

He punched me hard in the gut and I lost my breath, tears streamed from my eyes. He stood at the foot of the bed watching me for several minutes, as he did so he became more engorged. "No, please stop, don't hurt me anymore" I sobbed.

He smiled at me; the look in his eyes was of a savage, a ruthless man who was going to take what he wanted. He simply smiled. "See, nice and ready" he said.

I thought, "I am nobody."

I grunted in pain, his hands around my neck. "Take it bitch" he whispered and then he bit at my earlobe. I lay there helpless, waiting for it to end, for the pain to stop. The other two orderlies came in the room and started whooping and hollering as they watched their friend rape me, they moved closer to watch

He finally finished and breathed out with satisfaction.

"When you are here longer, you guys will get a turn. Hey, did you bring the ice and the medication?" I held my eyes closed and turned my head away from them.

They removed the restraints, and one of them picked me up and off the bed like a rag doll. He carried me to the shower, ripped my dressing gown off, and stood me under the nozzle. The water was freezing cold. I just stood there, my hips quivering, my body shaking from shock; I pulled my arms up and around myself.

The men roughly dried me off and put another hospital gown on me. I was so sore I could barely walk; I stumbled as they led me back to the newly made bed, I was in so much pain. There was a bucket of ice next to the bed, they wrapped the ice in washcloths and shoved the ice packs between my legs and butt cheeks.

One of the orderlies gave me an injection, and the room began to spin in a funny way.

It must have been several hours later, the room was still dark; someone came in the room and removed the ice packs, and the basin. I awoke with a start, feeling that same familiar feeling of being watched. I drew my knees up, surprised I was not in restraints on the bed, and I buried my face in the pillow, pulled the covers up and around me. My backside hurt as did my crotch as I drew my knees upwards.

I became aware that someone was in the room watching me; I grunted and moaned as I turned over away from the wall. I was shocked to see Dr. Gentlesse sitting in a chair next to my bed. I began to shake and tried to move away from him even though I was wracked with pain. Terrified by what the other men had done; I started to wretch with fright. Furiously pulling the covers towards me, I hugged the tiled wall next to the bed.

I laid in a fetal position with my face positioned to the wall. I did not trust anyone in this place and had no reason to.

Gentlesse sat watching her. With the full moon that night, he was in a desperate situation and was on edge due to the changes already beginning in him. His wolf smelled the sexual activity that had occurred. He had to force down his impulse to rampage!

This was his soul mate! The one he had breached time to find. She was here now! This woman who he should have protected had the scent of Hayward Sterling and the orderly Mike on her; his heart was heavy with dismay. Rage was beginning to take him over.

He knew that in his human form, he could not take her from this place of torment. As strong and skilled as he was, his human form could be overwhelmed by force of numbers. His wolf was just below the surface. He could barely stop himself from acting on its demands.

"Mrs. Young, may I call you Mary?" The doctor asked. He was greeted by further contraction by the terrified woman. "I know what is going on, but I cannot prove it. We need to work together to help you or there is no hope for you. Please look at me?" he asked.

I began to shake in fear, but I was struck by these words. I glanced at the doctor. I was surprised at the change in his appearance. The formerly immaculate and prissy professional seemed almost disheveled. His formerly clean-shaven face and head were stubbly. He still wore classic oxford clothing, but they appeared too tight for him.

He seemed more massive and animated. Was his voice slightly deeper and did his irises sometimes appear yellow? I looked at his hands and noticed a sort of old ring on his finger, a golden knot that I couldn't place but it seemed I knew it well.

"I have no reason to trust anybody here" I spit out tears streaming down my face. The therapist looked at me attentively. "Look at these bruises", I showed him my forehead and arms. "That is …unbelievable. You got those here?" the doctor asked. "Of course, you fool", I replied. "Look at this!"

I ripped open my robe and showed him my bruised breasts and turned around to show him my buttocks my body in pain, I sat back down on the bed pulling the covers over me.

The doctor averted his eyes and said, "I have seen enough! Please listen to me."

"I apologize in advance. I do not have time to choose my words so please excuse me if I am blunt. I will not be quite myself over the next three days so I will not be at work. So, I need to tell you now and there is a lot of information I can give you that you might have to believe on faith.

I have been suspicious of Dr. Sterling and his associates for several months

There have been several wives like you who seemed a bit submissive and who Sterling's claims are 'selectively' mute. They all seem to have particularly brutish husbands who are a little too friendly with Sterling and the administrative director. Their actions remind me of the communications of secret societies or cults. All these women have been horrifically afraid and have been unable to talk with me.

They are here for a few days to a month and seem to get steadily more withdrawn and more paranoid. They have always been in restraints, so I could never interview them. Many of them have committed suicide. For the survivors, after a few days, Sterling has recommended lobotomies. They have left with their loutish husbands, more like robots than people."

I snuck into the room on the night before the last poor woman's lobotomy and saw evidence of fresh physical abuse. As she seemed especially uncomfortable in her hips, I looked at her hips and buttocks and saw packed ice bags on her bottom and between her legs. I looked beneath them and saw terribly abused backside.

"I insisted with the threats of going in person to the state's medical licensing board to interview you while you are unrestrained for this short time.

I am convinced that the Director and Sterling are in a conspiracy with a group of… let us call them "sadists" for now, to make their wives mindless slaves. I am sure that they are part of a demon worshiping cult that infiltrates and corrupts pious churches and enjoys despoiling the innocent.

I have no concrete proof, but I know the doctor and certain orderlies sexually had amused themselves with those poor women.

I think, aside from their pleasure, this has the effect of breaking the women psychologically and thusly justifying the lobotomies.

The operations appear to be demonic sacrifices.

Mary I can save you, but you need to be prepared to see some. otherworldly things and some awful carnage. You will have to see them before you can even believe they could happen. I am sorry."

"What do you mean? Are you the crazy one?" I blurted out.

"Has anything I said fit your situation?" Gentlesse's voice was becoming deeper and more guttural.

My mind reeled when he said this. "These men have raped me, beaten me, they make me sick. The nurses savaged me." My eyes went to the wall, unable to linger on his soft brown eyes, tears falling from my own. "Let's say I believe you. What is in it for me? How are you going to get me out of here?"

The psychologist gave her an ironic laugh." You will avoid being a mindless slave for your husband. You will have freedom like you have never known and..... vengeance. The cost is that the moon will give you a burden. Further, we will be tied together closely forever".

I took a few minutes and assessed the situation. "O.K., the consequences of not trusting you are worse than trusting you." I asserted.

"Let us begin" Gentlesse said."

"At sundown I will come to you through that window". He indicated a window that had a mesh cage around it. You will be frightened by my appearance, but you will recognize me. I will give you a gift that will allow you to free yourself within 24 hours. But I am afraid that you may have one more night of torture."

"What do you mean?" I queried. "How can you get through a steel reinforced window? What will you look like? And how will I know you?"

Gentlesse sighed and shrugged his shoulders. "You will have to see it to believe it. Now this is going to seem strange. Do not let what those fiends did to you put you off."

He went to a corner of the room, turned his back to me and urinated in the corner. "Come here", he requested. I did so tentatively afraid of the doctor's actions. My nostrils were assailed by a pungent mixture of urine and an odd, savage animal musky smell.

An image of a wolf came to my mind.

Did his ears move almost imperceptibly in the direction of the door? "They are coming now. I hear them" Gentlesse said. "Play along. I will come in the middle of their abusing you. It won't be long. I cannot intervene until after moon rise".

The door opened and Dr. Sterling and his cohort of orderlies entered the room. "Well Van, any revelations from psychobabble land?" The physician sneered. "You are looking pretty scruffy. Didn't you shave this morning? And you smell like you haven't showered".

"I am…not… quite myself today." The psychologist offered and his eyes gleamed. "I didn't get any information that could… help you, Hayward. But I have a feeling that this case will have some surprises for you.

I'll be back." He gave them a wolfish grin as he slipped out the door.

Once the door was closed, the orderlies moved in a trained manner. One of them locked the door and the other two grabbed my wrists and threw me on the bed

Being slammed on the bed hurt my back and buttocks, the welts were soft and tender. I yelled out in pain. "Doctor, please don't do this…. I will be good. I will be whatever you need me to be…just please stop beating me…please doctor don't let these men hurt me again I'm begging you"

I looked pleadingly at Dr. Sterling. He gave me a mocking little laugh and said, "I'm afraid that there is no mercy here, my dear. 'If thou dost not speak to warn the wicked from his way he shall die'. It is time for another lesson in pain or compliance".

Dr. Sterling set down his files and took his white coat off and handed it to one of the orderlies. "You will do as you are told. The first thing I am going to tell you is to shut the fuck up or I will have to report that you have been found dead by your own hand…" he said.

I swallowed hard and looked around the room, there was no escape, and two of the orderlies were holding me down as he walked closer to me. He grabbed me by my hair and swirled it around his fist so that he had a good solid grip on it, he pulled me close to him. I could smell his aftershave, the coffee on his breath.

The pain of him pulling my hair took my breath away, "Damn you doc-tor" I whispered. He doubled up his fist and hit me in the ribs, my knees buckled at the pain as the air shot out of me, and I held onto his hand that was holding my hair.

"Now…Mary, you are not being a very compliant woman, surely you can do better than that" he said as he let go of my hair and I fell onto the cold tile floor. I grabbed as his feet and looked at his Nettleton wingtip black leather shoes. I held on to his legs and began to beg for mercy… "Please Doctor" I sobbed… "please, please don't". The doctor sneered, "Mike and Doug, could you please pull this little whore off of me, and show her how to comply with my orders?"

The orderlies pulled at my ankles, and as they dragged me away from the Doctor's feet, they began kicking at my ribs, I balled myself up, I could hear my ribs moving and cracking as they kicked at me.

"Enough, strip her clothes, the two of you kneel on her wrists to pin her down if you could make sure that you are facing this way, I would appreciate it. I want more of this whore; to explore some of my favorite games" Sterling said.

The orderlies pulled my dressing gown off, the necktie was on a little tighter and as they pulled at it trying to get it off me and it began to choke me. I clutched at it, and finally it came off over my head.

I lay nude on the floor, the men pressing their knees into the bones and flesh of my forearms. I drew my knees up, though it pained me to be on the hard floor, crossing my legs at the ankles.

"Mike…Mr. Big, that's what we like to call him; the man with the…ahem…unusual gift. You had a chance to meet him last night. Will you hold one of her legs for me?" The same man, Mike, pulled at one of my ankles and yanked it over at an angle, pinning my kneecap to the hard floor.

"Augh…the pain…Doctor…stop" I said breathless still from the torment. "Shut your slut's mouth, when I want to hear from you, I will tell you" said Dr. Sterling as he got on his knees behind my bruised and sore posterior.

He pressed his fingers into my hips and pulled me closer to him, he pushed himself up to me. I screamed out in pain, and he hammered the back of the head.

I tried to crawl away from him, just then there was a clamoring and the sound of glass shattering from the window above us…

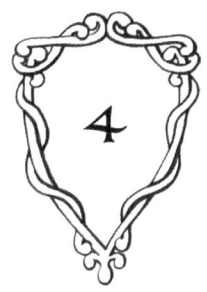

Blood Moon

*Even a man, who is pure in heart and
says his prayers by night,
May become a wolf when the wolfbane blooms and the
autumn moon is bright The Wolf Man (Movie, 1941)*

At the sound of the breaking glass, everyone in the room froze and looked at the window.

It was about 8 feet above the floor and was approximately 8 feet by 12 feet. There was a mesh cage around it that resembled a chain link fence, but about twice as thick.

An enormous black fur covered hand or paw easily spiked through the meshing and then pushed it aside as one might crumple a piece of aluminum foil. It sounded like nails scratching on a blackboard.

The large window was blotted out by a black form and then a head over five times the size of a human poked through. Sterling and the one called "Mike" shrieked, "Noooooo!" My and Doug's mouths opened in silent "Ohhhs" and the third orderly screamed like a primate.

The gigantic head oriented its face to us, and we could see a short snout and blazing yellow eyes. Blood dripping from me as I went, I scurried across the floor over towards the bed and pressed myself against the cold wall my legs barely moving beneath me.

Did it actually smile right before it slipped through the window as graceful as a gymnast?

The beast landed on its feet without making a sound. Amazing! It stood as tall and was as heavy as a large male Grizzly Bear.

I smelled something pungent, musky and suggesting a very dominant male. It was the same smell as Gentlesse's urine! I felt like I was in a dream, all the physical action seemed to slow down while my observation and thinking became incredibly clear.

I thought, he had been suggesting that he would return as a wolf. I had thought he was mad. But…NO… much more than a wolf. No wolf man movie had prepared me for this. He was not Lon Chaney Jr. in a fright mask and a black shirt. He was not a wolf hunkered down on four feet.

He was about twelve feet tall and upright and looked like a cross between a bear and a wolf. But he had the perfect proportions of a human being. His hands resembled paws but were prehensile with opposable thumbs.

On each finger and toe was a claw about three to four inches long. He was covered in thick black fur and, like a gorilla, it was everywhere except his face, abdomen and chest. He had a heavy brow; huge yellow eyes and his mouth formed a short snout. When he opened its mouth, menacing canine teeth were visible.

Within less than a second of landing, the beast closed the distance with the first orderly, grabbed his arm and shook him like a terrier would a snake; the man whimpered and groaned. The animal looked like a toddler mopping the floor with a rag doll. The right side of the orderly's face collapsed with a sickening crack and blood shot almost to the vaulted ceiling.

Next, with another sweep, the top of his head was smashed in like the shell of a boiled egg. The arm the monster was holding ripped off at the shoulder and a stream of blood followed the rest of the lout's body as it sailed across the room to crash with a smushing noise against the wall.

The Lycan stood for an instant looking at the bloody arm he held.

Mike and Doug stood between the beast, Dr. Sterling and I on the floor. Sterling pulled out a snub nose revolver and fired all five rounds in rapid succession. The timing of the shots was precise; this told me that the surgeon was an expert marksman.

The sound of the gun's report was both startling and disorienting. My ears began to ring; I covered my ears with my hands. Although he was less than ten feet away from Sterling three of the bullets wildly missed their enormous target.

One bounced off the brute's massive chest and ricocheted directly into Doug's head. I could see a geyser of bone, blood and brains erupt from the back of his head and he dropped like a stone. The final bullet hit the beast in the right shoulder, flattened and dropped harmlessly to the ground.

Mike fell on his butt, arched his body, and tried to crab walk backwards away from the creature. More quickly than the eye could follow the werewolf was on him and grabbed both of his arms in one oversized hand. "Please no!" The trapped man cried.

The giant animal looked and pointed at me and shook his head gesturing "No!"

Lifting the large man off the ground as if he were an infant, the monster jerked his arms abruptly outwards. Mike's body simply was torn in two with his head parting with his left shoulder. There was a shower of blood and internal organs and the victim's heart was thrown a few feet in the air.

Quicker that the fastest martial artist, the creature caught it in his mouth bit and slowly chewed. He then looked at Sterling and me. He slowly swallowed his grisly snack, and his chest and shoulders went up and down. Was he silently laughing?

The huge beast licked his lips and eyed Sterling. Sterling covered his eyes like a small child at a horror movie and let out a high-pitched scream. The were-beast was on him in the space of a thought. He grabbed the doctor with his left hand by the breast of his jacket as he lifted him and brought his face up to his own savage visage.

The doctor was whimpering and had his eyes closed. The Beast seemed annoyed by the doctor's cowardice. He found his voice. The room rumbled with the depth of his voice and the doctor's well-groomed hair was blown backwards.

The behemoth sneered, and mocking the surgeon's words, said "Open your eyes, Sterling. It would be a shame to have to cut your eyelids off"! The werewolf made a satisfied laughing noise. His voice was like rumbling thunder.

Sterling's eyes popped open.

Suddenly there was a darkening at the crotch of his pants followed by a flood of urine. The wolf took the claw from his right forefinger and made a long slash across Sterling's forehead. He then pushed the physician out the door.

I heard a scuffling as Sterling crawled away and then a panicked running down the hall. A trail of blood followed him.

The beast turned to me, kneeled and had a look on his face like a smiling dog. He waggled his jaw and opened his mouth and his face transformed into a gigantic version of Gentlesse's. His voice was another worldly Basso Profundo. The room resonated with his eldritch words. I could feel them vibrate my body.

"I know this has to be beyond your understanding. There is no earthly explanation for it. If you agree, I can make you like me. It will require a mild bite. However, if you do, you will never be the same and we will be mated for life.

For the three days of the full moon, you will be like me. You will retain your cognitive ability and even have speech. BUT, you will need to eat human flesh on one day of the full moon to survive.

You can leave now as a human with or without me. I will hoist you through the window, but you will have to run and hide, and your survival will depend on your remaining strength. In your weakened state, it is doubtful you can live.

I can begin the transformation process and take you out of here. Or we can follow a course that will end this injustice and give you and all the victims' revenge. I can begin the process and you can stay here until tomorrow night when the moon rises.

Your first "turning" will occur then. You will be much better than you are now. After the bite you will see.

They will take you to a surgical amphitheater where Sterling is planning to lobotomize you at 8 P.M as a sacrifice to the demon they worship. They usually have the theater filled with their many of their cult. The director, financial backers, the involved orderlies the abusers and lobotomized wives will all be there. No matter the circumstances, the demon compels blood at that time.

An orgy always follows the operation.

I learned this from your husband just by use of "intense interrogation". He cried like a baby. I turned and left him in a shallow grave in the woods. You will turn at exactly 8:10 tomorrow evening when the moon fully rises. You will become energized and ferocious, but you will remain in complete control of yourself.

You will feel euphoria, perhaps mania. But you will be able to direct your actions.

There will be just enough time for them to bind you and gather the medical instruments. You will have more than enough time and strength to break through your restraints. I will join you through the front door, the only entrance and exit, to the amphitheater.

We will have to slaughter everyone, even the innocents. Leaving the wounded alive would cause them to also transform like me. And it is also the only way to not leave any evidence.

Tell me which option you prefer."

I looked at the behemoth that was waiting calmly on bended knee. I had never been so frightened. My heart felt like it would beat out of my chest.

I thought of Sterling's sneering face. Suddenly I thought of all the years I was afraid and had no choice but to be meek and bullied. All the indignities I had suffered from cruel and thoughtless people. Men who had leered and catcalled me. Anger welled within me when I flashed on Sterling's smirk and something snapped.

With a wicked smile, I said, "Vengeance".

The gigantic beast grinned viciously.

The were-beast took my left hand in both of his and in a gesture resembling a proposal of marriage, bit into the fleshy part of my left palm. Blood gushed from the one-inch gash until the wolf licked it and then only a small dimple was left.

Then I saw his ears oriented to door.

The werewolf said, "They are coming. It begins. Courage!"

The creature gave me another dog like smile and uttered a guttural, "To- morr-oooooooooooow" as he leaped out the window as adroitly as a circus lion jumping through a hoop.

I felt a strange sense of wellness and energy filled my body. I noticed that the dark bruises from the restraints that had been on my wrists were gone. There was no pain in my shoulders, legs or bottom.

I sat against the cold tile wall beneath the window and smiled.

I sat and looked at the puncture mark in my hand and could feel my body healing. The pain being erased as if by some form of magic; I thought about what he said.

What I just saw… could it be possible? The carnage on the floor was proof enough that the magnificent beast that had come in through the window was offering to save me, to end this, and show me a way to relief.

I scooted back towards the bed, knowing suddenly that Sterling would soon be back with a team of men. I gained courage by savoring the actions of the were-man, his strength and agility, how he tore the men in two. I thought about his carnal beauty, his incredible size, and his promise to come for me.

Could I really become like him?

Yes! And then Sterling will be at MY mercy.

I looked down at my thighs and the welts of the beating were gone; the bleeding had stopped. I grabbed at the sheet on the bed and wound it around myself. I was cold and shaking and had wished that he had not run off so quickly.

In a flash, I discerned the clicking of metal tipped shoes striking ceramic tile at the beginning of the hall.

The door burst open and Dr. Sterling and a team of men rushed in. Two of them slipped on the blood by the door, falling over onto each other. I laughed.

Sterling held a straitjacket in his hands, "Get this murderess up off the floor, and put her in the straitjacket" he said watching me. "Then take her down to the padded room by the amphitheater hallway so that I can observe her until tomorrow night's procedure" he declared.

The men picked me up off the floor, pulled the sheet from me, and pushed my arms forward into the jacket; they secured the back buckles and crossed my arms to secure them in place.

As they put the jacket on me, I could my sense of smell became more acute. I was flooded with odors, like discrete ribbons floating through the air. I could smell alcohol, and Sterling's fear as it started to permeate the room.

There were other scents as well, aftershave, soaps, detergents, sex, hormones, the copper smell of blood on the floor. I could smell the lingering odor of my monstrous wonder, his musk still in the room. I felt the sudden sting of longing and attachment.

My pulse quickened with Dr. Sterling watching me with his beady shifty eyes; I defiantly met his gaze every time.

They walked me barefooted down the corridor, through a maze of steel mesh cage doors that operated by buzzers. After some time, we finally came to the outside of a door with a padlock and slide bolt lock. There was a narrow rectangle of glass on the front of the door for viewing what was inside. The men unlocked the door and threw me in.

I knew they intended to hurt me with that throw. The floor was white and bouncy, and I rolled as they threw me. As I bounced off the back wall, I let out a deep moan. The men snickered as they slammed the door, and I could hear the slide lock find home. A light covered by a wire mesh was on in the room.

I flipped my head back to get the hair out of my face and eyes, rubbed my face on the padded walls wiping the sweat off. The room seemed warmer than normal; I could hear the scuffling of feet outside of the room. I thought I could hear men breathing. I had to lay my head down on the floor; the barrage of odors and feelings was too much. I tried to wiggle free of the straitjacket, it would not come off.

First the hunger came and then the thirst. An ache, a cavernous hole of need, every fiber of my being became famished and alive with a primal need. I inhaled the air in the room and tried to calm myself

I could smell the fear and confusion of people long since gone from this padded room. I could smell the sorrow and grief. I laid there and looked at the door, the way shadows were moving in front of it. I rubbed my tongue against my teeth. They felt sharp and pointed. At some point in the night sleep took me.

Upon waking something inside me shifted; awareness… someone was coming towards this room. I could hear it in the vibrations in the floor moving up my arms and legs. I tensed at the new awareness. The sliding of the long metal bolt grating against the housing was like nails on a chalkboard. I winced at the sound as the door was unlocked and opened.

It was Dr. Sterling, looking more composed, and his head was bandaged, his clothes changed. He directed the men to bring a chair in the room and stand by the door outside.

Sterling's face abruptly became hideous. He leaped to me and grabbed me by the front of the straitjacket. He screeched, "What was that thing? That…that… monstrosity?"

Suddenly, I felt giddy.

I tried to sound like caricature of the Angels and sang "My boyfriend's back and there's going to be trouble…"

Sterling slapped me across the face and menaced, "We can do the operation with or without anesthesia!"

I rejoined, "If you see him coming better cut out on the double."

Sterling said disgustedly, "Why you ARE out of your ruddy mind. I didn't think you would crack so soon. No sense trying to interrogate a raving lunatic.

"What a minute, Gentilesse…he said…I would find this case 'interesting' And that name, RavenWOLF. Could he have…Bah! All that milquetoast can do is send reports to important people that I make sure are never delivered."

His voice became frightened, "It will come out eventually. How long can a secret like this be kept?"

I giggled and said, "Long enough."

Sterling sat down on the chair and crossed his legs. He resumed his usual supercilious manner. He sighed deeply for a moment and took out his pen and began writing on his clipboard. "Mary, I have decided to help you." He said as he scribbled on his paperwork.

I tried to prepare for some trick.

"There is no use in your fighting or being worried anymore. After tonight you'll see, all that is you or ever was will be gone…I am just finishing up the paperwork that prescribes a full-frontal lobotomy." The surgeon said with a smirk.

He calmed and became his usual arrogant self.

"I did want to offer my very own parting gift, something special from me to you" he said. He knelt on the soft padded floor and put his paperwork on the chair by the door. I could smell the blood, the wound on his forehead as he came closer to me. Due to the straight jacket, I was unable to grab him out.

"I will be coming for you later, you bastard" I hissed at him, the back of his hand found my face, but the usual sting was gone. He pinned me down by sitting on my chest and shoulders, pulled his pants down a little, and began to masturbate in my face.

"I want you to watch, so keep those pretty eyes open" he said as he stroked away in front of my face. It only took him just a few minutes.

Dr. Sterling stood up, buckled his pants and grabbed his clipboard. He sneered at me and said, "and everyone who would not seek the Lord, the God of Israel, was to be put to death, whether small or great, whether man or woman."

I said, "You're quoting the Holy Book is blasphemy!"

Before the door slammed, I laughed and murmured, "Kill ya later, Speedy Gonzalez."

Although I knew I should be frightened, my mood increased as the day went on. I could see by the mesh covered clock on the wall that it was approaching 4 PM. Over the past eight hours I went from feeling desperate to feeling stronger and healthier. I noticed that there were no bruises on my body and that rather than pain I felt an electrical current running through my limbs.

All my senses sharpened dramatically. My ears actually moved to follow the direction of the faintest noise. I could hear the squirrels playing in the woods outside of the building and the rustling of leaves on the trees. When I focused on the grout in the tiles of the room, they appeared to be huge furrows. My nostrils flared as I noticed the smell of the dust in the room; antiseptics the very smell of the tiles the scent of everyone who had been in the room with me and even of prior occupants.

By 5 o'clock it appeared I was growing in length and girth. I am an average sized woman. By 6:30 PM there was a noticeable lengthening and widening of my entire form. By 6:45 PM, I was aware that I must be about 6 feet tall and weighed about 190 pounds.

Although I am relatively hairless, any of the blonde body hair I did possess became noticeably darker. By 7 PM, I was approximately six foot four inches tall and the straitjacket was beginning to pull apart at its seams.

My body growth continued to gradually increase. By 7:30 PM I found myself in an almost unbelievably elated mood. I was incredibly ravenous, but it felt good.

For some reason, a silly old Warren Zvon rock song came into my mind. It was one of those songs that my strictly religious father would not allow me to listen to. Around Halloween, I and the other kids would sometimes hear it on shopping trips. It had made me laugh then. I tittered as I sung it out loud.

"I saw a werewolf walking in the rain, with the Chinese menu in his hand.

He was looking for the place called Lee Ho Fook's going to get a big dish of beef chow mien.

Ahoooo, werewolves of London, ahoooooo. Ahooooo, werewolves of London, Ahooooo!"

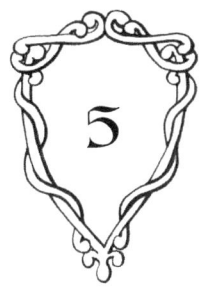

A Big Bowl of Beef Chow Mein

Feel what it's like to truly starve, and I guarantee that you'll forever think twice before wasting food. Jami Criss

My ears twisted imperceptibly to the door. At the head of the hall, I heard the click, click, click of a woman's heels walking towards me. I smelled the scent of the red headed woman who had abused me two nights ago. At this point I had no idea of my strength or power of the gift he had given me.

A thought leaped into my mind: "Rip his lungs out, Jim… Gonna have a big dish of beef chow mien". I chuckled manically. I found myself salivating. But then my reason kicked in. I struggled within myself. "Must wait… revenge…. end this all. And Sterling! Yes Sterling!!

I began singing "Dum, dum …dum dum,…dum da de dum… Ahoooo, werewolves of London…Ahoooo……

Just then the redheaded aide opened the door and blanched at what she saw. She slammed the door and I smelled fear. It was like rancid sweat. I could hear her running back up the hall.

I laughed and continued singing. "Dum, dum …dum dum, Dum da de dum…Ahoooo werewolves of London…Ahoooo….."

At about 7:45 PM, Sterling opened the door and entered with ten large male orderlies. "What the Hell!" He uttered. That dumb bitch Angie wasn't exaggerating. What could have caused this? Some pituitary imbalance brought on by stress. Perhaps Excited Delirium?"

The men with him hesitated. I could smell the putrid odor of fear. It excited me! I pretended to struggle against the useless straitjacket. "As big and scary as she looks, she is helpless in that jacket. But watch her legs!" Sterling proclaimed. "Get that big bitch strapped on to the gurney and wheel her to the operating amphitheater. We still have a show to perform."

It took six of the men to lift me on to the gurney. They strapped me down, and it took of their full strength to wheel me out to the corridor. I knew I could snap the heavy leather straps on my arms and legs like strands of wool. I smiled, broadly…manically.

Then, amid the kaleidoscope of lights, noises as subtle as the mice in the attic, and smells of the men's' colognes, the cotton of their uniforms, their sweat, the newly painted corridor and all the antiseptic was a stream of an unmistakable scent. Gentlesse!! Gentlesse was near; something in the blood made my heart sing out. Revenge was near!

I laughed out loud and screamed in my put-on floozy voice, "Mr. G is here!"

One of the men said, "I told you she is cray -cray!"

The six men struggled to push the gurney up the corridor and into a well-lit and proper looking hall. The orderlies and Dr. Sterling, with his hands folded behind his back, followed behind. They wheeled me to a large wooden double door. When they opened it, I could hear the applause and hoots of a large crowd of people. The lights and smells overwhelmed me for a second and then I came back to razor sharp clarity.

I knew that, despite the full change not having happened yet, I could break these restraints and do heavy damage. Sterling was dead already and he didn't even know it. I smiled broadly as I thought, "They think I am helpless inside with them. But….they are powerless inside with me!"

As they began the laborious task of pushing my ever-changing form to the circular center of the amphitheater; the clapping, hooting and now cat calls continued. "Look at the big bitch!" someone shouted. "I like long legs, but she could be an NBA center!" one wag offered.

Once on center stage, Sterling came close to my head. Orderlies positioned themselves four on each side of the gurney, and four more behind them. I could see a digital clock projection and the time said "7:59". Sterling cupped his hands around my ear and said, "They like you Mary! This is all for you! You're the star". I thought, "What the Hell, a star should put on a good show! I replied, "A bloody good show!"

I laughed out loud and then began to sing out in what could have been a low man's tenor voice.

"Dum, dum ...dum dum... dum da de dum...Ahoooo werewolves of London...Ahoooo...... and continued the verse over and over.

I continued my loud singing. By 8:01 PM I was over 7 feet tall and weighed over 350 pounds. The gurney creaked with the strain. I felt better each moment that passed a rush of adrenaline. However, my heartbeat was steady. I experienced an eerie calm and a focus – and a hunger.

I glanced overhead and could see tiers of church- like pews spiraling upwards that were fully occupied by prosperous fat men, vacant eyed women and male and female orderlies. They all looked like people at a horror movie frightened but enjoying the show.

Dr. Sterling lifted his hands and shouted to the crowd. "Ladies and Gentlemen! Ladies and Gentlemen! Please quiet down and let us begin!

The physician lowered his head as if in prayer and said, "Let us begin this offering to our Lord."

"Wives submit to your husbands for man was not created for woman's sake; but woman was created for man's sake!" This was met with a resounding chorus of "Amen" from the audience.

"Former Governor Hathforth, Senator Waylens, Mr. and Mrs. Huges, Mr. and Mrs. Rocfoiler, the Wellington brothers, James and George, Police Chief Ramford, Sheriff Jameston, with your gracious financial and logistical support, we present another of our little shows.

Fellow members of the New Earth Church, Pastor Mathers thank you for your fellowship and contributing the subjects for our presentations. Unfortunately, Charles Young, our subject's husband is not in attendance. I suspect he will be along shortly."

I thought, "Yeah, by now he is being chewed on by rats in the woods somewhere". I noticed that I was about seven and a half feet tall and over 400 lbs. This made me laugh out loud. I then continued the song.

"Ahooo, werewolves of London, Ahoo....."

"As you can see our subject is .... howling mad! Some unknown factors have caused this unusual growth in our subject. We will have to retain her for further investigation and probably vivisection. Considering how unrestrained she is, this full-frontal lobotomy will give this poor wretch much needed relief.

Now, Mary here has caused us considerable...err.... inconvenience. CONSEQUENTLY, and we all do love our consequences" .... Applause and hooting erupted from the crowd. Sterling held up his hands to indicate the need for silence; 'An eye for an eye and a tooth for a tooth.' We will administer the procedure WITHOUT anesthesia!"

Dr. Sterling laughed and then raised his hands for silence. He signaled to eight orderlies and they braced my arms and legs. Sterling turned his back and gathered his instruments.

I noticed that it was 8:09 PM. I began to feel a sense of expanding. My head, body and limbs felt like they were shocked by electric currents. An intense pain started in the center of my body and spiked as it worked its way to my extremities.

Just then, from the front doors a sound like a cannon firing blasted. One of the big oak doors exploded across the room almost to the stage. Three rows of people in the pews were sloppily decapitated. Blood gushed as high as the ceiling from jagged severed necks and with meaty thuds a dozen heads showered the center stage.

Three of the distinguished guests in the lower pews were crushed between the detached door and the railing to the stage. They shrieked and desperately tried to hold in their erupting internal organs. With a splat, a huge gut pile formed at their feet. Looks of shock were painted across the faces of people sitting nearby.

In the doorway was the silhouette of a giant ogre, as big as a male grizzly and like a cross between a wolf and a bear. His eerie yellow eyes shined like taillights. I smelled the pungent musk of Gentleness's scent.

8:10: My body began to thrash; the pain was intolerable, the expansion of my bones creaking and snapping in my body; I began to scream – this scream soon turned into a howl.

My body convulsed under the restraints. Then my mind went white and then I didn't feel a thing. Within the space of a minute, my body exploded in growth. Snapping under too much pressure the straitjacket and heavy leather restraints flew off my body like rubber bands

I was about 10 feet tall and weighed about a thousand pounds. Except for my face, chest and stomach my body was covered in a black downy fur. My naked breasts were perfectly shaped as if sculpted by one of the old masters. My face, except for top protruding canine teeth, was unchanged.

The eight orderlies circling me recoiled away and stepped back. Sterling dropped a medical device that resembled ice cream scoop and his mouth opened and eyes widened. He screamed as he inhaled and went ashen white.

I didn't need any time to orient myself. I immediately kicked out both feet and the four orderlies at my legs were propelled the fifteen feet across to the rail that separated the seating area from the stage proper. Three of them were killed upon impact while the fourth cracked his head with a huge surge of blood against the rail. He would die in moments.

The were-woman that had been me found herself laughing. I grabbed the orderlies on the left and right of the restraint table by their arms and smashed them together like a toddler crushing her dolls together. The one on my left hit the other one with the top of his head in the face and it was crushed in a spray of blood. The other's face was pushed into the back of his skull killing him instantly.

I sat up and saw Sterling paralyzed in place with his mouth frozen in an "O". My vision took on a red haze and with cat-like speed I seized him by the back of his hair with my left hand. I laughed and in a deep unearthly voice said, "The devil will quote scripture to his own end" and I shoved the fingers of my right hand in his eyes and my thumb in his mouth.

I jerked my hands forcibly in opposite directions. The bones supporting his face and his and upper row of teeth came off in my hand. The stream of blood followed my right hand – I smiled a little at the sound and feel of his blood in my hands.

I immediately popped it into my mouth and chewed. It tasked like an exquisite combination of veal and pork.

Sterling dropped to the floor in quivering in a heap. He was still alive but in shock. I could see his exposed brain, the meat inside of his head, his naked eyeballs dangling from their optic nerves, the triangle where his nose had been and his lower jaw. Every time his heart beat, blood gushed from his face.

The rest of the orderlies were frozen in place. I sat up snarling and thrashing. Marveling at how easy it was, I smiled to myself. I grasped two of the orderlies nearest to me by their soft heads and squeezed my clawed hands into their skulls; they popped like grapes in my hands. The hot gush of blood sprayed across the stage floor.

The crowd shrieked and gasped in wonder. I looked at my own blood and brain-soaked hands and jumped sprightly off the gurney.

On my haunches I growled and snarled at the other two orderlies, I wanted to taste their blood, to rip them apart. I grabbed one and pulled him close to me while moving towards the other. I bit and chewed at his face while I had the other one by the leg. As I killed him the hot gush of blood in my mouth and trembling of his body fascinated me. I ripped off the face of the other one snapped his neck and licked the hot blood.

Angie, the red-haired orderly that led my female abusers was in the front row and tried to turn and run. I seized her by her right leg and hoisted her to my shoulder height. I grabbed her other leg and then paused to look in her face. Her eyes were wide, and her mouth was opened in a look of disbelief.

"Make a wish", I rumbled to her. And then I ripped her legs apart.

I found myself holding Angie's legs in my hands. Blood from her torso flared up to the tiled ceiling, staining it brownish red and showered my head and shoulders. The rest of her body fell to my feet. Her face was frozen in a gruesome, open mouthed death mask.

I laughed. I threw her legs at her black comrade who ran as if she could get away.

I could hear Gentlesse at the front of the crowded amphitheater, smashing and rampaging through the terrified crowd. He had started a stampede. He crushed and mauled, shook the onlookers as he made his way through the crowd. Snapping women and men as if they were mere twigs, throwing them along the walls, blood spattering everywhere.

I turned to the crowd of onlookers, those that had jeered and laughed at my form. I leapt into the crowd, slashing and decapitating as I went, pulling out kidneys and lungs, rolling in the viscera. The crowd shrieked and moved away from me as I galloped though, slashing and chopping.

The electric current of excitement and feeding made me euphoric. The more I killed the more I enjoyed it. I had only just started to satiate my desperate hunger.

I slowed my pace and watched Gentlesse as he worked his way through the crowd. He was a beautiful killing machine; every move was absolute precision. He ravaged the crowd; everyone was screaming and pleading for their lives. He was an artist; his physical strength was unsurpassed.

Growling and moving towards a group of three people, he ripped open two of their bellies. With looks of awe and shock on their faces the people toppled over their own guts. Biting and ripping the flesh from thighs and hips. Blood was dripping from his enormous mouth and canine teeth. His eyes flashing yellow as he moved from person to person.

I let out a "Hawwrooooooooooooooo" in admiration of his work. He turned and looked at me; did I detect a wink?

I snatched the sheet from the gurney and wrapped it around my chest.

I moved into the remnants of the crowd where Gentlesse stood over some of the fools of this cult,

I clutched a remaining man by the throat, moved my snout close to his face, and growled in it. Even as it escaped my throat I was shocked at how deep and reverberating the sound was. The look of fright in the man's eyes was ecstasy.

I licked at his face, and then bit down hard over his mouth. Feeling his muffled scream as I slowly bit down on his cheeks, crushing his jaw in my mouth. I pulled at the flesh of his cheeks, sweet soft fleshy meat. I swallowed it down and licked my lips. I crushed his windpipe as he let out his final gasp.

I paused and I took a moment to look around

. My counterpart stood in front of the open door destroying anyone who attempted to escape. Some of the police officers had fired their nine-millimeter Beretta 92s at him. A few people had been killed by the ricochets from his body.

There was a pile of bodies around him of the people who had the courage, or the fear, to rush him. Blood splatter literally covered the wall and the floor behind him. There were torsos without limbs or without heads. The great beast was in the process of knocking off the head of a police officer who had gotten to close.

About three quarters of the spectators in the theater were slaughtered carcasses. The governor and senators and their wives were in the rear. The rich people were pulling women orderlies and some of the lobotomized wives if front of them.

Gentleese approached them from the right and I from the left.

The Pastor hid behind one of the lobotomized wives and was shouting prayers. "It is with the finger of God that I cast you out! My Lord casts you out!", he shouted and made a pointing gesture.

The giant stopped, looked him in the eyes and rumbled, "You don't serve Jesus! We know who you do serve!" Gentlesse hit him on the top of the head with a hammer fist. His head collapsed like old time top hat and blood erupted in a circle from the area of his shoulders.

I shouted at my former pastor, "A man cannot serve two masters!".

Gentilesse noticed that he had slightly gashed the lobotomized woman. He said, "I am sorry. Sleep child" and sighed. He gently took the woman's head in his hands a sharply twisted her head so that it was facing her back and moved on.

I looked at the faceless Sterling and saw him rise to his knees. With a quick movement reminiscent of a frog biting a dragon fly, I snapped off his head. Blood spurted all over my head and the body dropped. The taste in my mouth was like the most luscious silky-smooth blood pie.

Six of the dignitaries cautiously approached me. The two in the front produced Charter Arm Bull Dog 44 Special Revolvers from their front pants pockets. They stood in Weaver stances and quickly fired their 5 rounds each. Their aim was better than Sterling's had been the night before. Six of the bullets struck me at the center of my mass.

"Those are Buffalo Bore bear loads" one of the men in the back chortled. I felt a slight pressure where the bullets impacted, but those that didn't bounce off me, simply flattened and dropped to the ground. I was amazed.

The six corpulent men froze and two in the back shuddered. In less than a heartbeat, I was on them and knocked the head off the man in front and back handed the man next to him crushing the side of his head.

The three remaining men began to turn to run. A thought came to me. "See how they run like pigs from a gun, see how they hide". I bowled into them cutting them to slivers with my claws.

I watched Gentlesse finish off the others, the room was still… the coppery smell of blood thick in the air…" Ahrrooooooooooo" I howled and curved my head backwards; blood dripping from my mouth. I ran to him sniffing the air as I went.

I decided to stay back several feet from him, giving the massive beast a wide birth as he feasted upon the plump thigh of a random administrator. He pulled and snapped at the meat. He looked up at me; licked his bloody chops and howled a deep gurgling howl. He snorted and looked around the room.

Gentlesse snatched up my medical record. "Let's go" he rasped.

6

Free in the Woods

As if the world and they were hand in glove William Cowper

I ran behind the enormous man-beast towards the deep woods that surrounded the facility. I was filthy with viscera and blood, gore dripping from my body and fur. We sped through the underbrush in a blur until we reached the shores of a large, serene lake.

Dawn was breaking over the water. The wolf turned and looked at me, his yellow eyes glowing like the moon that was descending further in the morning light. As I stumbled towards the lakeshore, I could see something inside of him shift, and I felt it too

Crawling forward as dawn began to break, I could feel myself shrink, my bones crunching back into their original places, body losing mass and hair receding. With the setting of the moon and the coming of dawn, I watched him return to human. I could see his fur retreat into his muscular body. His transition back into the doctor was smooth.

I moved closer to the edge of the water, closer to him. I cried out in pain as my body transformed from an immense beast, back to itself. My heart raced as the transition happened.

I pulled myself closer to him as I crawled along the shore, and we moved into the water together, washing each other's body. I let myself sink letting all the air out of my lungs as I sank deep into the dark water. Moving my hands through my hair to wash the gore out,

I rose to the surface to find Dr. Gentlesse washing his perfectly shaven head, and staring at me, as if the wolf that he was had retreated inside of him.

I swam closer to him in the cold water, shivering. "I don't know what to say to you…you saved me and set me free. I am in your debt forever." I said to him.

He smiled just a little and reached through the water and pulled me close to his warm body. "We are connected, forever. We have always been." he breathed into my neck as he pulled his body closer. I could feel his warmth pressing against me.

I looked into his eyes. His gentle caresses and soft kisses were comforting as he moved his mouth along my pale collar bone; he lifted me in his arms and took me back out of the water.

His car was nearby. He carried me trembling towards his car; he opened the door to the black sedan. "Here my dear, wrap yourself in these towels", and he handed me exceptionally large beach towels. It felt soft and warm, and I could detect just the faintest odor of almonds in the fibers. He dressed, as I watched, beach shorts and a pullover, and some flip flops. I studied his body as he dressed, his muscles rippled as he did.

Watching his penis sway as he dressed made me blush. He opened the door to his car and drove me along the causeway away from the island. I pulled the towel around myself as we pulled up to a small white house sitting on the beach.

"I am bringing you home, where you belong" he said as we pulled into the driveway. "Come with me, and rest" he said. He took me into his large and opulent home.

It was marvelously serene, with the scantest number of decorations. Katana swords hung ceremoniously from the walls. Japanese art and white marble floors; fine oriental rugs with simple patterns. He led me into a large bedroom that had a bathroom off it.

The room was massive with a view of the beach, the pink light rising in the morning sky. He began to draw a bath for me. He seemed to watch more than talk. He even put bubbles in it, which smelled of almonds.

"Drink some wine, it will make you feel better, more relaxed after a night of carnage" he said. As he handed me a glass his eyes glistened with some interior light. I sipped at the wine and looked into his eyes.

"May I pin your hair up Mary?" he asked in a very calm voice. "Yes, please doctor" I said. He wound my hair up very gently, and pinned it up off my neck, and used a loofah to wash my neck.

I finished my wine and emerged wet and soapy from the tub. He approached me with a fresh towel and began to dry me off. He smelled spicy and warm, his every touch with the towel excited me, brought some of that beast out in me. There was a need, something in the blood, an ache for him now. He picked me up and cradled me in his arms and took me to his bed.

He laid me on my back still swaddled in his towel, he had his shorts on, and his shirt was off. He hovered over me, looking into my eyes. I moved my mouth towards him, a desperate longing to kiss this man, this savior

I could feel his teeth, his canines with my tongue. I could almost taste the people he had feasted upon earlier in the night. He breathed hard as we kissed, and he pressed himself against my pale naked body. I was so much smaller than him, his muscular frame, and his broad shoulders.

"Mary", he breathed in my ear, "I need you" he whispered. I pulled at him, building his excitement.

I moved my legs so that I was now sitting on him; he was so regal beneath me. As I leaned over to kiss his mouth, I could feel the stubble of his face, very slightly.

'Quando tu Gaius, ego Gaia.'" he sighed. I moved my hands to my breasts then into my hair with the pleasure of riding him.

I growled as I started crying out – "OH…please…OH…" He quickened his pace. He caressed my hips and kissed my back as I shivered.

I collapsed, shaking with pleasure; Van on top of me, sweaty from the force of our passion.

I slept away the next day and a half.

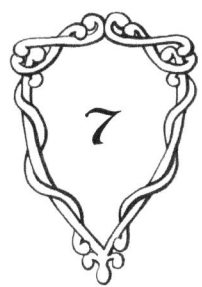

Ghosts in the Darkness

"... it was written I should be loyal to the nightmare of my choice." – Joseph Conrad, Heart of Darkness

On the last night of the full moon, we slipped effortlessly into the forest. We moved as easily as squirrels skipping along tree branches. Although we were as large as some mini automobiles, we made no missteps, left no tracks nor broke any branches. There was no evidence of where we had been, and we made no sounds. We defined the term "ghosts in the darkness".

Everything was surrealistically sharp and clear to me. I could see even the tiniest insect on the leaves, hear the quiet snoring of birds in the trees and the world was filled with the pungent bouquet of life. My arms and legs were where they needed to be, and it was if I and my mate were one body. We each knew exactly where the other was.

There was a sense of gliding. It was almost like floating. There was no strain, no jarring or labored breathing like running.

Time seemed suspended, as we passed startled deer that were only partially aware of us after we were gone. Just a little ahead of us, I smelled distinct scents that smelled like sweaty locker room, mixed with soap, perfume, cotton and leather.

I could discern six distinct heartbeats swishing and beating at different rates. From those sounds I could detect exactly where each one was. Then I saw a small party of people wandering the woods in search of something.

From perhaps a mile away, I could see four men and two women inching their way through the woods. I noticed that two of men and one of the women had motion picture cameras. Another's camera was infrared.

At about a half a mile away, I heard one of the men whisper, "What's that glimmering ahead?" Immediately after, I and Van playfully barreled through them knocking them around like bowling pins. Van turned back for a millisecond to deflect a man before his head could be shattered on a small boulder. We then sped on into the night.

From about a quarter of a mile, we could hear the party hitting the ground with various thumps and whacks. We heard a baritone voice exclaim, "I think I got it! I got a picture of Big Foot!" A woman's alto voice cried, "Look for evidence! Scat or tracks!" I heard a soft laugh from my mate.

I saw light coming up at a bedazzling speed. It was the New Earth Church, my old congregation.

I caught a scent of several dozen distinct men and about 20 women: and old wood and brick. I could smell gasoline and the exhaust from many cars. There were 50 heart beats arranged in rows inside of a wooden and brick structure.

There was the smell of two men in a car close to front of the building and a man and a woman in a car behind the building. We stopped just short of the thinning of the woods. From about three quarters of a mile away we could hear the two policemen talking inside their patrol car.

There was another, more familiar scent. I knew it was my youngest sister!

"We drew the easy job, Bill", the first officer said. "We just have to babysit these people in their memorial service while the boys finish up the job".

"I don't know, Jim," the other man replied. "The nut house was a really creepy scene. It looked like my Uncle Earl's slaughterhouse in there. If we had found any explosive residue, I would have sworn that bombs were set off. There were no witnesses, and obviously we don't want to get Homeland Security involved.

More parishioners are arriving."

"Well, we've got to clean up all the loose details now." Jim said casually. That Mary Young woman sounds like she had something to do with it. Some of the boys said she did some strange things while she was hospitalized. From the shape of the bodies, we couldn't tell if she was one of them. The others got her family tonight. We didn't get anything out of them. "

"Yeah", Bill replied casually. "They cut their father's throat in front of them, then the oldest sister's. The women didn't know the truth and then they raped the mother and daughters. Afterwards, they strangled them to death.

Jim said, "I wish I could snap the smallest's neck like a chicken. I like to hear them choke." They both laughed out loud.

Suddenly, the interior of the patrol car was blotted out as massive dark forms appeared on either side. "Oh, my God, the windows are open!" Bill screamed.

Van and I each pulled a deputy by their heads out through the windows of the sheriff's cruiser. I sat on the one called "Jim" in what is called a mount position in Jujitsu. Despite having a thousand pounds of were-beast crushing his upper body, the lawman seemed hypnotized by the gigantic breasts swaying above him.

"Men!!"

"Choke?" I growled. I held his forehead with my left hand and pushed my enormous fore and middle fingers into his mouth. I pushed them into his larynx and held them there. I smiled as I saw his eyes widen in panic as he began to gag.

With one huge hand, Van was holding the other deputy by his hair just above the ground. The pain kept the man from screaming and flailing made the captive's body agonize more. Van gave him an evil smile and pointed to me and his partner.

The man pinned under me began to squirm and struggle and made desperate choking noises. His eyes filled tears and bulging pleaded with me. I pushed my fingers harder and, in an eruption of blood, bone and tissue, his head exploded. There was a shower of gore that rose about eight feet in the air. I looked towards them and like a child might slurp the frosting from a cake, liked my fingers.

Van put the man down but held on to his hair. In a voice that made James Earl Jones' sound soprano, Van whispered, "Tell the truth and I will not kill you. How many and where?"

The smell of feces filled the air. The serial murderer named Bill appeared to have regressed to the psychological state of a scared little boy. "Golly, you won't hurt me Mister?" He pleaded. Van shook his head "No!"

Jim was shaking and sputtering. "Only the senior adepts are in the church…twenty…maybe fifty.

"What about the officers at the back of the church? Are they in on it?"

"They are newbies. But yeah, they know a little."

The huge werewolf put him down and backed off. What passed for a smile came to his lips. Jim fell to his knees and cried softly, "Thank you…thank you…thank you…"

In a quarter of a second, I had crossed the distance between them and tore out his throat. His body dropped hard; a torrent of blood flooded from its neck. There was that taste of pork and veal again, but much more exquisite than the previous night.

Van smiled. "It tastes better every time. It can become addictive. You come to crave it all the time". I was startled. "Your parents and sisters are already dead.

My heart dropped and tears rushed to my eyes. I was murderous. I reared up and pounded the policeman's body to mush.

Fortunately, my wolf mind was tougher and could accept the inevitable. My soul screamed in grief and vengeance.

"Let us plot our own little surprise for these murderers. But we must do something about your appearance. Your sister and congregation members will surely recognize you. Just seeing us might make your sister end up in Creedmoor. We will have to be stealthy".

I knew what he said was true; the salty taste of blood in my mouth and the power that I could now wield was like a drug–an aphrodisiac and stimulant.

I swallowed hard and spoke to him, "Van, teach me." With my stomach half full all I wanted to do was walk into the building in a blood lust, paint and decorate the walls with their entrails. To slash their throats and watch their surprise and the light fade from their eyes as they fell still begging to be spared.

I copied Van as he prowled through the underbrush along the perimeter of the building, staying low and following him. For such a massive creature he was extraordinarily light on his feet. We paused for a moment; I could hear the scuffling of feet on the hardwood floors inside the building. Some sort of tonal moaning coming from the inside, like a chant but dour and sinister.

"Two doors, locked, but six windows".

Van said, "Let us do something about your appearance. He instructed me to push out my jaw and raise my nose up. Amazingly a muzzle formed on my face. He cradled my face in his hands and said, "Che belle. Who couldn't love a face like that? Kind of sweet and silly; in a terrifying sort of way." He mused.

His touches were like little electric currents, I wanted to grab him, but he was monolithic in his current state. I wanted to kiss him but could not imagine the logistics of doing that with a 12-foot-tall wolfman.

I followed him in the underbrush towards the white painted front door. As we approached the chanting got louder and more rhythmic. It was neither words nor any language I had ever heard. I could pick out the scent of my youngest sister inside the doors.

I felt the hackles along my back rise. My family, my beloved mother and father, my precious sisters were dead. They were murdered by this cult. My kid sister was a captive inside this desecrated church.

To my advanced senses the scene was surreal; I saw the light coming through the church's windows like a photographic negative. The lights were the figure, and the building was the ground.

I could smell my sister's scent and their heartbeats told me that they had encircled the child. Her breathing was labored. I smelled a man behind her. There was the smell of an old woman and her weakened heartbeat suggested supreme age. She wore sickly sweet talc. There were two men at the front door.

There was car exhaust and the purr of a police car in the front of the church. Inside were two officers, a man and a woman.

What panicked me was the source of the light. It was being emitted by a source under the old woman. I could hear a throbbing and crawling, mewling sounds coming from it.

I was about to charge inside when a huge hand, half the size of my head covered my mouth. Van looked concerned. "Careful! Sheath!" he said. "We must try to avoid letting the girl see us unless it is absolutely necessary".

My ears oriented to the building and I heard a rhythmic chanting. "Maga Um…Maga…Um…Maggay Arga Agga Maga Um", the men repeated and built to a crescendo.

The crone was screaming exhortations that were indiscernible.

As gigantic as we were, we moved as stealthy as cats. We crept up to the church window. Our attention was immediately drawn to a crack in the empty air in the center of the floor.

Light was emitting from it and it appeared to be cracking like a chick might chip out of an egg.

My youngest sister, Sarah, was bound to a prayer bench and cinder blocks with her hands tied in a praying position and as a man stood before her. The crone was standing behind him with a serpentine knife and a golden goblet. She seemed to be exhorting the creature to break through.

I knew that, once the creature emerged at a certain point, my sister would have been garroted. And just as she died from strangulation her throat would be cut and her blood would be offered to the creature.

Just then, it was like a portion of empty floor, separated into a crease and a brownish yellow talon the size of a human hand emerged.

Van shouted, "Push has come to shove. I know what this is. Kill the deputies!", and he shoved me towards the police car.

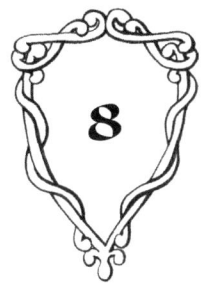

All Hell Breaks Loose

"Demons are like obedient dogs; they come when they are called." – Remy de Gourmont

Van shoved me hard against my flank and towards the police car. I bared my teeth and charged; my feet barely touched the ground.

A single clawed finger from my right hand scraped against the side of the patrol car, shaving metal in my wake. Both officers turned to see. I had their heads in my left hand before they could gasp in fright. Blood spurted out of necks and their bodies slumped over, hearts still pulsing blood onto the dirt pavement glistening in the moonlight.

I could hear the odd cacophony of mixed sounds and human voices. Men and women chanting and intoning non-synchronously. They were tapping their feet off beat. I could detect no words, only harmonics, the soft tapping of shoes on floors, heart beats and the smell of incense. The vibrations made it seem like I was rocking from side to side.

In milliseconds Van had breached the distance to the entrance, his unnatural form exploded through the double doors shattering wood propelling and smashing it against the adjoining walls. A few people were impaled by the wood splintered from the door. There were screams, muffled, gut wrenching cries as I approached the broken door.

Then I saw what they were doing inside.

There was a massive burning crevice in the floor, black smoke and embers strobed fiery red into the room. A deep moan came from its middle that shook and rattled in my diaphragm. The very floor trembled from the sound.

My naked sister knelt blindfolded and bound to a prayer bench and cinder blocks. I scanned the room, and Van was making quick work of the people dressed in red robes. I pounced on one and slashed and bit his throat, savoring the salty warm blood in my mouth.

I grabbed the arm of a woman, ripping it out of the socket; her shrieks were a delight as she tried to crawl away from me. I bit down on the back of her neck, feeling the vertebrae snap and pop in my mouth.

Everything in the room was chaos, many of the robed figures were dead, bodies mangled, blood gushing from faces, viscera steaming in the cool night. Van reared up on his haunches, slamming and killing with speed and godlike strength.

I moved towards him slipping slightly on the blood on the floor I plowed into the pews, pulling off arms, slashing open bellies and watching as their intestines poured onto the floor, others slipped and tripped over the viscera.

I felt euphoric, insane, and ultimately alive! I laughed aloud, pounced upon a man, and put my index finger on his lips and said 'Shhhhh". Then I ripped the rubbery skin off his face, peeling his scalp backwards off his head, his eyes in a panic, blood seeping into the sockets, bloody tongue searching for lips that had been torn off. I pulled out his windpipe and threw it across the room, his legs twitched under me .

I quipped, "Ya gotta be cruel to be kind!" to no one in particular.

Towards the back of the building, I found a woman cowering. I tugged off her red robe. She was naked underneath. I wrapped her hair around my fist and pulled her head close. I held her as if she were an infant.

I menacingly laughed. I said "There, there. It will be over soon. Go to sleep my little baby". As she closed, her eyes, I slashed her carotid artery, the hot spray of crimson blood running down her tanned body. Her mouth slackened and she went limp; her eyes vacant and she slipped onto the floor.

Something in the room seemed to shift; I could smell and feel it. The hairs on the back of my neck stood stiff and hard. The massive crack in the floor, that burned and sizzled, began to move. I backed away in fright and started to growl. Van continued, biting, clawing at the red robed, they fell in his wake.

I could smell the skinny, wirehaired crone, moving as if she were slithering approaching the vertical, glowing pit. Her face was deeply wrinkled, and her eyes were vacant milky white. She was the last of the clergy.

The witch looked strangely familiar. A hunched figure with a sourly leather face. She had a large nose with small black eyes and wore a white robe with a wide blue stripe and two smaller ones as a trim. She reeked of self-righteousness and hypocrisy.

I could swear I had seen her on the News. She smelled like "old ladies' talc" She held a serpentine Athame high above her head. She spoke words in a hissing raspy voice. In perfect Slavic laced English, she said, "Suffering is the most holy of acts!"

The hag then gave us a defiant look and plunged the dagger into her own chest. She grunted, and then fell forward into the pit; her body was enveloped in thick black smoke. A small tendril of this smoke settled like a garland in my hair.

The building quaked, the room quivered, floorboards buckled, and bodies rolled away. As the hole pushed wider apart, two large golden hands pulled a massive, gilded man up from the yawning pit.

He was bigger than Van, and absolute perfectly proportioned. His face was that of a classic angel. Jutting out of his shaven head were two amber, crescent shaped horns. Once he was out of the abyss, hundreds of perfect little people fluttered out on butterfly wings.

"Well, you Old Dog" his melodious bass intoned. "Still doing penance for the Sabine whores. You might have bitten off more than you can chew this time. I see all and hear all. Do you think you can best me?"

Without a word, Van rushed him and was greeted with a staggering upper cut to his jaw. Van grabbed the golden man's legs and knocked him crushingly on his back. Van crawled on top of him and began raining blows on the demon's head. Each punch was seismic.

The demon arched his hips and thighs forcibly upwards and Van was tumbled over his head.

I grabbed my sister, lifted her like a baby and began to run to the door. When the demon saw this, he waggled his finger and said, "No, no, little were- ling, we have plans for that virgin."

The demolished front doors flew back into place and reassembled themselves. I knew that they could not be opened by strength alone. Van staggered and put himself between my sister and I and the dark angel. He snarled a deep, furious growl.

The golden fiend moved with preternatural speed and grabbed Van in a headlock. Van tried to bite only to find that demonic skin was every bit as impenetrable as his own. The werewolf pushed his huge outer arm over the demon's head, placed a massive leg behind both demon's legs and twisted toward his rear. He smashed the fiend onto to its back.

Van managed to roll the golden beast over and grabbed the evil being's great horns. He put his right foot into the demon's back and heaved. Just at that point, the butterfly people began pelting both Van and me. I huddled over my sister and took the burning blows onto myself.

I could hear grunting sounds and managed a peek at the wrestling match going on. I could see veins bulging in Van's forehead and neck. He simply ignored hundreds of impacts from the tiny beings. I observed every muscle in both of his arms standing out in bold relief from his effort. Using all the might of his legs and back, he repeatedly wretched backwards.

With an abrupt, deafening roar and explosive crack, Van ripped both horns from the demon's head.

The devil's shrieks were like peals of thunder.

Van took advantage of the demon's freezing with pain, to shove the horns into the abomination's eyes. "What are you going to see and hear now, filth! "Van thundered" What are you going to see now!"

Immediately, the butterfly demon-lings all flew into Van. Dropping the horns, he backed up waving his arms as if you might swat swarming bees. The great amber devil managed to clench Van's neck and together they slowly, but steadily inched towards the gaping maw in the middle of the room.

Van expected the stench of sulfur but was greeted by the smell of frankincense and myrrh. His head and shoulders were in the yawning pit and the demon made himself deadweight while Van was continuously pelted by the lesser demons.

Van could see a bottomless swirling tunnel that became brighter red as it descended.

The golden fiend clasped his hands together and hung from the wolfman's colossal neck. He kept jerking his legs up and down to weaken Van. At the same time, each feeling like a shot gun blast, the swarm of butterfly winged imps smashed themselves into Van. He showed no reaction. He knew that their end game was to get him below where they could torture him forever.

Van had penetrated the powerful claws of his left hand and feet six inches anchoring himself into the front of the pit. He was methodically punching the demon on its lacerated left ear.

Each punch sounded like a pile driver incessantly ramming home. Except for jarring from each blow and a slight deformation of his face, the golden devil showed no sign of being hurt. Occasionally, Van crushed one of the small demons against the canyon's walls. It was a matter of endurance and pain tolerance for both.

Soon the demon's ear looked like a lump of chopped meat.

I could see Van's behemoth legs, waist and back protruding from the hellhole. My mind raced to find an escape. Cradling my whimpering and still blindfolded sister like a football, I thought to pull him back up to safety. I eliminated that choice.

I needed both arms to pull him out.

I clenched my sister and frantically looked around. A sense of fatalism and fear began to clutch my heart. I desperately cast about the room for something to use to help. Wooden boards, furniture, pews. Nothing seemed helpful.

Then I remembered! The horns! The horns had been able penetrate the evil brute!

I looked on the floor where Van had ripped those appendages off the golden beast and glimpsed a golden tip poking out of the debris and dust. I grabbed it with my free hand and felt a sting in my palm as the horn's tip tore a small puncture in my impenetrable hand. Rich thick blood dribbled from the wound.

I smiled as I realized I had a weapon.

I pulled out the great horn from its hiding place and took a quick look at it. It was about four feet long and inestimably sharp on its outside curve. It became less sharp as it approached its base. It would make the bulky scimitar for a normal person. At my size, it was like a large Arabic Jambiya knife. As I picked it up, I noticed its mate poking into a side wall.

My mouth twisted into a vicious smile. I stifled a howl so as not to startle my sister. With my sister cradled in my left arm and the horn held in an ice pick grip in my right. I leaped towards the pit and its desperate fighters.

In the flaming mouth of the chasm my eyes and nose burned. There was a sickly, thick smell of spices and the burning seized at my chest, my heart raced with fear that I might fall and be swallowed by the endless underworld.

The smell soon turned to the wretched odor of vomit and excrement. I leaned into the ferocious maw of the pit and slashed at the golden fingers clasping Van. The winged imps noticed me and flew into my face, arm and shoulder. Each contact was demolition but didn't break my skin.

As I dug the makeshift weapon across the demon's fingers, I prepared for a spray of blood. To my amazement, the fingers simply dissolved with an eerie hissing into steam. The Demon screamed and began to fall back into the ruby glow. The imps seemed to be spiraled down in his wake. He shouted "RRRRRROOOOOMMMMMUUUUULLLLUUUSS" as he fell.

Together, we pulled ourselves out of the crater. Van was enormous and had been hard to pull up, especially with only one arm. I tumbled back onto the floor with his weight crushing me. The hole quickly shrunk like a constricting pupil and then disappeared altogether. In his right hand, Van had one of the small imps. Its wings were practically torn off and it was either dead or unconscious.

I breathed heavy, and watched him rise to his feet, his eyes burning with intensity. Somehow, he seemed larger, as if the struggle had made him more formidable in size and bulk. I noticed that my sister, Sarah, who was nestled in my left arm, seemed noticeably smaller as if I had grown as well.

I nestled up to him shaking, holding the horn in my hand, I offered it to him. "A trophy my love", I whispered gutturally, and handed it to him. He considered the offering, took it in his and turned to me, "Thank you, my monstrous Beauty".

He spoke. "I never bested him strength for strength before. This and the other horn will be useful when we are not in this form. There are many enemies, supernatural and other about. They will want to avenge this defeat".

"We must go. The sun will rise soon enough. I have much to tell you…come, bring your sister. We must go". I turned to Sarah and gathered her up in my arms, and given my massive size and strength, she was light as air.

Van pulled the drapes off the back of the altar. In what were obviously well practiced movements, he carefully wrapped the horns. After licking the small evil thing, made a full body wrap for the demon-ling. We made crude back packs from the remainder of the drapes and attached them to our backs. Van carried the horns and imp while I carried Sarah.

I attempted to talk to Sarah, but she was in shock and unable to respond. Van licked her forehead. "That's better than what the cult had in mind for her," Van offered sympathetically. "That lick will repair any physical damage. There are good treatments for this kind of psychological trauma. The best we can do is to get her out of here."

"What about cell phone pictures", I asked. "They will be unusable. We blur out photographs." Van replied. "We need to set this place on fire to cover as much of the evidence as we can".

Van spilled as much ceremonial oil as he could find on the floor, wooden pews and bodies. We then ignited them with candles from the huge candelabras all around. I followed Van out of the burning church building weaving my way through bodies and slippery pools of blood. My claws scratched at the wooden floors as we made our way out and melted into the night.

I heard the church explode as we reached the woods.

I ran following close behind, snaking through the underbrush and out into the thick pine forest. It felt good to be outside, to feel the cool dirt under my feet. We felt like we were skimming along the forest floor. We were so swift that, although I could discern the slightest blemish on any leaf at the same time, things seemed like a blur coming towards me.

My sister made muffled noises as we ran along. We did not follow the same path back, we were on some sort of deer trail, headed towards water. I could smell the moisture in the air. Moving steadily behind him I feared the approaching dawn, being caught nude by strange eyes and not having the strength to complete our mission.

We reached a sort of campground, and paused at the edges, I began to pant from stress, "Give Sarah to me" said Van, I looked into his bright yellow and reddish eyes, "But, these people are strangers" I whispered doubtfully to him. "Trust me" he said, and I handed her over to him."

"She needs a hospital. This is a forest ranger training camp. They are all trained paramedics. They will awaken very soon. We will keep track of her and take her later if we need to."

He walked slowly forward, sniffing the air as he moved, the campers were lined up, and all was darkness. I could hear the steady breathing of sleeping souls inside each of the campers; twelve young and one middle aged man. He disappeared behind a truck that said, "State Forestry Services" and moved like a phantom through the park. I sat down, listening for him. I could not hear a thing save the normal sounds of the night.

Van slapped the forest floor, which caused a rumbling thud. This would awaken the rangers.

A light breeze moved the leaves, a heavy tiredness started to envelop me as I waited. I could hear him approach me, his dark shape moving from the left. His arms were empty.

"Follow me, we must hurry now, time to rest my darling" Van said. I stood up and followed him back through the rugged forest. I was confused and hurt, but I understood the need to get my sister to a hospital. In my form, she would only have been more terrified than she was already.

The sky was changing from black to deep azure when we approached the clearing that was adjacent to a large wine-colored lake. I noticed the morning star. I followed Van, fear gripping at my chest and nagging at my mind.

"The sun is coming up…and soon we will change, our wolves gone until the next full moon". Van said. I sat on the cool ground and flopped down. The running and fighting had exhausted me.

My stomach full, my mind spinning with the shock of what I had done, my loins ached, and skin burned for his touch. All that I had seen took its toll on me, and then I began to shed my beastly appearance.

My bones shook, cracked and rocked back into position, my skin tightened down on my body, the hair that had covered me seemed to implode. I curled inward against the pain; my eyes locked again on the form of Van.

He shed his beastly appearance as if shaking dust from his shoes. Tears welled in my eyes; I felt disgusting, filthy. My hair matted with blood, gristle, brains and mud. I pushed myself up, my breasts bobbing as I sat up and looked at Van.

As we descended into the cool, dark lake to cleanse ourselves of the gore, I was aware of a faint craving. It was like an appetite for something that couldn't be specified. As I cleansed myself, a remembered taste came into my mind and my mouth watered. What was it? Pork chops, leg of lamb, bacon, rack of lamb, veal cutlets? The craving became increasingly more intense.

The burning hunger was intense from head to toe I craved something; my belly rumbled and ached, but I was distracted by the cool waters, the way the last of the moon lingered on the surface of the water; dawn broke softly in the eastern sky.

I watched Van out of my peripheral vision, his smooth skin, his shaven head, dark eyes. I watched the way he washed his face with his powerful hands, his muscles glistening in the soft dawn. The way he watched me when he thought I wasn't looking at him. I submerged myself, raking my hands through my hair and washing my face.

I swam towards him my dark hair slick and wet against my face and shoulders …" I must look horrible; I need some soap and I am very tired" I said as I swam towards his chest. The pangs of hunger returned; my body ached for something.

Waves of sleepiness washed over me, and tears welled up in my eyes. I was afraid to ask him for anything because he had already given me so much. I reached out for him, and he took me in his arms, his body warm and slick in the water.

I looked up into his deep brown eyes moving my hand to his neck, my legs wrapping around his waist, the hunger hit me again. I nestled myself against his strong chest and began kissing his neck and collar bone, soft kisses of adoration.

I wanted him, controlling this sudden urge did not possible. I kissed his mouth, our tongues caressing. I could feel his teeth with my tongue I sucked on his bottom lip and sighed as I became more aroused by him. His hands explored my behind moving up my waist and cupping my breasts.

"We should return and rest Beloved" Van breathed in my ear as he kissed my neck.

"I don't feel very well" I said as the lake began to cock sideways, "and I'm terribly hungry".

"Let's get back and rest" Van said. He carried me to the shore in his arms, and set me down, and grabbed the sacks, leading me along and through the forest. I was worried about the horns, what they meant, and the strange creature that Van had with him.

How could he seem to be so nonchalant about them?

I followed him through the morning light.

Refuge

*Come away, O human child! To the waters and the wild
With a faery, hand in hand.
For the world's more full of weeping than
you can understand. - Yeats*

We walked into the house, hand in hand through the cool of the morning, my feet damp from the dew. Van said, "I want you so badly, that I ache. But we have things to do before we can shower, enjoy each other and then rest. We are actually in more danger now, and in these forms, we are vulnerable".

"How can you be so casual about those awful things you have in the bag?" I asked in a trembling voice, my fear was rising. I could not meet his eyes. Van chucked my chin, and said, "Because, I have lived an exceptionally long time and have encountered them before. Although you have seen things that most people could never believe, I have much more to show you." He led me to a steel door, and we stepped on to the landing of a sturdy wooden staircase.

As we entered the door, on the right wall I saw a modern type finished basement with a well-equipped workbench and a functional machine shop. There was extraordinarily little clutter, but there were large but neat selves and cabinets stocked with food and survival equipment on the left. There was also a large gun safe. The adjacent walls were clear of any storage.

"We are both very tired, so I will just give you the essentials now, and when we awaken, I will elaborate. These are things you have to understand well to ensure our survival."

"The first is the hunger. Once you become like us, you will constantly crave human flesh. When the moon takes you, you will need to eat it at least one day. Giving in, in our human form, is like indulging an addiction. You need more and more and live like a ghoul. It will always lead to our discovery and we will be constantly hunted. Do you understand?

Our beasts are cruel. Sometimes we cannot restrain them. They enjoy the killing as most carnivores do. Enemies are prey. Our human psychology turns this into a mean and sardonic humor. It allows us to distance ourselves from our horrible deeds. You will find that it becomes part of your personality."

Even though he had warned me, and I had already eaten parts of people my mouth gaped in shock. As the impact of what he said hit me, I began to understand my craving and a sense of revulsion overcame me and I began to feel like I wanted to vomit. I was unsteady on my feet at this revelation. Van put his arm over my shoulder and then hugged me. I nodded that I did understand.

"The next is that sorcery and magic do exist. I think it is ultimately science and will be considered technology in the future. I am well acquainted with a sorcerer who is much older than I. You will meet him soon".

I tried to take this in. My Bible conditioning rebelled and I recalled verses that warned about the abominations of sorcery, witchcraft and divination; and all the punishments in Hell that awaited those who trafficked in witchcraft.

It was supposed to be all nonsense anyway. Not biblical or scientific; the beliefs of primitive people.

Considering what I had been through over the past four days, my mind reeled. I had been forever changed into a creature, I had seen a demon, it had talked, flying devils bit and tore at me. "But... but" I began–I had millions of questions.

Van put his right index finger on my lips to silence me.

"Forgive me, My Love", Van said sympathetically but urgently. "Your Bible references during the Exodus the Hebrews when asked by Yahweh to hear and decide whether they would accept his law, said "we will agree and then we will hear"".

"This house has conjures on it that makes it several minutes behind actual time. This means that we will have time to prepare for any external attacks. Also, at all the crossroads that lead to it, there are spells that compel humans and less powerful supernatural entities to go in the opposite direction. We are almost invisible while we are here."

The knowledge of this made me feel safer, although I did not understand how much danger we were in.

"For now, try to suspend your thinking and trust me. You will soon understand." Van held my hand he moved forward and appeared to walk through a solid stone wall, his hand pulling me forward and we simply walked through the rear wall of the basement. I turned and saw the wall behind us, it appeared solid. "This is our "safe room". There are wards that prevent others from entering here. You will learn them. Now we have little time, and we must rest soon."

My mouth dropped in awe at the stone edifice that lay before me. The cavernous room was indescribably massive. There were endless piles of boxes covered by tarps in neat rows. The walls had suits of shining armor and weapons from various periods in history hanging from them. Bronze and silver war shields, with dents and dings in them neatly hung; helmets, leather chest plates emblazoned with eagles; samurai swords, spears and staff weapons and others I could not understand the use for.

Among the shelves and tarpaulin covered crates were separate piles of gold and silver neatly stacked as high and as I am tall. I could discern at least a dozen beds along one of the walls deeper in the cavernous room. My eyes lingered on the sheer number of things before me.

We walked for several minutes and we came to a barred gate which Van unlocked. Van reached into the back, and produced the imp, laying it on the floor of a silver cage; he muttered words as he locked the cage door:

"Kal amatusha malla-a sseri Ina qibit iqbu-u ilani mushitum"

"That should hold him, he will awaken in a few hours" Van said. "I placed a binding spell on the cage, he will not be able to get out nor harm us."

His words were gibberish in my ears, yet his confidence made me feel safe. I felt weak at the knees, my stomach ached. I started to topple over with exhaustion. "Come my love let us go back upstairs" Van said, and he led me back through the cavernous warehouse and up the steps.

I followed him through a hallway into a large shower room; plush rugs upon the floors and towels stacked neatly by color in open faced cabinets, the glass was frosted in a Greek motif. The nickel-plated shower heads were very high on the marble walls. He closed the door behind us as he turned on the hot water.

The room became steamy at once as the hot water ran down our bodies, Van handed me a bar of almond scented soap As if wishing to remove my sins, I scrubbed myself with desperation. The hot water soothed my sore muscles.

I turned and watched Van lathering his chest and muscular biceps; the way the water pushed the evening's filth off his body. Van came closer to me, and washed my hair, his large fingers gently massaging my scalp, I could feel his hard body next to mine. I closed my eyes and felt the soap running down my back.

I felt pangs of the hunger again, and an unreasonable irrational desire to devour him. I shook off an urge to bite off and devour his cheek. The famine roared in me. I was desperate to control myself but found it almost impossible. I turned to him and kissed him hard on the mouth pushing my tongue into his mouth.

I fought down the desire to bite off his tongue.

Without conscious decision, it turned into another appetite. I grabbed him in my hand; I clutched at him and forced him toward the marble wall of the shower. I moaned and sighed. I need to feel him.

Just as quickly as my need erupted, I felt ashamed and blushed before him. I stepped back from him and looked at the floor. "I'm sorry, I don't know why I did that Van, I'm so hungry for something…I didn't mean to …" I was choking back tears of shame as I said this to him. "There is nothing unreasonable about need Mary; I will teach you how to control it. Now rinse your hair and come to me" he said.

I rinsed my hair as he stepped out of the shower, I could see him through the frosted glass, drying his body and wrapping a towel around his waist. He left the room, I turned off the tap and stepped out naked and wet.

My skin giving off faint traces of steam as I moved through the room to grab a thick black towel. I dried off and wrapped the towel around myself and could hear the faintest sounds of him somewhere in his large abode.

I wandered down the hallway; I could smell wine, meat – feeling the movement of his feet on the floor and hearing the clinking of glasses. I found him in his kitchen. "I have something for you Mary" he said with his back turned to me as he poured the wine into two glasses. He presented me with a large black box.

Opening it I found a black silk Japanese kimono, it was heavy, at the bottom embroidered in gold and silk threads were warriors and dogs the pattern ran along the bottom. He pulled the towel off me and held up the kimono for me to wear. "It's beautiful Van, one of the prettiest things I have ever seen in my life. Thank you so much" I said as I put it on and wrapped it about me. Van's eyes watched me turn. I sipped at my wine and sat down on a kitchen stool.

He gave me a plate of bacon and pork chops, "Here eat this but slowly, sip your wine. Tomorrow I will give you some training on how to control yourself, but for now eat".

I ate and sipped the smooth red wine, he sat across from me watching me eat; sipping at his own glass his eyes sparkled, from deep brown to almost a red. I was still hungry for something I couldn't name. As the meat and wine that Van poured for me went down, I grew sleepy.

"Come my love" Van said, and he picked me up and cradled me in his arms carrying me to his large teak wood bed. He set me down and pulled the comforters down. The room began to spin just a little, and extreme exhaustion took me again

He ran is hands through my dark hair and kissed me softly on the lips and cheeks.

My hands explored his torso, and I pulled him close to me as we kissed deeply. I moved onto the bed, crawling towards the middle.

"I have missed you for so long, Mary" he breathed as he followed me onto the bed, his hands on my hips caressing my behind. He kissed and nibbled on my shoulders and back as he mounted me from behind.

We made slow, exhausted love

I moaned into the bed sheets and gripped them tighter.

I breathed into the bedding, feeling satisfied. "I love you" I whispered into the bedding, feeling the weight of him on me. He slid off and pulled me towards him, kissing my sweaty brow, "I love you – I have scoured endless ages to find you again", he said.

I nestled up beside of him and all too soon sleep took me.

11

Two Dreams

These dreams go on when I close my eyes
Every second of the night I live another life
These dreams that sleep when it's cold outside
Every moment I'm awake the further I'm away
Martin Paige These Dreams That Come

Early morning on the next day, Van slept on his back. His closed eyes began to follow the action of a dream.

Moving in corridor, everything cloudy and indistinct. Angry and frightened. Opening doors, and watching wretched men in rags, Running away. mumbling words of thanks. Feeling desperate; frightened for another.

Indistinct words. Melodious baritone. "You are elder". "Not his place". "You will be disgraced". "He will have honor." " Quod licet Jovi non licet bovi!"

Cloudiness.

Strong wooden door. A face like I see in mirror. Relief, love.

Name not spoken for extremely long time.

"Remus?"

Large bronze hands on his shoulders. Huge bronze head behind him, murmuring in his ear.

"Come, brother!"

With joy, I say, "Brother". No return looks of love. No relief. No loving greeting. Expression on that beloved face that I have never seen before. Sourness, disdain. Hate?

"Quando podeces te regi eorum fecerunt!"

Pushed aside, Remus exits first. He shouts orders. "Sicage ut frater tuus!" Large bronze man sits down and gives mocking smile.

Cloudiness.

Fear need protection. On Palatine Hill. Loyal men building defensive wall. Eagles soaring overhead. Hope, Maybe a great city?

Good stone wall. High. Hard to breach.

Goat on a marble altar. Squealing, plaintiff cries.

The holy man, with hands bloody and filled with entrails. Predictions of great city. A center of the world. A place of equality and learning. But no one must breach the wall or the death of all follows.

Shouts from below. A group of rowdies, challenging men. Remus in leather armor with spear and wooden shield. "Pudor tu!" Tu es stultior quam asinus ! Es mundi excrementi!"

Aventine Hill is superior. Six eagles seen overhead." I shout,

"But, brother, we have seen twelve". "Spucatum tauri!" A threat to tear wall down. Must reason with twin.

Face to face outside the wall with Remus. "Oracle says Palatine must not be breached". "Flocci non facio"! I am thrown hard to the floor. Grab brother's rear leg. Explosion at the side of head. Frantically grabbing, wrestling.

Grabbing Remus' wrist, a steel sword in his hand. A frantic push, he spills and falls flat on face.

Kneeling by him, turning him over. Sword in belly. Blood gushes from mouth every time heart beats. Look of love. Not seen in years. He whispers, "Simul ridemus, simul lacrimus":

The golden man....the golden man...renidet! " Eyes close forever. Nooooooooooo!

He does not rise! HE DOES NOT RISE! Spread of crimson.

Mary giggles in her sleep. She was lying on her right side.

The Disney cartoon of: "The Three Little Pigs". They are so cute. They have little bow ties. One has a sailor's hat. They play and sing. Flutes and fiddle.

Uh, Oh. The Big Bad Wolf is coming out of the woods. He has a floppy, patch work stove top hat and a carpet bag.

She sees the house of straw. Oops, he blows it down! They run to the house of wood. Oops, he blows it down! They run into the house of bricks. He huffs and he puffs. Not, good enough, Wolfy. He climbs to the roof; they prepare a huge kettle of water in the fireplace.

She has the three terrified piglets cornered in front of her. She reaches out and grabs one by the leg. She delights in their squeals. She grabs his opposite arm and bites his bulging belly. The sweet taste of flesh and blood fills her mouth. His stomach and intestines spill out.

She rips off the legs and savors the raw meat of the piglet's rump. She rips off the swine's head and sees the slack jawed head of her sister, Sarah.

She laughs and sees the faces of her mother and father on the other pigs.

Meat! So good!!

Van continues to dream.

In the late night, golden man with beautiful voice comes. A god? Offers consolation, then good advice.

City grows. They give it my name, "Rome". Growth, progress. Pride.

"Why give up control?" You are power. All due to you. Dress like king! Be king!

On the battlefield. Group of friends approach fast. Smiling faces. Friendly greetings. Rough hands grabbing, piercing pain. Wet sticky blood flowing down torso. Slipping, falling hard.

Face of darling wife. Bella!!!!

Whiteness.

The rising of consciousness. Smells of rot, corruption. On back in garbage dump. The moon is full.

Voice like thunder. "Romulus get up and look at me".

Enormous red man in complete armor towering as high as defensive war.

The god Mars!

"Death no refuge for you, Romulus. You have let yourself be corrupted by an old one. The Adversary! The Corrupter! Killed brother, valued golden man over Olympians. You are guilty of hubris! You lose everything!

Jupiter, King of Gods, curses you to walk earth until its end. You will hunt archfiend to eternity. For three days of full moon, you run on all fours as wolf. You will eat human flesh or shrivel into worm.

You will be ravenous. Your will never be able to be satisfied. You will never be able to conceive children."

Alone, amid rot and stench of garbage. Pain wracking body. Bones shifting under skin. Joints popping out. Tearing inside.

Smells so strong. Vision so clear. Rats skittering sound like war horses.

Smelling smoke from fires. Smells like sex. Incredible kaleidoscope, cacophony from city.

Hunger, starvation. Need to eat.!

NEED TO EAT!!

Travelling at blurring speed to city.

11

Meat is Murder

*When the truth is found to be lies And
all the joy within you dies
Don't you want somebody to love
Don't you need somebody to love Jefferson
Starship Somebody to Love 1967*

He had been thrashing around in his sleep, speaking a strange language, and growling from deep within his chest as we slept. I reached to touch him as he slumbered, his body was cool and he slightly perspired. He growled at the touch, and I curled myself away from him as he dreamed.

It was the words more than anything that frightened me; the feeling of almost being able to make them out, but the more I listened, the more the words slipped away; Spanish? Italian? Portuguese?

Later, I awoke and stretched out in the bed. Seeing the room through my hair, feeling across the bed for Van, he was gone. I slipped out of the massive Scandinavian bed. I carefully smoothed the pillows, sheets and covers. I heard the faint sounds of working coming from the basement.

I was so hungry, my stomach growled, and I started to feel weak, it was as if I had not eaten for weeks.

I was naked and found my way to the bathroom; sat on the toilet and urinated. I noticed that my urine had a stronger, aggressive odor than I was used to. Usually I would shower first, but a biological imperative called me.

I padded into the kitchen looking at the austere layout of this room, the large metal appliances. I opened the high-end large silver double-sided refrigerator door and was surprised and pleased to find it almost completely stuffed with uncooked meat. Mostly it was lamb and pork. But there were at least a family of four's monthly supply of veal and beef.

I pulled out a double portion of veal cutlets. I was unfamiliar with his kitchen and wondered where I could locate the pans and cooking oil. I looked at the meat.

The meat looked so good; I could smell it – smell the blood; even tell what the animal had eaten. Van seemed to have a knack for finding the choicest cuts. How could it smell so good without even being cooked?

I moved my nose and face closer to the veal to savor the delicious aroma. My mouth watered, and my stomach grumbled louder and harder. Without thinking I took a bite. I had never tasted anything quite so delicious.

Before I knew it, I had devoured the first cutlet, and then I snapped up the second, and the third and the fourth. Eating the meat calmed the urge, the hunger, and the empty hollow spot inside of me.

I snatched at the meat in the refrigerator and piled a bucket sized portion of meat packets into my lap. I sat naked and cross legged on the floor in front of the fridge, shoveling as much uncooked meat into my mouth as quickly as I could. Rolling my eyes in delight and making guttural noises as I satiated the need inside. In my haste and hunger, I even ate good amounts of the cellophane coverings.

I jumped as I heard Van say in a kindly, amused tone "Why, there is a beautiful naked lady wolfing down raw meat in my kitchen". I still had part of a veal chop between my teeth. He was standing at the basement door in blue jeans and a black T shirt. I could see how the clothing hugged his frame and the muscles of his forearms rippled under his skin. "I have been in my workshop, doing some maintenance".

I looked up at him guiltily, moving my hair from my face, I was aware of blood and morsels on my cheeks, hands, arms and chest. "Van, I..... I....." stammering in a horrified and contrite voice," couldn't help myself! I was so hungry…I don't know what came over me" I said tears welling up in my eyes.

"Sweetheart, it is perfectly normal for our kind", Van said sympathetically. It is usually better to let someone discover this by himself. You would not have believed me. It is hard to conceive of rationally. I stocked that refrigerator just for you. You are a light eater. Eat your fill". He said.

"Thank you, Van, this is delicious, the meat is exquisite, tender like butter almost" I replied.

"May I join you, My Dear? Scoot over." Van said politely. I gave him a bloody, embarrassed smile as he squatted ape style beside me. I scampered over a little for him.

Van took a boneless porterhouse steak and began to take a bite. As he did, I became angry. A bristling greediness arose in me, and I found myself stifling a growl. I wanted to push him away; to bite at his ears and nose. This impulse brought me back to rationality.

Van looked in my eyes and he began. "In order for us to control our craving for human flesh, we must eat a lot of raw, red meat. We will always have the hunger and the urge but eating large amounts of raw animal meat can keep us rational and from attacking humans", He said as he chewed on the porterhouse.

I watched him and thought about what he said, I had so many questions for him," But, Van. It is gluttony and cannibalism is...is... just ...wrong", I returned.

Van looked away from me like he was trying to find the right words. His eyes filled with sadness. He sighed and said, "You are no longer a human being, sweet little Mary. You are now a different species. You are what I call a "Other-Human".

With the wolf inside, you will always be the same size, but you will become increasingly more muscular. You cannot die. You will always revive at the full moon." He chewed some more, exploring me with his eyes as he sat next to me.

Cannibalism has been a primary taboo in most cultures. Times have changed.

There are restaurants in New York, London and Paris that specialize in entrees of human meat. Not especially the nicest thing to think about, but sometimes values loosen.

"Regarding right and wrong", Van mused, "to paraphrase Shakespeare's 'Hamlet', 'There is nothing right or wrong but thinking makes it so'. All the laws, and cultural conventions and even religions are just inventions so that humanity will not constantly be killing each other. They are arbitrary made-up rules; mainly to keep the poor from rising up and overthrowing the rich."

"I have discovered over the years that it is best not to eat people when the moon has not taken me. Believe me, I learned the hard way and I was a slow learner. It required ghoulish stores of body parts and it gave me less control. I always needed more.

I became more of a ...thing, than a person. I was always discovered and forced to run and leave everything behind. You know, peasants with pitchforks and torches like in the old 'Frankenstein' movies.

It is just too disruptive to constantly feed on humans. I have had to dig myself out of too many shallow graves. What a pain in the ass. As I have become older, I have come to believe that it is morally wrong. For me, it is anyway."

"So, you are telling me that you are immortal, and that there are ways of controlling this...this hunger that I feel...what about the other hunger that I feel?" I turned to Van, and offered him a morsel of steak, his lips lingering on my fingertips as I placed the plump meat into his mouth.

"Yes, you will come to understand many things in a short period of time. Many things you thought of as being final truths will be destroyed, and you will have to replace them. Mary and I will help you" he said.

I eyed his jeans, and as if he could read my very thoughts, he pushed the plate of meat aside. I sucked the blood off my fingers as he moved more closely. He grabbed a chunk of veal and offered it to me. He dangled it above my mouth teasing me with it, blood dripping onto my lips.

I reached out and unzipped his pants, "But I am going to get you dirty Van" I breathed, as he pushed the morsel into my waiting mouth. He kissed me, pushing his tongue into my mouth; I reached for more steak, found the plate and offered him the rare meat. His mouth biting at it and the smallest bit he left dangling I started to eat from his mouth.

We kissed deeply; he pulled me closer to him, being pressed between his clothed body and the cool of the marble floors.

"There is a desire inside of me Van, it frightens me", I breathed out as he moved his hand down towards my behind. "Do not be frightened, I am here…" he said, and he kissed me again, harder with more urgency. I pressed my body into his, and pulled up his shirt a little, and unsnapped his jeans.

Suddenly I felt panicked. I felt that I couldn't breathe and wanted to run. I became hysterical about those men at the facility. What if they or that monster, Sterling had made me pregnant. I gasped and saw their mocking faces. I closed my eyes and moved my hands in front of my eyes so that I could not see.

Van nuzzled closer to me, kissing at my neck, "Mary…do not think about this. While the wolf spirit is within you, you cannot conceive. Do not cry My Sweet", he said as he kissed my salty tears. I hugged him close to me, digging my nails into his back and shoulders.

He was soft and tender with me, kissing my body.

"I love you Mary" he whispered in my ear. As he said this, I dug my fingers into his back through his T-shirt tears welling at my eyes. "I love you my dear Beast, my dear Beast that saved me" I said, "Go shower Mary, I will clean this up." Van offered.

I entered the eloquently decorated, Greco-Roman style bathroom. It seemed to be marble with gold fixtures. It was white and had a blue accenting stripe by the ceiling. It had crown molding. There were small marble Roman statues strategically placed. Everything was upper end.

There was a bidet next to what seemed to be an especially heavy-duty toilet bowl. The bowl had a magnificent mahogany seat.

I moved over to the shower stall which had built in marble seats. It seemed strange, but it had an industrial strength garbage disposal. The shower doors had scenes like those on Grecian urns. Frescos of heroes and ladies provided the occupant some modesty.

There was a vanity with three basins and a mirror going to the ceiling. Oddly, one of the basins also had an industrial strength garbage disposal.

As I slide aside the shower door, I couldn't help but to see myself in the mirror over the vanity. I was a bloody mess, but I noticed that my face seemed leaner somehow. My black hair was shinier and seemed more luxurious than before.

My body was different. I could see the beginnings of defined, corded muscle rippling under my shoulders. There was a line running down my stomach and a faint line demarking my middle and lower abdomen muscles. There were also lines at the sides of my thighs. Could it be the lighting?

I closed the shower door and turned on the water. Water streamed from all directions. The touch and aroma of the warm water was one of the most sensual things I have ever experienced. The water felt like dozens of gentle tickling fingers on my flesh. The smell of the water was vaguely salty and had an aroma like an earthy perfume. I found myself uttering a soft moan of pleasure. What kind of water had Van discovered to feed into the system?

The almond scented soap smelled so fresh and nutty, that I almost wanted to take a bite out of it. The cool shampoo trickling down my scalp and hair were a cascade of dribbling pleasure.

I was shaken out of my reverie when I noticed a few chunks of meat about the size of a quarter to a nickel flowing towards the garbage disposal. I was repulsed, inhaled sharply flailed about until I turned on the electrical switch. The wet grinding sound was at once irritating and reassuring.

I turned off the water and wiped down the shower stall. I saw Van holding out a large royal Turkish towel in front of it concealing all but his hands and the lower half of his face. I pushed aside the shower door and rushed into his arms as he enveloped me with the towel.

"I see you understand our need for the garbage disposals and the ultra-sturdy facilities", Van offered good-naturedly. "We tend to be enthusiastic gourmets. It can be...messy. Even though we will wash in the lake outside, sometimes when the moon is ripe, we need them. It's a simple fact of life."

"Van", I asked. How can you afford such luxury? Do psychologists get paid that well?" He looked at me with a gleam in his eye and said, "Pretty well, but not that well. I just put a little away every month for an exceptionally long, long... long time. He looked up and to the left and seemed amused with himself. We see such horror, that we deserve luxury."

He was back wearing his blue jeans and black shirt. They clung to him as they would to a male model. "Come, lie with me, I have more to tell you. I know you have questions." He said. I wrapped myself in the towel, and another around my hair, and we lay on our enormous Scandinavian bed.

Questions and Answers

*"The past actually happened.
History is the stories they tell about it. Samuel Clements.*

We laid in our king size Scandinavian bed, wrapped in each other's arms. There was a large bay window on the wall across from our feet with its tasteful maroon drapes drawn. A large Flat Screen T.V. sat across from the foot of the bed.

Large teak lamps rested on the night tables beside us shown upwards towards the glossy white ceiling giving us indirect lighting. I noticed crown moldings. There were reading lamps on the headboard. On the floor were several lambskin rugs. Abstract paintings lined the walls. The door to the bath was slightly ajar and a gentle light was peeking out.

Van began talking, "We have known each other for only about a week, and you have seen things that would have driven most people catatonic. That means you have an inner strength that is exceedingly rare, my darling". Now I shall try to give you answers.

I cuddled a little closer to Van and then moved slightly away and looked into his now gentle brown eyes. "You talked in your sleep last night. I think this all has something to do with Rome.

I know, you are a werewolf and, to save me, you have made me one also. I crave human meat and must eat it to stay alive. And we will be alive until the end of the world.

I have had a glimpse of another.... reality. I have seen a demon and other supernatural beings and you have told me there are other types. You have shown me that black magic is real", I offered.

Van gave me a smile... "I know it is hard to believe, and might seem like a lie, but I started out life as Romulus." He pronounced the name "Rom-U-Loose". I am the original Lycanthrope, cursed to be so by he who you know as the god, Jupiter".

"But Van, I was always told that those were myths! Belief in other gods breaks the Ten Commandments. They were just fiction! And that would make you.... about three thousand years old!" I blurted out.

A concerned look came over Van's face. "How do you feel about older men? Moisturizing is the key." He quipped. "Actually, more like about two and a half thousand years give or take a hundred. Soon you will meet one who is even older than I."

"I was turned when I was in my early forty's and we do not age after our transformation. I have read the myth of Romulus and Remus and the main points are generally accurate, but of course it has been embellished.

Like so many things, changed to glorify the dirty acts of Rome. You see, the actual events cannot be observed or re-experienced, so the victorious produce self-aggrandizing and justifying narratives; one that better suits their ambitions and politics. It is what 'history' becomes.

Your history is always influenced by preternatural entities, not gods, but with amazing powers, to further their own political and selfish agendas. Why would your god forbid the worship of other gods unless he didn't want the competition?

As for sorcerers, in the Bible, in Numbers 22 there is a black magician named Balaam sent by the king of Babylonia to curse the Israelites. He even had a talking donkey. Yahweh was worried about his power. If the truth be known, all historical narratives would be similar to the Iliad".

The Olympic gods are what are known as 'thought forms.' Natural forces that were named and given personalities by ancient people. From human intention and worship they took on consciousness and independence. After thousands of years of worship, they attained tremendous power.

My jaw dropped at these new revelations. I tried to speak, but my mind was reeling. "Shall I go on, or do you need a moment?" Van asked, lovingly.

Van put his hand over mine and gave it a reassuring squeeze. I asked him to go on. He seemed to get caught up in the narrative.

"My twin brother Remus (which he pronounced "RayMoose") and I were the unknowing heirs to the small city state of Abla Longa. Our uncle, Amulius, deposed our grandfather Numitor and condemned our mother to be a holy prostitute. We are said to have been suckled by a she wolf, but in the vernacular of the time, a prostitute was called a "Lupa"- she wolf.

Our mother was taken by the Olympian god Mars and we were conceived. Amulius would have killed us as newborns. At our birth, we were concealed with a shepherd and his wife in a nearby community."

"Our childhoods were idyllic. Our adoptive parents were wonderful and liked having two strong sons to help with the work and care for them in their old age. We grew up playing naked in the sun and without a care in the world. We were inseparable and loved no one more than each other.

Although we would be considered just slightly tall by today's standards, at a time when most full-grown men were just five feet tall, we were considered incredibly large. We did everything together and, as we grew, we became the leaders of a loose band of boys from the neighboring villages.

"The rigors of a shepherd's life caused us to grow strong and muscular and we were almost telepathic as many twins are. We learned to hunt. We learned the ways of the spear, bow and sword from the men of the villages.

Remus excelled at wrestling and I at boxing. We taught each other these skills. Some of the old people even taught us the basics of reading and writing. We seemed to always agree, and we never said angry words to each other. We always talked way into the night."

"Just as we were beginning to grow beards and found girls... interesting... Remus became more withdrawn. I would awaken in our room in the middle of the night and hear him talking and receiving responses. Soon, he would frequently not be in our room when I would awaken from a dream.

Remus began to insist he was the better of us and that I should follow him. I did not care because he was still my loving brother.

He became more and more of a bully and was soon the leader of the more aggressive teens. They began demanding tolls for travelers crossing our roads. They went around to villages farther away from our union of towns, and extorted money from merchants and fought with local toughs.

One night, I awoke and Remus was not in our room. From the window, I heard him talking outside. The responses came from a sweet but deep voice. Curious, I arose and, using my hunting skills, sneaked into our garden. There on a large boulder, sat my transfixed twin with an enormous bronze man kneeling and talking in his ear. Shaken, I withdrew. I kept this knowledge to myself.

Soon, Remus and his group's activities drew the attention of the people of Abla Longa. He had raided some of the villages allied to that city. They set up an ambush, killed some of Remus' companions and took him to their fortress.

I raised a force and we infiltrated Abla Longa. I freed Remus from the dungeon, but he seemed to resent it. To my horror I found the bronze giant in his cell with him. When I saw the giant, he smiled. It chilled me to the bone.

Remus left the cell and took over our force. I turned to the bronze man and he was somehow gone. Rather than sneak away, Remus boldly took revenge on many of the innocent citizens of that city. Later, we learned that the city people overthrew Amulius because he could not defend them from us. They restored Numitor and there were rumors that they sought revenge on us and our townships.

There were frequent skirmishes with the Abla Longans, and we began to arm ourselves with steel and armor. There were a few deaths, and the atmosphere was very bad. We outnumbered them, but they had the stone fortress, now reinforced, to hide behind.

Because of Remus' arrogance and contrariness, he alienated most of the people of our group of towns. The "bully boys" preferred him, while the remainder followed me. We were all of about sixteen years old.

He and I agreed on nothing anymore. He seemed to willfully do the opposite of what I wanted and took glee in undoing what I had done. We frequently almost came to blows over various disagreements.

By this time, our sweet gentle shepherd parents had passed on so there was no one who could intervene.

Everyone in the villages agreed that the general well being called for the safety of defensive walls. There were seven hills in the area, and most of the wise old ones agreed that a hill named "Palatine" offered the best defensive position. The town's folks proceeded to quarry stones and construct a fortress on the top of that hill.

We were amazed to see eagles, twelve in all, while we were building the wall. We took this as a good omen. We built a fine, effective fort; one which could house the general population and allow storage of food and supplies in case of an attack. There was even an underground spring that could supply water.

Meanwhile, Remus and his people were constructing walls on nearby Aventine Hill. He and his followers were impulsive, and jerry rigged a wall from inferior materials. It seemed more important to him to have his own structure, separate from ours, than to have an adequate defense.

I was angry because, if we had worked together, we would have finished earlier and had an even superior defense. As it was, Palatine was a good, but not superior fortress. While Aventine looked like it was constructed by toddlers.

Our council thought it best that we do not confront Remus and his followers. They were tough and would keep our outer borders safe. They would continue to raid, and we thought that this would put fear into our enemies and might reduce both their and our enemies' numbers. This would also give us more time to prepare.

They became our outer guard. We thought they would come around in time and once their pride cooled. We went about improving our fortress and stocking it with weapons, armor and supplies.

We were as pious in our worship of the Olympian gods as people today are about Christ. We dedicated our fortress to them. We made Jupiter our patron god and conducted blood sacrifices. An oracle saw that our new city would be the center of the world for hundreds of years. It would be a center of learning and democracy and a light of civilization; but only if its founding spirit remained unsullied and the walls remained un-breached. We began a three-day celebration.

During our second day of reverie our sentries rushed to the council and reported armed men approaching the gates. We locked the inner and outer gates, put on our chain mail armor, helmets and donned our shields. We hunkered down and waited on the walls with our bows and great ballistae.

To our surprise, Remus and about two hundred followers staggered up to the front gate, stumbling drunk: but armed and armored.

Remus issued drunken and slurred challenges. He was cheered on by his inebriated mob. He threatened to tear down our walls and wanted to take us to Aventine.

The council conferred and it was decided that I should go down and reason with my twin. I took off my armor, announced my intentions to Remus, and walked out the front gate. As a show of good faith, we left the portcullis open.

Remus stepped up to meet me. He was falling down drunk and crazily angry. My soothing words were met with curses and threats. He told me that his golden man insisted that we comply or that he take Palatine Hill by force.

I cautioned him to sleep and come back sober. This infuriated him and he threw his spear at me. It was clumsy and I easily dodged it. He stepped within a few feet of our open gate. I could not let him breech it. He began to draw his sword and I closed with him.

I grabbed Remus' sword hand and we struggled. To disarm him I spun him around and pushed him. He lost his sword and fell face forward on to it. I heard the slurp of the weapon piercing flesh and Remus screamed in pain. I notice blood surging onto the grass in saw him violently twitch.

I screamed "No!" and kneeled beside my fallen brother. At that moment, a thousand armored and well-armed men surged out of the gates and surrounded Remus' rowdies. Several of the hooligans began to attack and were summarily dispatched. The others surrendered their weapons and sat down.

I turned Remus over and held him in my arms like a mother holds a baby. The sword had pierced his lower abdomen below the navel and had cut a large slice across his pelvis. We both tried to hold his intestines in. Hot tears formed in my eyes as his hot blood pumped into my hands.

I looked into Remus' face and I could see it was contorted in agony. Blood gushed from his wound and mouth. He looked in my face and seemed confused. Then he softened and said, "My beloved twin. My Romulus! I have missed you. Where have you been?" Then he winced and stiffened, and his death throes were upon him. He clutched my shoulders and said, "The golden god, he…the golden god…he is smiling."

He became silent forever.

I cried unashamedly as memories of our childhood flooded me. But then, I heard cries from the Palatine's defenders to slaughter the attackers. I shouted that there had been enough death that day; that these were cousins and old friends. I asked them to bring the defeated men to the dungeon. Once they sobered up, we would let the council decide their fates.

The next day, the council decided that those of Remus' men who wanted to join us would be welcome. Those who wanted to go could leave unharmed. Most chose to remain. Remus was to be given a hero's burial.

I was to be honored by having our citadel named "Rome".

I delivered the eulogy at Remus' funeral. I described him as a hero of our people who pushed us to move beyond our comfort level and forced us to create a splendid city and an enormous fighting force.

I offered my vision of a great empire modeled after Athens' democracy. I talked about being heroes for the least of the people. I finished to the repeated cries from thousands of, "Hail Romulus! Hail Rome!"

That night was hard, I struggled to fall asleep. Memories of childhood mixed with the horrors of watching Remus die finally faded into blackness. I was awakened shortly before dawn by a melodious, deep voice calling my name.

I bolted out of bed and grabbed a dagger. But no one was there.

All Roads Lead to Rome

And the youth, mistook by me, Pleading for a lover's fee.
Shall we their fond pageant see?
Lord, what fools these mortals be!
William Shakespeare A Midsummer's Night Dream

I was mesmerized by Van's tale and he appeared to be "on a roll". He put his hands behind his head and stared at the ceiling. I could see the drifting emotions play across his face and he seemed to be mentally seeing much of what he talked about. I determined to remain quiet, unless I really couldn't understand something he was saying.

"After that, the city grew unbelievably fast.

People of all types were welcome. If they followed our laws and respected our customs they were accepted as citizens. We had to spread out across the Seven Hills to accommodate them all. Tents were replaced by stone structures and the needs of the people required more and more attention. Cow paths were replaced by dirt roads only to be replaced by cobblestone roads.

People think of ancient Rome as the bleached white ruins they see today. But houses and businesses were painted many bright colors, blues and reds and yellows. The statues were painted to seem lifelike. Speculators made incredible fortunes. The Council had artisans plan the permanent houses so that it would not be a hodgepodge of clashing styles.

Late in the night, I kept hearing my name being called. I shook it off as bad dreams caused by my beloved twin's horrible death. But then, I started seeing mist like formations in my room and eventually these became so dense as to cast shadows.

Being a worshiper of the Olympians, I sought council from an oracle. She told me that it was possible that one of the gods might be trying to contact me. When I asked the Council about it, most were impressed but the oldest seemed skeptical.

The grey heads and bald pates had seen too many self-serving tales of interactions with the gods to not be skeptical. Soon, they made me Head of the Council and we began to formulate laws and a governing body. We formed a confederation and established a rotating leader. I was about twenty-two years old at the time.

The Senate struggled with what to do with the growing population. Most of these were men who had a rambunctious nature. There were few women except for prostitutes and slaves. We established a caste system and strict laws and a force of guards to keep order and administer justice. Except in the Middle East, our justice would be considered brutal by today's standards.

One night I was awakened by being called in a deep, beautiful voice. I could see it was coming from a large, dense mist that approximated the shape of a huge man.

"Romulus," it said, "Young men need purpose and discipline. Their nature is to either defend or tear down. They need to be a team and have an outlet for their aggression.

Recruit an army of fighting men in groups of six thousand. Teach them to fight behind their shields and as a unit. No individual combat for personal glory. Put those not fit enough to serve militarily to work on construction projects for the public good."

Then I found myself awakening near dawn as was my habit.

Upon awakening, in my mind, I saw an image of a warrior in full red armor.

The Senate was impressed. With the brilliant minds in that group, we quickly established several public works to benefit the people.

Primary among these was the defensive wall around the whole area, an aqueduct system and paved roads. Ursicinus, an old commander, was chosen to head the army and he went about recruiting men who were the worthiest.

We were surprised when he had collected sixty thousand men and organized them into ten "legions." Their early efforts were more like blacksmiths, making the armor and weapons they would need. Once that was accomplished, they learned to fight as a great machine rather than warriors for personal honor and glory.

I slept with the peace of a man who believed he was blessed by his gods. One night, I awoke again to my name being called; this time by a solid black shadow. "Are you one of the gods", I asked in awe. "It is always as you believe" was the answer. "You need allies, go to Abla Longa. Beg an audience with the ruler, Numitor, and his daughter Rhea Silva."

"But we have fought and killed each other in the past. Why would they want to see me?" I asked.

"Things have changed, and they need allies now. Sue for peace. You do not understand now, but Numitor and Rhea Silva need to see you. They fear your growing strength and could hinder you. Trust me."

"I will propose this to the Senate", I replied.

"Use your influence to force it through the Senate. Many of them are old and timid and will not understand. You need to do this thing. Shame them if they disagree." The dark man demanded. I nodded my agreement.

Then I could see a smile on the face of the dark shadow. And it lingered after the figure dissolved.

I fell back to sleep and dreamed of a warrior in full battle armor all in red covered with the gore of many battles. He seemed to stare sternly at me. I thought it was just a dream.

The Senate, particularly the older more experienced Senators recommended wariness. Vincus, a fifty-year-old ex-soldier, expressed the most doubt. As an old military officer as well as a strategist, and an extraordinarily rich man, his opinion was highly respected. He argued that we had been enemies for ten years and it is likely that such an approach would incite new violence. Also, he said that my last supernatural inspiration could have been a simple dream with lucky consequences.

The Senate was generally against my proposal. I told them that, like fearless Leonidas and his bold Spartans, I would take my personal guard and go under my own authority. I mocked Vincus for being afraid and shamed the old warrior into accompanying me.

A few brave Senators volunteered to also come along.

We sent envoys to Abla Longa. They agreed to host a diplomatic meeting. Within a few days along with an armed escort, we took the short march to the city state.

As we approached the city walls, I thought that they seemed much less imposing than they did that night we rescued Remus. Their armed guards were older men perhaps in their late thirties. Soldiers usually retired about that age.

It all seemed small and sad. So, unlike the mighty citadel that my 15-year-old self so feared.

Our armed escorts remained outside of the walls and set up camp. I, Vincus and a small retinue of senators and bodyguards were ushered through the rundown courtyard to a building about as large a rich merchant's home in Rome. Our Senate building dwarfed it.

We walked through the poorly maintained corridors with their thread worn rugs and into a throne room that was only a little bigger than my living room. On the throne sat a proud, grey haired man in his early sixties. At his side was a small woman in her early forties with salt and pepper hair.

I was stunned to gaze upon the faces of Numitor and his daughter Rhea Silva. I was familiar with those faces. They strongly resembled a face I had seen most days of my life: my beloved twin, Remus! We noticed my unmistakable resemblance to them and were nonplussed. Hurried questions and delightful answers were given.

My mother had found her twin boys who she had saved from her evil brother. I had discovered my grandfather and mother! We cried wretched tears over the death of Remus. So, it seemed that I had two mothers and five grandfathers!

I was told of my uncle Amulius' treachery and how our raid to free Remus had freed them as well. However, he still had power in the city.

My mother cried and my grandfather hugged me. There was no question that we would be allies. We had come at a time of desperation as Rome was drawing all the immigrants, the new blood and the trade and Alba Longa had languished. Now, they no longer needed to fear us.

Numitor asked me to assume his throne, but I told him I had sworn responsibility for Rome. Alba Longa would become part of Rome but remain under Numitor's leadership. This also added their thirty-thousand-man army to our sixty thousand army, and we were both safer. We could direct excess citizens to my grandfather and mother.

Vincus said. "You must be truly being guided by a god. And so, I shall say to all of Rome!"

The night was one of feasting, celebration and family reunion. Over wine, lamb, goat, dormice and succulent fruit we laughed and talked. We all joked and became truly fond of each other. Vincus seemed like part of the family. Rhea Silva said she refused to leave me again and we agreed she would live with me in Rome.

We would immediately share trade and security with the city. We would leave troops and artisans there to begin to solidify our union. We made endearing promises of frequent visits.

We left the next morning and our retinue was swollen with diplomats and tradesmen from Abla Longa. My mother was in a carriage and I rode next to her. We talked most of the way. She told me of my family history. She said that my father was a god, probably Mars; that Olympus was with me.

Vincus, cast admiring eyes at my mother, and she returned them. We were all feeling very genial. The accompanying senators drank wine, told jokes and sung. We rode into Rome jubilantly, settled my mother into my house and then called a meeting of the Senate.

Within hours, Vincus and I shared the great news with the Senate. After the details of our visit to my grandfather's city, the members seemed captivated.

My nocturnal visitor's counsel had paid off richly. Vincus shared his conversion to my side and discussed what he admitted he considered miraculous. "All of these marvelous events that Romulus has caused to happen, could not have happened without direct intervention of Olympus", he said. He put his hand on my shoulder as a father might. The senators were jubilant and cheered without restraint.

In gratitude and led by Vincus I was given tribute and proclaimed King. I appointed these men the "fathers" or "Patricians" of Rome. Senators who had accompanied us to Abla Longa heaped praise upon my head, but some of it seemed slimy and forced. In a few minutes, I had become rich and powerful beyond belief.

On our way out of the Senate, Vincus told me that, deception and deceit are always the real ways of government. "Those who cheered the loudest for your elevation were the ones who have called the loudest for your death. The noblest sounding senators have the blackest hearts and perform the foulest of deeds. The hidden things they have done to advance themselves would justify condemning a poor man to be flayed alive.

It is a game of power of greed, played out with secret, dirty deeds. If it has a stench, it could kill a herd of swine.

They would have your blood if it can make them richer or more powerful. Those who claim the most patriotism and concern for the common man are frequently the least to be trusted. Slithering reptiles, those. We will need to prune that ugly garden. Politics requires compromises, but compromise for personal gain corrupts. We must watch our backs; very carefully. My men will add to your own to protect you as of this hour" He said.

"With your permission, My King, your treacherous uncle Amulius, who caused you and your mother so much grief, will be assassinated by the end of the night of tomorrow.

It will not seem to come from Rome. It will seem like an accident or heart illness. It will consolidate our and your grandfather's positions", the old warrior offered.

"Yes, it is the only way he will meet justice", I replied.

I returned home and we supped with my mother. We lingered over our wine and appreciated our good fortune. "I have seen few women of childbearing age" My mother remarked. "How can your city survive without children to carry on?" I commented, "But surely,

Alba Longa has many women who will need husbands." "Oh, there are hundreds, but you need thousands", she replied. "We have made invitations to the surrounding communities, but have had very few positive responses", I stated.

"Trust a woman and a politician that this is not happenstance", my mother replied." They envy and fear Rome's growing strength and would starve us in any way they can. We will have to consider these things" Vincus added. "I have to leave to set up a night guard for you.

When I return perhaps, as experienced politicians, your mother and I discuss this further and advise you in the morning." Vincus added. My mother gave me a sly smile. It seemed that Vincus might become more than a good ally. Taking their cues, I retired to my bedroom.

Once I got into my bed, without being half asleep, I heard for the first time that familiar melodious, baritone voice beckoning. On my porch, I expected to see the deep black shadow. But this time there was the large figure of a man. I knew he was my patron and rushed to greet him.

I was shocked by his appearance. I was surprised by the strong smell of incense, some of which I recognized as frankincense, which we use to purify holy temples. He was perhaps a head taller than I and had golden skin. The smell of the holy, purifying incense comforted me.

His body was like one of our celestial statues. His face was the very definition of beauty. His head was shaven clean. His smile was at once beautiful and hypnotic.

"Are you a god? I have heard descriptions of golden Apollo...." I sputtered.

"It is always as you believe it to be" with a wry smile, the golden man answered soothingly. "You have a problem with obtaining women...breeding sows. The other cities are starving you in this way. Please sit down".

I felt mesmerized. I found myself sitting obediently on a marble bench. The golden god knelt behind me. I felt weak, unable to move or think for myself. He alternated speaking in my left and right ears. This shut my reason down, but I could remember everything he said.

I believed it without question.

"A king does not think small. A king must be bold. Aggressive! Imperious! The other cities withholding their women are passive acts of war. They seek to starve you to death.

If they don't respect you, they need to fear you. They will only respect you if you give them active war. Only blood and death will set this straight. Like daring Alexander, always lead your troops and be in the forefront of battle. War is a good way to eliminate usurpers of the throne and rival patricians.

Raid your neighbors and take their daughters. Sabine to the south is more powerful and richer than Rome but has the largest number of nubile women. An act of deception is called for. They are mostly merchants. Fortunately, they are timid and, through political infighting and jockeying for power they are slow to react. By the time they do, you can prepare yourselves to best them. Time will also change…other things.

How does a man take a hesitant woman? By seduction or rape. Seduce the Sabines, and then take them. Invite them to a festival, and when they are sleeping off their drunkenness are nauseous and have headaches, seize their daughters. Drive the rest out and then rape their daughters.

In two months, you are celebrating the Feast of Neptune. Flatter the Sabines and entice the noble and rich families into joining you in a lavish feast and celebration.

Many on the Senate will resist this plan, but you are the king now.

Decree it!

If there is a lot of resistance from the Patricians, arrest the weakest of them and execute them summarily. Secretly kill their entire families, particularly their sons so there will be no ideas of revenge. Give their land, wealth and slaves to supporting senators and they will be assuaged. All will then understand that your rule cannot be questioned".

The next thing I knew, I was awakening as if from a dream. The red warrior was shouting at me and pounding his spear on the floor. I did not know why I could not hear him. But I was sure that it was my father Mars, encouraging me to war!

14

The Rape of Sabine Women

Vice is a monster of so frightful mien
As to be hated, but needs to be seen
.But seen too oft, familiar with her face, we
first endure, then pity, then embrace.
Alexander Pope Essay on Man Linedm 217

The next morning, at breakfast mother shared with me that she and Vincus had come to a similar conclusion. The aim of not responding to our generous invitations was to destroy Rome within one generation and that women would have to be forcibly taken.

She advised against rape as an initial strategy if we wanted to win the women's hearts. She recommended kindness and seduction. "We will need to make allies with their families, and, if they are treated well and have Roman babies in their bellies, this will be much easier." She stated.

When I told her of my visit from Apollo, her jaw became slack and she suggested that we contact Vincus immediately.

I sent a runner for him, and Vincus was with us within the half hour. The smiles between him and my mother suggested that a romance was blooming. He reported that my uncle Amulius had "died" unexpectedly in his sleep. He laughingly offered his condolences.

Vincus heard that Apollo had identified himself and what he had told me.

Vincus offered that the strategy was sound. He reasoned, "Your visits from the god have only brought us success and good fortune. We cannot risk angering him by not complying. But we need to gather our allies in the Senate first and make sure that there is no dissension. Now, who can we count on?"

We reviewed those that had always been supporters and those who had accompanied us to Alba Longa. We settled on those that had been both. Quintus, Arilius, Lycinius and Melbius fit those categories and had personal fortunes and their own guards. They would take an active part. It would be necessary to recruit Ursicinus the head of the army. As he had served with Vincus, was his friend and had prospered greatly under my leadership, we were virtually certain of his loyalty.

The less wealthy and influential of our companions to Abla Longa would be informed so that they could lend congressional support and so they could retreat if violence should occur.

We took the rest of that week to gather our allies. My head almost split from the aching pain of simply decoding the hidden agenda of each. Fortunately, Vincus, Ursicinus and my mother were well versed with the convolutions of diplomacy and we were able to come to a compromise. We were all fervently religious and believed that I was favored by the gods and being guided by Apollo himself.

After what they had seen with their own eyes, they did not want to defy the Olympians. This and having gratitude from their king, their army commander and the richest man in Rome were imminently persuasive. It would be much better than our enmity. We settled for prestige, power and fortune to be determined later and to have their pick of the daughters of Sabine. All but young Quintus, who had the eyes of a serpent, made demands. He agreed without conditions.

Two days after, we met with the senate. Vincus, Quintus, Ursicinus, Arilius, Lycinius an Melbus and I concealed short swords. They all had men hiding in the streets outside. I told them of my meeting with Apollo. I announced my decisions. We would begin raiding the surrounding areas and that the women were to be kept as honored guests for three months. They must not be raped and should be immediately released if they wanted to go.

We would take the daughters of Sabine at the next Festival of Neptune. The same rules concerning treatment of the women, applied to them as applied to all Roman men, Patrician and Plebeian.

As there always was, there was immediate division and squabbling. I shouted them down and told them that I had decided, and it was not up for debate. Vestus, Quinones, and Lucius, rich and powerful men refused to be silent and became animated. Vestus cried, "How many times will you come to us with tales of orders from the gods, Apollo no less, and expect us to fall into line?" Quinones argued, "Every unmarried bitch whose womb becomes ripe claims she was taken by a god. Let us not be fools!" Lucius scoffed, "And we will make enemies of all the surrounding states because of a wine dream or an undigested piece of meat!"

Vincus, Ursicinus and Arilius rushed forward to them grabbed the back of their necks with their left hands and viciously and repeatedly stabbed them in the stomach and chest areas.

Shouting and screams erupted from the Senators. Many of the Senators tried to run out of the building and moaned when they were stopped by armed soldiers at the exits.

The foul smell of fear filled the building.

Ursicinus shouted, "The King has so proclaimed! The army will obey and enforce". Cybius, Acostis, and Ligginius had vocally supported me and I granted them the lands and fortunes of the murdered men. Seneca stepped forward and said jovially. "I will personally rip my prick into every foreign cunt that we take!"

I leaped forward and with one sweep of my sword, I took his head. It went spiraling, gushing circles of blood into a group of senators. His headless body took a step forward and then crumpled. "I said no rapes!

Even if we must kill to take them, the women are to be honored guests and not molested. Those that cannot be seduced will be sent back to their families with honor. Aggripa now owns Seneca's' lands and fortunes." I bellowed.

The others seemed shocked but dropped their heads and shoulders in compliance. Their silence screamed. "You all will have first pick of the women", I consoled. This seemed to assuage some bruised egos. I pleaded for peace and compliance and acknowledged that it was hard for former equals to accept a king. "But", I added, "It is what YOU wanted. And you MUST accept my sovereignty".

Quintus and Arilius agreed to have the mess cleaned up and Vincus, Ursicinus and I left under heavy guard. I was glad to leave, the Senate smelled like shit and blood and it had all been…disgusting. Four good men were dead, and their families would soon follow: simply for opposing me. However, Apollo had commanded me. And my father was Mars himself. The gods were on my side.

Melbus and some of our lesser allies remained behind to snoop out other traitors, and sly conspirators. Ursicinus said. "I will assure order while my old friend Vincus is better at making the families of the traitors …. er… go missing". Vincus laughed, "It will be completed by tomorrow morning… or the morning after that. We have been successful, but now we are the most vulnerable."

Ursicinus suggested, "We better give something to the soldiers because they are fickle and like to grumble." Vincus and I opened our own coffers and agreed to give them bonuses." The old general responded, "That will help, and I think that giving them wine and a cause against enemies will help even more".

I said, "The raiding will begin tomorrow". Ursicinus pounded his right fist to his heart as a salute and acknowledgement. He offered, "We have a carrot, now we need a stick".

Vincus offered, "Those who rape if they are Patricians will be publicly beheaded. The Plebeians will be whipped to death until their skin flays" I thought for a moment and said, "Our symbol will be an ax with its handle surrounded by rods. As a warning and show of authority, one of our men will carry it whenever we are in public. Disobey and get the ax or the rod."

From that time onward a large guard carried Fasces whenever any of us were in public.

Soon, women were being brought into Rome in ever increasing numbers.

Single women of Abla Longa became the wives of Roman men. We treated them like royalty. Soon the word was spreading, "Romans treat their wives like queens". I sent envoys to Sabine with tribute and invitations to join us in the Festival of Neptune.

Unfortunately, some of our neighbors had been killed in the raids. An army from the northern city of Veii rose against us to punish Rome.

We rode out into the field with Ursicinus commanding. As Apollo ordered, I was in the forefront in full armor. On a white war stallion and in charge of our elite cavalry; my helm trailed white and purple standards. I was easily identifiable as the king.

We traveled for a day and confronted an army of perhaps thirty thousand in a great open field. Our side was professional soldiers while their side was part-time militia; tradesmen banded together to exact vengeance and retrieve their daughters and sisters. Following them were about five thousand irregulars armed with clubs, pitchforks and other farming tools.

They were significantly outmatched in numbers and skill. But they had courage and were filled with rage.

When they fired their missiles at us, our troops quickly formed a "testudo", a roof or hut, of shields. They had seen similar formations, but they were shocked when we advanced upon them in this formation.

Our archers took their toll. We advanced to the point where we were almost with in closing range when we formed a "false middle" formation. Three squares of legions, with the center line consisting of a single line of men formed the middle. The first and third were backed up by six lines, and those were backed up by four more legions.

As they rushed us, the middle retreated, and they were swallowed by the other two lines. The men of Veii fought as a single men looking for glory while we fought behind our shields and stabbed while covered from head to foot. It was not a battle, we simply butchered them.

As I think back, the scene reminds me of a great harvester machine cutting down wheat.

Their king was on a hill behind them. He was too entitled to fight beside his rank and file. Like most cowardly leaders, he thought he was safe behind his great hoi polloi. He was obese and was eating grapes and meat while his soldiers were dying.

Our cavalry had maneuvered behind him and his personal guard. While our troops fought, we attacked their rear flank. We broke through the easily surprised and bored elites. I caught up with his chariot as he ran like a rabbit. I drove my lance through his lightly armored back. It was more jewelry and pretension than armor.

The king of Veii had never considered the possibility and inconvenience of personal combat. He screamed like a small child and farted as my lance ruptured his heart.

When he fell tumbling out of his chariot, his generals surrendered and signaled their troops to stop fighting.

Ending the enemy king so quickly saved untold numbers of lives on both sides.

Cries of "All hail the King" arose first from their side and then from both sides, and they became my subjects and citizens of Rome. "Hail to the King who leads in battle!" Our causalities were minimal, and we added twenty-five thousand to our army.

I took the king's armor. When we returned to Rome, I held it up for all the people and the Senate to see. Some of the younger senators, those who were suspect, we had put on the front line of the battle. A quick spear to the back prevents a lot of possible problems. We ensured that they did not return and were given heroes' burials. We would provide for their families.

I ordered that a Temple of Jupiter the Slayer be erected and that the armor of defeated kings would be displayed there.

Our joyous citizens and army celebrated until dawn; many fat rams and oxen were slaughtered, their fat and viscera roasted on coals for the gods.

We had one more similar battle soon thereafter. The results were the same. In the end we had the new territory of Lavinium to send us tribute and I had another king's armor as a trophy; minus the shoulder and arm I had amputated in acquiring it.

I commissioned kingly armor for myself in pure black with a skull like faceplate to let my kingly opponents know that they faced death. I found a spirited black stallion was my war horse. Part of this was a tactic to instill fear but it also reflected my growing arrogance. After all, was I not a demigod, the son of Mars and favored by Apollo?

Ursicinus told me that in it I looked like Pluto himself.

We began making preparation for the great Feast of Neptune and abduction of the Sabines. We brought in huge tables, tents and a store of food and wine.

15

The Feast of Neptune

"It's better to get something worthwhile done using deception than to fail to get something worthwhile done using truth." Carlos Castaneda

Soon the Feast of Neptune was only a week away. We began receiving, thousands of members of the Sabine families.

We accommodated them in Roman homes according to their stations. Our senators and generals got to decide which Sabine daughters they wanted to claim. Their wives and especially the prepubescent girls were strictly off limits.

After a night of drunken revelry some besotted legionnaires and local thugs raped three women, one of them a Sabine. The night guard took them and the next noon we brought them to the public square. The Plebian mob was joyful and there was almost a sense of festival in the event. The Sabians looked forward to the spectacle. The crowd cheered and jostled among each other for a better view.

The condemned were tied to building columns. Large muscular legionnaires in groups of five carrying thin rods were assigned to each man.

As the public gathered, I, Ursicinus and Vincus officiated. Our bodyguards held up Fasces over their heads.

"As we have commanded if you rape, you are condemned to death. Patricians meet the headsman while Plebeians are flayed alive. Victims will have silver to compensate them. If you are so aggrieved, tell a centurion and you will have justice. You will see your attacker bleed.

If you make a false report, you will be fed alive to hogs. You will die screaming.

My people and guests enjoy today's entertainment", I announced. Ursicinus gave the signal and the legionnaires began slowly and enthusiastically whipping the men, rotating turns as each became fatigued. The cries of the condemned started out angry and defiant and after an hour, became pathetic squeaks. The crowd cheered each blow at first.

The skin of the men being executed began to roll off in sheets. They began to whimper after two hours and then could not vocalize at all. The crowds began to flinch and moan as each blow was struck and the blood splattered on the ground and columns.

After two hours, a centurion stepped forward and put his sword deeply through the collar bone into the heart of each and the crowd, looking shaken, slowly dispersed.

We had demonstrated our resolve and made our point. I was surprisingly unmoved by the condemned's pathetic suffering. When I told this to Vincus, "He put his hand on my shoulder and sadly said, "You have become a king".

Then he punched my shoulder lightly and said in jest. "Good! Now we need to decapitate a Patrician to punctuate the sentence. The Plebeians would like that, and it will show that the law applies equally to all."

Ursicinus laughed, "I can make that happen. I have one in mind. And it will make me feel so much better." I shrugged, nodded and said, "Make it so".

The next morning offered a similar scene. The mob gathered in the public square and the young son of a senator was marched in under heavy guard. Behind him was a large legionnaire with a thick belly and a large war ax.

The young man was the son of one of Ursicinus' political and business rival. He was courting one of the women from Alba Longa and had lost control and forcibly raped her. She had complained to Ursicinus' daughter, her friend. I formally condemned him to death. Our guards held up our Fasces over their heads.

I announced. "Lothius has been convicted of raping a daughter of Alba Longa. She is being escorted home with silver as we meet here. Rape in Rome means death! Will the father, uncles and brothers hold the condemned legs and pull his hands forward so that he does not struggle and can die bravely and cleanly." It was both a mercy and an additional punishment.

A patrician could demonstrate one last act of courage in this way, and his family would have the agony of holding him down to receive the death stroke. Otherwise, the executioner would end up catching him as he could, essentially slowly hacking him to death.

The youth was on his hands and knees and his relatives stepped up to him and with tears in their eyes offered their extended hands. An uncle and brother tightly held his legs. He could not find the courage to extend his arms, and his father Scrotius and mother pleaded with him to do so. The parents and uncles ended up coaxing him like a child who would not eat his peas.

The crowd hooted and jeered, and the executioner stepped forward. His father and uncle had to resort to wrestling with him to get his arms and the crowd laughed as if this was the world's best comedy. They finally pulled his hands forward and away from his body.

The condemned's brother stepped forward and handed the headsman a purse of coins. He said, 'Strike true". The executioner took a wide stand, lifted his ax over his head, and then forcefully swung in down. A wavy-haired head fell heavily from a kneeling body. His father and uncles holding his arms were showered with blood.

As his head hit the ground with a meaty thump, the crowd winced and turned away. His family women started wailing. Ursicinus put his extended pinky to his lips and stifled a laugh.

One of Ursicinus' commanders walked over to the grieving family and offered loud condolences. He whispered to the father, "Next time you will vote with the general. And you will lower your price on beef. If you are thinking of vengeance, remember you have other sons." Then he promptly walked away.

Ursicinus looked at Vincus and I and shrugged and said, "Its only business. He was a spoiled, mouthy and entitled little prick." Vincus laughed and offered, "He was not the heir and Scrotius has more sons. Now we have had one of each, Plebeian and Patrician. The crowd is shaken and impressed" We then went about our respective days leading up to the great festival.

On the day of the festival, I greeted the best families of Sabine. The senators casually walked up and touched the shoulders of the women they claimed, and scribes took notes on who selected whom. Once they were done, the high-ranking army officers did the same, then wealthy trade's men, then the soldiers and the plebeians.

Of course, we did not allow married men to choose.

We did our ceremonies and sacrifices to great Neptune; and then huge street festival ensued, and private parties were held in wealthy homes. There were tables and canopies everywhere and all of Rome resembled a modern-day Italian street festival. There was raucous music, bawdy singing and dancing, the best of local foods, and a river of wine.

The nobles of Sabine and Rome of course were at the King's palace. Ursicinus and his generals, the Melbius, Quintus, Arilius, and Lycinius, now elevated to advisers, my mother and her escort Vincus, now Regent and I were the formal receivers.

Many of their daughters were beautiful but seemed vapid. It was wearisome to greet hordes of affected and fat nobles until the representative of their king, Tatius, made her appearance.

She, however, was a strong, sturdy woman with flowing wavy black hair. Her face was the epitome of feminine charm. There was animation in her features and shining intelligence in her eyes. She had wide hips and a big bosom. Her arms and shoulders were muscular.

She wore a red, Greek style gown and the light seemed to follow her. My mind was taken away, and I imagined a woman in a Greek dress with her hair pinned up, sitting on a three-legged stool looking into a volcanic crack in the earth.

She gracefully offered me her hand and her grip was incredibly strong.

She said "I am Bella Aguinius, the great King Tatius' cousin. I am his envoy; I represent him. Tatius apologizes but the business of state keeps him from attending." She was aptly named as "Bella" meaning "beautiful" in our common language. I felt unreal, as if in a dream, as I reached down and touched her shoulder. My mother gave me an approving smile, while Vincus raised his eyebrows in a knowing manner.

We all circulated and then, as people do at parties, we settled into amicable groups. We ate the feast that we had been preparing for weeks. I started liking these people. Many of them were articulate and intelligent.

Of course, I managed to separate Bella from the crowd. We talked and laughed. She knew many amusing stories of the gods. She was astounding at coming up with spontaneous poetry that was both beautiful and poignant.

She was taken back when I told her of my vision. She shuddered and said she had that exact image when she was a girl of six or seven. We pondered what this concordance meant and agreed to consult the Oracle the next day.

Wine was a wonderful social lubricant.

As we drank, we began to giggle like toddlers. The attraction between us was palpable. I could not help but sport a huge erection, which was embarrassing and hard to conceal. She noticed it and made tentative and ambivalent approaches and avoidances to touching me. She seemed to unconsciously rub her breasts and licked her lips several times.

We lavished our rich red wine on all the Sabines and drank very lightly ourselves. We even foisted wine on their slaves. Outside the palace, the scene was being duplicated all over Rome. Their guard was encouraged to drunkenness by our soldiers. Soon spirits were high and vast numbers of our guests were vomiting and passing out. We let them sleep where they fell while we prepared for dawn.

Bella consumed as much as most men could and fell asleep at a great dining table. I carried her to a bedroom and lay her on the couches and posted guards at the door and under the windows. I wanted to take her right then, but I managed to go back to the party.

Vincus and my mother approached me and smiled." I see you have made your choice and it seemed to be a good one", my mother said. I was amazed that I was still erect, and the pair noticed it. "Take one of my female slaves or you might break your own law." Vincus jested while pointing to a stunning young woman in his retinue.

"Drusilla, she specializes in that".

He and my mother laughed. At that time, sex, toileting and bathing were not private acts as they are today. I motioned Vincus' female slave over to me, I bent her over the table, pushed her skirts over her head, put my phallus into her.

"You have a horse cock" my mother commented. Vincus offered, "That's it, Majesty slowly".

She then bent there stoically, and I finished almost immediately. In my drunkenness, I slipped and knocked us both to the floor. In getting up, my foot caught in her long skirt and she fell heavily on top of me. My mother and Vincus laughed hilariously making raucous comments. Mother said. "Does she specialize in that as well? You must really like Tatius' cousin, my son!" They tittered like children at my expense.

Those comments as much as the sex act shriveled my penis to the size of a small mushroom.

I purchased the slave girl from Vincus and gave her a pouch of coins and jewels that would set her up for life. Then I granted her freedom. Vincus and mother thought that was extravagant and not necessary. It made me feel better. I had never forced myself upon a woman. She left under protection of my best personal guardsmen with a young legionnaire making puppy dog eyes at her.

I learned later that they wed and set up a tavern and bawdy house on the outskirts of Rome. I discovered years later that Drusilla had become one of the mothers of Rome's premiere crime families. It is said she only said the best things about King Romulus, even into her old age.

In the years to come she granted me the greatest favor in my life.

We prepared all that night. Just before dawn, our legionnaires were let into all Roman homes housing Sabines and separated the entire group of young single woman from their families and escorts.

The young women were confined in the most luxurious room of the citizen's home. However, guards were posted as I had done. I sent a group of legionnaires to escort our head-achy, fatigued and nauseous fellow partiers to the knoll just before Sabine.

In the evening of that day, I enacted a scene that was again being repeated all over Rome. I approached my reluctant guest and entered her room. Although her eyes were glazed, she was unsteady on her feet, she was outraged. "How dare you detain me", she roared.

"I am King Tatius' envoy. This is an act of war".

I said soothingly. "You are badly hung over.

I find you so amazing and I merely wished some more time with you. We are going to see the Oracle about our shared vision, remember?"

"If I am a guest, then I am free to go!" she demanded.

"I put you in here to preserve your dignity because you passed out from a little too much wine. You seem nauseous still", I offered. "Then why the armed guards?" she protested. "Standard precautions to protect a guest of your high standing", I replied.

She started heaving, and I grabbed an unused chamber pot and held her hair back as she vomited into it. I dabbed the remnants from her mouth and offered her a cup of water to get the taste out of her mouth. "Oh, I am seeing double and my head is splitting open!" she complained.

"You are just not used to our strong Roman wine. Sleep sweet lady and I will stay with you this night to attend to your needs". Before she could protest, I said, "I will ask a woman to stay with us if certain things you need will be more comfortably done by a female." I told the guards of my plans and one of my middle-aged women house servants came in a few minutes later with a water basin, pitcher of water, soap and towels.

"Lay your sweet head down and I will put a cold towel on your forehead." I offered. She relieved herself in another chamber pot and lay down. Within a moment, she was fast asleep. She looked like an ivory statue of a wood nymph in the moonlight. However, I laughed when she began to snore as loudly as a mule hauler.

"What is it in our Roman wine?" I mused to the servant woman. "Yes, our guests only drank about a gallon each," She chuckled. I laughed and said, "They are lucky to even be alive". Then I spent the night beside my black-haired Bella, the Beauty.

We awoke in the morning and Bella was feeling much better. Bathing was also not a private thing at the time, and we went to the baths in the palace. I was taken aback by her body. Nudity was commonplace in those days, so we did not get so easily sexually aroused by nudity as people do today.

She had a muscular body that was round in the right places and hard in the right paces. I could see her looking me up and down admiringly as well. We chatted and flirted as the slaves scrubbed our backs and washed her hair. I found her so intelligent, attractive and desirable, that, like a 13-year-old boy I found myself again sprouting an erection. I flushed a little and tried to hide myself.

I pulled away and said "I am sorry, my lady, I mean no disrespect. This hasn't happened since I was a young boy. But I am so attracted to you."

I motioned to move away from her and get out of the bath, but she pulled me forward and took me in her hand and put me inside of herself. She kissed me wildly on the mouth; our passion let loose; we copulated like wild animals in the warm water.

The body slaves in the room were there to ensure my absolute pleasure as king; a slave licked Bella's nipples and while the third spurred me on.

That afternoon I collected tribute for the Oracle and arranged for a 12 man and horse lectica to take us to Pythia. We were to travel to the slopes of Mount Parnassus just beneath the Castalian Springs. We both wore plain white robes in honor of the virgin Oracle.

We walked together up the slope, and upon entering the cave saw the words carved in the stone "The Voice of the Gods", and we offered tribute to the priests of the Oracle.

We whispered our query to the Oracle who sat upon a three-legged stool, shrouded in the darkness of the cave. I could hear a slight hissing, as if a viper were nearby. She seemed to lurch and wobble as if she were drunk. She held a simple bowl and a large sprig of bay

After I had asked her about our similar visions, she swooned, and was bobbling around in the chair, nearly tipping over! She began to speak in an incompressible foreign tongue. I felt the hairs on the back of my neck stiffen at the strangeness of it all.

One of the priests moved forward his face hidden by his gritty tunic. He interpreted her speech, "Pythia says: "Apollo is moving… but not all smiles are friendly …behold a stone, you and she are the substance and the result, bound to each other through time and pressure, two that make a whole…await not in quiet the coming of the horses great King, the marching feet, the armed host upon the land…turn your back and you will meet in battle anyway…prepare thyself for black moons risings… the son of Mars is a great beast that devours all".

The oracle grew sweaty as she spoke and went into frenzy, her eyes rolling in their sockets. The priest moved us along and out of the cave and past the Oracle. In ancient days, what the Oracle had to say to us was as if the gods were speaking to us, this was important for both of us to hear.

We were a couple after that and enjoyed fantastic lovemaking several times a day. We swore our love to each other and agreed to plan a marriage. We gave each other knotted golden rings as a symbol of our union. She assumed all the trappings of the queen but didn't have the title yet.

The same results happened thousands of times all over Rome. By the three months limit, Bella was showing the child I had planted in her and Rome seemed a city of women with swollen bellies. But not all the unions were as happy. About four hundred women requested return to Sabine. We plied them with silver and arranged an escort and envoys to take them back to their home city.

About two days after their departure, ragged and bloody legionnaires appeared at the gates of Rome pleading to be let in. About, twelve of the three hundred we had sent returned whipped and mutilated. Some of them had had noses, ears or fingers cut off. Some eyes had been gouged out.

They had escorted the women to Sabine, but a large force of men spilled out of the citadel and took charge of escorting the women inside.

Marius, one of the troopers who had suffered amputated fingers reported, "The Sabine soldiers cursed us and formed a phalanx. They outnumbered us three to one, but our armor, weapons and tactics were superior. We quickly decimated them. But then, from over the nearby hills an incredible throng of armored men descended upon us.

They looked like ants flooding from an angry ant hill. We fought bravely killing perhaps twice our own number. But, in the end, there were too many and they overwhelmed us by sheer force of numbers.

They killed all but thirty of us and took the survivors into their fortress. There we were met by King Tatius, who had us bound and, in front of his mob, mutilated our bodies in the ways you see. Your envoy's heads are decorating his ramparts. Some legionnaires died from the torture and some died on our way to deliver this message to you. We twelve are all that remains.

Tatius said that he would be sending a special envoy to you, My King. That Rome's surrender would be negotiated, or it would be burned to the ground.

They hurt me the least so that I would give you the following message: "Their convoy will arrive tomorrow morning."

We then sent the wounded soldiers to the healers.

Vincus was with my mother and I as we heard this. Moments later Ursicinus and Crassius, his sub- commander joined us. Vincus shared, "This is an exercise in dominance and submission. We did violate guest etiquette by abducting the women and Tatius has lost face."

My mother offered, "We need to make a dramatic response to counter this." Ursicinus thought out loud, "If they are going to demand surrender, they will send people of power and authority." Crassius added, "Someone who is important to King Tatius."

I thought for a moment and then said, "We will need an example and it will have to be good theater". Ursicinus chuckled and added, "I learned a cute little trick or two while I was serving in Macedonia..."

The next morning, two open wagons accompanied by forty soldiers dressed in scale mail, leather helmets, and carrying iron weapons sued for entrance into Rome's gate. Two young men in slightly better armor and plumed helmets rode in front. They came into the large open square for the city and were met by Ursicinus, Vincus and my advisers and three hundred of our most seasoned veterans. All our men stared directly and unflinchingly in these envoys' eyes.

One of young men announced imperiously," I am Crown Prince Moribuis and this is my brother, Prince Oblerius.

Aggression against us is aggression against King Tatius himself. I have come to make a presentation of tribute to Romulus and to accept your terms for surrender. Where is Romulus?"

Bella stepped forward from between the veterans and Moribuis was obviously stunned to see her, especially in her pregnant state. "Are you sure you want to see him, Cousin?" She replied and then smiled. Although his confidence seemed deflated, he announced, "I am future king of Sabine and I will speak only with Romulus, himself. Defying me is an act of war!"

Moribuis and Oblerius dismounted and each went to the rear of each wagon. They signaled and two troopers grabbed the coverings on the wagons and quickly pulled them off. There were the heads about a hundred of our fallen soldiers in each of the wagons. The flies immediately swarmed, and the stench of rotted flesh filled the air.

Moribuis barked, as if to a great audience in a theater, "This is what you will get for opposing Sabine and Tatius."

At that moment, two hundred legionnaires in a wall of shields rushed out from all quarters and pressed their spears lightly into the chests of the Sabines.

"But...But, this is a diplomatic mission! I am the crown prince and rudeness to us is to declare war against the strongest force in the land".

The wall of Roman shields parted, and I walked forward. The princes were still built like boys and just over five feet tall each. I was wearing my black steel plate. In my full war armor to the top of the comb, I stood about seven foot tall. I wore my silver skull face plate.

The Sabine troopers and the princes were visibly shaken, gasped and could be seen to tremble. I could hear their troopers murmuring "Pluto" and "Tantos".

In a way, they were right.

I stepped directly up to the older prince and said, "I am Romulus! You dare to threaten us and expect us to cower at the mention of Tatius? You bring us the heads of our brave warriors who you cravenly overwhelmed and slaughtered. You offered them no quarter.

You killed my diplomats and tortured my surviving legionnaires! Now we will return the favor."

I walked up to Moribuis looking him directly in the eye. He turned his head away. "Rudeness?!" I shouted. How is this for rudeness?" I hit him with a right hook from my armored glove. It was like being punched with brass knuckles. I could feel his jaw break under the blow. He flew back against the first wagon. He crumpled on the floor and gurgled trying to speak.

"Ursicinus take them and do as we decided. All except you two", I put my right arm over Oblerius and a random Sabine trooper. You are guests of your cousin Bella and will be treated to one of our most extravagant shows"

The legionnaires marched the Sabine soldiers and Moribuis to a trove of trees just outside the front gate. They were stripped and hanged from the low-lying limbs with their toes touching the ground. They gagged and gasped for air as they were slowly strangled. The mob gathered and began cheering and throwing stones.

The legionnaires moved them back and Crassius rode along their line and announced. "Do not harm them! We have a three-part play for you today."

Towards noon, the half strangled and weakened Sabines were cut down and dragged by horses back into the main square. Their skin suffered terrible abrasions. The thirty-eight men were lined up with Moribuis at the end of the line. Then each man in turn had his arms and legs tied separately to four horses and the horses were given the spur.

The mob laughed, cheered and mocked the men as they were torn apart. My retinue and the remaining Prince and I watched from the elevated palace stairs.

Finally, after several hours the crown Prince's turn came up. He cried and whimpered as he was dragged to the binding place. As he was being tied to the horses, I shouted to him, "Ah, we saved the best for last. Any last threats you wish to make?"

The mob roared with laughter. Then he was quartered, the crowds dispersed and seemed pleased and amused at the show we had provided them.

I turned to Oblerius and asked sarcastically, "You don't have any threats or demands do you? Good. You will remain here as Bella's and my house guest. A legionnaire will bring us your brother's head in a box and your trooper will take it to Tatius. I hope he accepts my terms. The boy stood there stoically, but I recognized grief and fear in his eyes.

"Now, shall we dine?"

We were surprised when there was quiet for over a year and a half. We continued to take our neighbors' daughters and defeated the inferior armies of their cities. Tribute flowed in from all the conquered provinces.

Rome rang with the laughter and play of children; including my twin sons, "Remus" and "Numitor"; and Bella was expecting again.

Even Oblerius seemed to like his gilded cage.

The Fullness of Life

All Is Vanity
1 The words of the Preacher, the son
of David, king in Jerusalem.
2 Vanity of vanities, saith the Preacher,
vanity of vanities; all is vanity.
3 What profit hath a man of all his labor
which he taketh under the sun
4 On earth abideth for every generation
passeth away, and and other commeth but
the earth abideth forever. Ecclesiastes

Two years had passed and Remus and Numitor had a one-year old sister, Lucia. Bella was as beautiful as ever. I thought, even more so as she was carrying our newest child in her womb.

Our lives together were wonder and joy themselves. We saw things exactly alike and seldom disagreed. When we made love, it was always like the first time. The only thing that was difficult is that I was frequently away with the army repelling invaders.

My mother and Vincus were wed and assumed leadership of Abla Longa. Mother looked much too young and beautiful to be a grandmother and enjoyed the admiring glances she received at the public baths. Vincus was happy and became ever richer. My grandfather lived with them and we saw each other several times a week.

Old fierce Numitor, the terror of my adolescent fears, was a doting and loving great grandfather to our children. He tended to spoil them and would have died for them. He always had treats in his pockets for them and was their consoler when they were sad or hurt.

Numitor, Ursicinus, Vincus and my mother and I often sat on the toilet together and discussed affairs of state. During these sessions we decided who was becoming a threat and how they would be eliminated.

Often, we would simply put the young ones in the front line of battle and then assure that they were counted among the casualties. Sometimes "raiders" or "brigands" would lay waste to entire households. Most of the time discrete poison gave the appearance of natural death.

It was a game to try to finish first and not have to be the last one to use the common wiping rag on a stick. My sweet Bella was too genteel to join our group.

We continued to raid our neighbors for their women, and we insisted that of anti-rape laws were enforced. Rape was virtually eliminated among the Plebeians.

The Patricians were different, but we had to make decisions politically. I hated to do this, but we always exacted a dear price from the Patrician family involved. In the future if they opposed us or voted against us, the Patrician's heir was surreptitiously eliminated. Of course, there were still public executions and tortures. They were for murder, treason, heresy, theft and such. But even these were getting rarer.

Ursicinus opined that the executions were good in that they inured the mob to violence and death, and it provided them distraction. Numitor suggested "In Alba Longa, before funerals the rich are providing combats to the death by slaves. They are spreading to weddings and other celebrations.

Vincus opined, "I like them! The rabble decides the fate of the defeated. If a fighter is bested but has been brave and put up a good fight, they frequently let him live. The magistrate lifts his right thumb up if they live, or makes a throat cutting gesture if they die. "Ursicinus said, "That shows that bravery is rewarded and demonstrates basic armed combat techniques to the young.".

Numitor laughed, "Watching puts starch in your cock and the women love the bared bodies of the slaves. It is always funny to watch a slave in his death throes" He moved his head to the side and back, stuck his tongue out to the side and made gurgling sounds. He bent over guffawed and slapped his knee in emphasis. I was not so callus to death of anyone without good justification. But one learns to keep his mouth shut around older, more conservative family members.

That week, we bought two slaves who had been condemned to death by their masters and put them in the public square. We gave them swords and bucklers. The winner would have his life and freedom. The match up was between a cook and a wine waiter. Neither had any idea how to keep a guard up. They were clumsy and managed to inflict many minor wounds on each other.

The mob reveled in it. They hooted and coached the fighters and booed their mistakes. Bets were hastily offered and accepted. The combatants became progressively whiter in pallor and they each ended up dying of blood loss. But the public loved it. We continued these weekly, recruited paid fighters and expanded it to as many as ten combats per occasion.

It took on a life of its own and soon rich families were offering such entertainment at their celebrations. Schools for training slaves to fight arose and men made fortunes. It turned out to be a boon the professional gamblers of the city.

We had to go ever further afield to get the women we needed. None could stand against our army

When a city retaliated, I always led the cavalry in my black armor and skull face mask. I collected ten more sets of kingly armor. At first, the ignorant and superstitious among our enemies thought I was Pluto or Death himself. They came to realize that to face me was to face death. Soon, it was widely said that "Romulus is Death".

In my arrogance and vanity, I came to believe it myself. Lately, our enemies just surrendered and welcomed us in to take our choice of their daughters. We did not plunder but became still bloated with tribute.

Our Army swelled and we divided into two sub-armies covering out north and south. Ursicinus was overall commander of two armies each of one hundred thousand strong.

Our martial arts experts developed deadly and dominating style of combat. Legionnaires would crash into enemies with the bottom of their long shields. Then they would stab from behind the shield. Combat masters taught ways to swing around the back of an opponent and stab his kidneys and other vital organs or cut the back of his legs.

Our armorers and engineers continued to develop better and better tools of war. We crafted huge ballista, crossbows that with one bolt could take out a line of twenty enemies from incredible distances. Catapults that could throw horse sized rocks and balls of grease fire. Some had seen "Greek Fire", that would literally burn on water and we attempted to perfect it. It was the most feared weapon of the ancient world.

Then one night, I awakened from a dream and heard a sweet deep voice calling my name. I turned to look at Bella lying next to me, but I had never seen her in such a deep sleep before. I arose and went to the porch and there was the familiar golden figure.

"You have done well, Romulus. Has not my advice has caused you to prosper?" the golden one said. He was identical in appearance except for two small horns that were forming out of his forehead.

"My lord Apollo", I said. "It is always what you believe it to be", he replied. "I am a little confused by that statement, My Lord. Are you not the god, Apollo?" I offered. He gave me a sly smile and said, "How can men understand the ways of the gods? Have I not favored you? Have you not prospered greatly under my beneficence?"

I found myself confused and sitting on one of the marble benches without conscious volition. Apollo stood behind me, put his hands on my shoulders, and whispered first in one ear and then in the other. The result seemed to transport me into a state like a waking dream.

"Sabine is getting ready to move against you. Six moons from today, they intend to storm Rome's gates. Sly Tatius is preparing siege weapons and is recruiting mercenaries. His army is larger than yours, and the mercenaries are the best, most experienced, soldiers in the world. He will recruit a daughter of one of your commanders to secret his troops through a side door.

You will need a hundred more ballistae and as many catapults. The mercenaries will be easy to identify. They will not have identical armor as the Sabine regular army does. They are a hodgepodge. They have never seen anything like your weapons. Kill them at a long distance with bolts, rocks and fire. Try to eliminate Tatius, if you can. He is vicious and cunning. He will be in the rear, like the… um… "hero" he is…

Line up a moderate force at the gate, and have your main army concealed on the left and right flanks. As they close with you, bring the traitress to the top of the wall and kill her terribly. I have my favorites, but you Romans seem to be so inventive that I anticipate your creative choice.

Capture the men they sent to infiltrate your fortress and kill them in front of their comrades.

I will begin to reveal myself to some of your most loyal allies and advise them. This will give you more credibility. I will only giveadvice that is for the greater good of Rome."

I found myself nodding throughout his soliloquy.

He smiled and it was like looking into the sun. I had to cover my eyes. The smile blazed on after he faded away.

I dreamed of the warrior in crimson armor agitated and yelling at me. I could not understand him. He was shaking in rage, and I could see the veins in his forehead popping out. He put his hands on the foot of my bed.

Bella and I were awakened by our bed shaking violently and being thrown about three feet to the right. She grabbed my arm and screamed. The guards rushed in just as small objects, vases, face mirrors and other bric-a-brac, levitated from all the tables and shelves and flew at us.

To their credit, despite their terror the guards shielded us and hefted their spears. But there was no enemy to defend against. Everything became deadly silent in that early dawn, but a beacon of light shown shined in from the porch entrance. The guards rushed in and armed with a short sword, I followed them.

There was the shape of a smile, blazing like a lantern where I had last seen Apollo.

It glared into the next evening.

I brought in my advisers and soothsayers, and they all recoiled at the still blazing disembodied smile. There was much disagreement. Certainly, we should prepare for a siege and construct the war machines he advised. But what did the image of his smile mean; was he "smiling down on us?"

But then, what about the spirit attacks Bella and I had suffered. Surely the warrior in red was my father Mars. Was he trying to push me to action? And why did the ghostly attack feel like a warning?

We knew from our religious stories and the Iliad and Odyssey that the gods disagree. We could not find any answers. I found myself saying automatically, "How can men understand the ways of the gods".

The Invasion

But if our hopes are betrayed, if we are forced to resist the invasion of our soil, and to defend our threatened homes, this duty, however hard it may be, will find us armed and resolved upon the greatest sacrifices. King Albert II

We made good use of the six months Apollo gave us. On the day he predicted, our advance scouts gave us a twelve-hour warning. We moved our ballistae and catapults into place. These were alternated in two rows with additional 4 ballistae in the front. The northern and southern armies had been called close and were mobilized.

We had uncovered Lavidia, the daughter of the morning guard commander, Urripitus. He himself took her into custody and made the preparations for her execution. We knew to the hour when the Sabines and their mercenaries would arrive. Our preparation was almost casual.

The myths say that the Sabines took our citadel, but in truth, they never did.

Just before dawn, we spotted the touches of their advanced columns about two miles away. One hundred and fifty ballistae and catapults each were primed and ready. They had spare ammunition in the exact position for quick reloading. Some of the catapults were loaded round hut sized rocks, some with hundreds of fist sized rocks and some with Greek Fire ready to be ignited.

About two thousand legionnaires waited about a hundred yards before them. The two branches of the army surrounded the city with the majority hidden in the forests on our right and left sides.

A group of select soldiers waited concealed by the door that Lavidia was supposed to open for the Sabine commandos. I donned my black armor. I had had the silver skull face plate polished so that it would reflect the rising sun. This would give the impression of being a blur in the dawn of the sun, emerging out of the glare into a grinning skulled warrior. It would also make it hard to accurately aim arrows at me.

We knew no succor would be given on either side.

At about three quarters of a mile away, we could see a gigantic force of men approaching us. There were perhaps twenty thousand warriors in varying styles of armor, some in skullcap helmets, some in helms adorned with the horns of bulls, others in spiraled domed Persian helmets.

They were very disciplined and walked with grim purpose. These were the mercenaries moving forwards in a phalanx, their long spears extended. They were obvious intended as shock troops. Behind them was a main force of perhaps two hundred thousand Sabines in their inferior scale mail and bronze Corinthian helmets.

I thought of Marius the Legionnaire whom they had tortured description of "angry ants erupting from a disturbed ant hill."

In the rear of the infantry was their cavalry, and among them was Tatius surrounded by his honor guard. He was affecting golden armor which made him look regal but easy to identify.

I could see that their cavalry was intending to split up to attack our flanks. But they were boxed into the valley that led up to Rome and could not maneuver. Behind them, we could see siege towers and catapults slowly progressing.

The legionnaires in the front of the city formed their "wall of shields" defense. Their shields were also polished to reflect the morning light. This concealed what was behind them. The artillery was making their calculations and at a signal the first row of ballista opened fire. Fifty ten feet long, three hundred-pound missiles covered the three-quarter mile gap between us and the enemy in seconds.

Most of the bolts struck home and the first lines of the mercenaries' phalanx were penetrated pierced and plunged back to the twentieth man. Then the second battery of ballistae opened taking out the next lines of twenty. We repeated this one more time.

Then the small group of ballistae then let fly. Tatius' honor guard was decimated, and several missiles just missed him. He had luck, this golden armored ruler. He was no fool as he retreated with some of his generals to a hill behind his troops.

The catapults with the smaller stones opened up and several tons of fist sized rocks rained down and completed the destruction of Tatius' much vaunted mercenaries. They had been destroyed in less than twenty minutes.

To their credit, the Sabines kept advancing. At about midway, they paused awaiting orders from their king. At that moment, our wall of shields opened and their twenty commandos, who were to breach our door, were marched out and arranged in a line with a legionnaire behind each one.

In unison, the legionnaires swung their swords, and twenty Sabine heads flew in various directions. Blood spurted and streamed high into the air. Their bodies dropped before their killers' feet.

I walked out from behind the wall of legionnaires and picked up one of the severed heads by the hair. I could see the Sabines shielding their eyes to get a glimpse at me from behind the glare from my face plate and the polished shields. I pointed to the high wall above our gates.

On top of our twenty-foot-high wall, a squad of soldiers pushed up a large cross with Lavidia tied to it and set it fast. She and the cross were soaked with dry Greek Fire. Her father Urripitus stood a few feet away holding a blazing torch. He shouted at the top of his lungs, "Lavidia, the traitor.... Lavidia the traitor" ...repeatedly. I thought I could hear his voice break at the end of his rant.

As a father, I felt his pain and his anger. I had known and liked Lavidia.

I sadly guessed that money could corrupt anyone.

From below, our legionnaires shouted repeatedly in chorus. "Behold Greek Fire....Behold Greek Fire!" I motioned them to silence. I raised my right arm over my head and threw it down sharply. Urripitus touched the torch to his daughter.

There was a flickering of fire up to the top of the cross and then a huge explosive ball. When the flames leaped twenty-five feet in the air, we and the Sabines startled.

Lavidia let out a piercing scream that resounded and echoed throughout the valley. Even though this, I was glad that she was incinerated in seconds and did not have a prolonged death. I was even more relieved for her father's sake.

The ballistae and catapults were reloaded; distances were calculated. About a quarter of the large throwing machines contained wire cages contained tinder and Greek fire. These were always testy and unsafe to use to ignite until right before they were released.

Some had large round stones that would barrel down a whole line of men in phalanxes. Others had fist sized stones that would rain down on the Sabines defeating their "roof of shields". Our archers prepared to follow.

I was brought my black stallion and I rode up and down our line of defense challenging the Sabines. I bellowed, "'Tatius' over and over as I rode. He knew what awaited him if he faced me.

I lusted to add his gilded armor to my collection.

Seconds turned into minutes and silence fell that was almost deafening. Everything seemed to be suspended in time. Our senses became exceptionally clear and every color and sight was poignant. Every sound was like the ringing of a bell.

An incredible din arose from the side area when the Sabines were supposed to breach our wall. The opposing sides were stunned when thousands of our Sabine wives rushed between our force and the enemy. Once I recognized who they were I was not surprised to see my Bella in the lead.

I was immediately overwhelmed with fear for my beloved wife and mother of my children. My men seemed to feel likewise. The Sabines were literally taken aback. Many of them dropped their weapons. Just at that point Tatius signaled the attack.

The woman rushed to their Sabine relatives. They were appealing to their fathers, uncles, brothers, cousins that they did not have to be rescued from their beloved Roman husbands and children's fathers. They beseeched both sides to not hurt the men they loved. They rushed to the Sabine phalanx and it broke.

Tearful reunions were made. A great cry arose from our attackers. "They do not need rescue". When Tatius fervently signaled the attack the cry of "No!" arose from their ranks.

Both sides rushed forward. We hurried to protect and gather our wives and them to collect and defend their closest female relatives. At this Bella signaled and the woman raised a chant, "We are all family! We are all family! We are all family!" Both armies were stunned. Hastily, we dropped our weapons and met and embraced our Sabine in-laws.

Soon, Tatius and his commanders and I and my generals met in a large tent just outside the front gates of Rome. Tatius was their hereditary ruler. He was a small, rat faced man who had shifty eyes. He had pipe thin arms and a protruding stomach.

I was amused that he referred to himself as "we". At first, I thought he was talking of him and his companions. But then, I realized he was referring to himself alone. I did manage to quip, "We? Do you have fleas?" He was not amused and bristled. I tried to console him with, "No offense, Mighty King. The Roman way is light and to make humor".

He talked down to us, "Our men have no heart for this battle. Fortunately, mostly only foreigners and few of our own were killed; all were lower class. We are saved the payment promised to the mercenaries. We think it best, since we are the god granted ruler of Sabine, and your women and children are Sabines, that we assume kingship of Rome.

You, brave Romulus will be my regent and commander of the army. We can see you in the forefront of all out battles".

Ursicinus gave him a knowing look and replied, "Just as you were in the forefront today, great Tatius". Vincus offered, "We have seen too many of our dear and valued Patricians gloriously taken on our front lines to want to risk our king".

I looked at Tatius with an unflinching stare and said, "Romans earn their kingship. Our people will not accept another ruler. Perhaps a joining like we once enjoyed with Abla Longa is most appropriate."

Tatius turned his gaze away and retorted, "But we are bred to the kingship and have much more governing experience than you do. Hereditary kings are more suited to the rigors of leadership".

I moved close enough to him so that he could feel my breath on his face. I saw Tatius flinch and fear come into his face. I rejoined, "I have the armor of thirteen hereditary kings in our Temple of Jupiter the Slayer who might take issue with you." Hands went to swords.

My most beautiful Bella stepped in and offered, "For the moment the important things are peace and harmony. Why not settle for an alliance, each retaining rule of his state at least for now? Rome and Sabine will both benefit from the trade and mixing of cultures. In the future, we can negotiate these issues further".

As we watched the Sabines depart from the vantage point if our ramparts. Ursicinus remarked, "We'd better kill that entitled little bastard before he can kill us." Numitor make a throat cutting gesture by drawing his extended thumb across his throat. Vincus added, "It won't be easy, but I'll see what can be done". Even sweet Bella nodded her head in agreement. "I know him, and he only knows deceit and treachery", she said with sadness.

"We will have a great meal at our palace once the deed is done", my mother contributed.

"I shall need chicken, beef, clams and perhaps squid. Fresh fruit from that farmer you favor, Vincus. And cheeses! We will get or wine from Tuscany; both red and white. I shall need to get out my finest dishes and silver eating utensils. Of course, our crystal goblets...

I tuned out at this point.

The Field of Mars

*Naturally, when one makes progressive steps,
there may be some who see it as a betrayal of
their goals and interests. Louis Farrakhan*

By the end of the year, news arrived that Tatius had been assassinated by several ambassadors from Laverium. He had been conspiring with them to revolt against Roman rule. He was planning two front invasions. Apparently, they affectionately greeted him as best of friends, surrounded him and then just stabbed him to death.

Vincus gave us a sly look.

We all breathed easier, and we declared Rome the capital of the country.

Our former "guest" Oblerius was now king. He would retain his titular title.

My mother was in her glory, conducting the finest of feasts. She encouraged us to overeat becoming stuffed. She insisted that we were all too thin.

Over dinner, she started a conversation about the merits of the woman on top position for sexual intercourse. She opined that it was hard for a woman to bear the weight of a large man. She said that dog style had its merits but was too fatiguing on the arms and legs.

Bella stopped her from having two slaves demonstrate her points at the center of the dinner table. Numitor made amusing hand gestures to illustrate the conversation. Vincus pretended to mount the corner of the table. Ursicinus called a young slave woman over and she kneeled between his legs and serviced him under the table. He stood up partially and grunted as he orgasmed.

And then the wine loosened us up, and we prattled on into the night.

Ten years went by. Rome continued its campaign to dominate the area. Numitor and Ursicinus were in the Elysian Fields. I cried at the funerals of my grandfather and trusted friend.

Crassius assumed leadership of the military. Although he was a good adviser and commander, I never had the friendship with him that I had with his predecessor.

I could not be at every battle because there were so many, but I still led the elite cavalry in major engagements. To my chagrin, over time I needed several larger size suits of armor.

Bella graced me with four more children and my mother and Vincus were their doting grandparents. Our married and family life were the most joyful of my treasures. We started all the children on a classical instruction modeled after what we knew of great Alexander's education.

Our twin sons were twelve years old and were to sprouting body hair. We started teaching them military strategy and hand to hand combat. My mother delighted in pointing out changes in their bodies and, if they got a spontaneous erection in her presence, she would grab the boy's crotch and say, "chee, chee, chee, chee".

"I must take them to a whorehouse and get them properly instructed ", she mused. I was glad I had not had to suffer puberty with her.

Rome did not need more women, but my counselors advised continuing to expand our territory. This needed money beyond the tribute we received from conquered states. Also, we were beset by insurrections in the conquered lands particularly from Veii and Latverium.

We insisted on taxes from our residents and fees for various public services, water, collection of refuse, night guard etc. Senators were especially resentful of this, but placement of their sons in military service stopped the grumbling.

We also pressed them to donate funds to the army and named legions after them. I could see that they did it grudgingly. They were frequently sullen and seemed to be going through the motions of voting. They were always cliquish and secretive, but they were becoming much more obvious about it.

In their little circles, I could see those casting frightened and angry glances at me.

We received notice of a major advance of rebels from Veii. This would require dealing them a crushing defeat. We decided to engage them in the Field of Mars about two days march out. Because of the importance of this battle my advisers and the senate encouraged me to participate.

We set out the following morning and had a dull and dusty two-day long trek and approached the Fields of Mars. Just before dusk, we set up camp. As was my custom, the night before a battle, I walked around the camp greeting and encouraging the legionnaires.

I was surprised to see Quintus, one of my first allies and supporters. He was accompanied by Crassius, and several high-ranking soldiers and senators. I smiled when I saw them, and they smiled back. I motioned them forward.

I was greeted with salutations such as: "Hail Romulus", "Romulus is death to the enemies of Rome"; "Hail the Lion of Kings" and I was encircled by this smiling group. Why did it seem like they were smirking?

Before I suspected anything, they closed in. An arm encircled my throat from behind, I was bent backwards, and I felt a deep, sharp pain in my right kidney as a knife penetrated it. The pain was immobilizing. I would like to say I took a stand and fought back but I could not do anything. I tried to scream but nothing issued from my mouth.

I had a clear image of Bella's beautiful face.

Suddenly, I was watching the scene from above. Several of the soldiers closed in and violently stabbed my stomach with their daggers. Blood and organs erupted from my chest and stomach and drenched my attackers. Quintius stepped forward and announced, "Romulus, you have been a great king, but Apollo has told us that you must die for Rome to survive!"

Then the sky suddenly opened with crushing rain and blasting lightning.

From my position over the scene, I could see the group throw me to the ground, stabbing me wildly as I fell to my knees and then to the ground.

Floating across from me was the spirit I had known as "Apollo" and he gave me a smirk.

"What a waste of energy, you are already dead. They must really fear you.

It took a lot longer, and you were wiser that your impulsive brother. It was I who turned the sword so that he would fall upon it. For the son of a whore, you have done well for me. You were a good puppet.

You should have no complaints. I let you have wealth, position and a wonderful wife and family. These conspirators will spin tales of you being spirited off to Olympus to sooth the masses. You will become a myth.

Quintus will be my new puppet king. I have been grooming him since before you reunited with your mother.

And you took my lies in like a babe suckling on its mother's teat!

No, I am not Apollo.

I am far older that those high-minded Olympians. Indeed, I am older than the Titans that preceded them. I am from the chaos that spawned the earth. I am decay, illness, corruption, domination of all kinds. Some call me "the Adversary".

I dine on low behavior, hatred, violence war and rape. Since women give life and I delight in death, I am a connoisseur of their degradation and rape. Had you raped the Sabine women as I told you to, perhaps you would have lived and prospered a little longer?

It's a pity. I had planned an exquisite rape and murder of your wife, mother and daughters and horrific torture of your family. Your wife foresaw it. Your father-in-law, that pain in the ass, found out about my little party. I had planned and spirited most out of the country. He is clever that old snake. Even I don't know where they went.

Vincius sent messengers to warn you, but I made sure they were intercepted. No matter, Rome will go on to be a ravenous devourer of nations that will bind the minds of its followers to rapine for millennia. You have set the course.

The poor will be devoured by the rich. And they will believe they are serving god! It will set the tone of dominance and suppressing the weak that will go on forever."

My blood boiled and I wanted to tear this deceiver, this brute to pieces. I was paralyzed, my limbs were deadened.

The golden man gave me an arrogant dismissive look, grinned wickedly, and then made a "be gone" gesture with his right arm.

I sank into a white oblivion. T h e n, I slowly stirred. I reached my left arm for Bella as I did every morning when I arose. My hand touched something, and it scurried away from me. My nostrils were assailed by the stench of decay, rot and corruption. I bolted upright to find myself naked in one of Rome's garbage heaps. Everywhere there was decomposition and the foulness of excrement and decay.

Suddenly, a voice like the pounding surf assailed my ears. "Romulus!! Romulus! Look at me!!" My ears began to bleed from the power of the voice.

I turned and towering above me was the red armored warrior from my dreams. He stood as high as Rome's defensive wall. He had a humped nose like mine and his teeth were white pearls.

"I am your father, the God of War! Your mother is not one of those vacuous women who lay with a tradesman for a price and then claim to be impregnated by a god! She was one of my most favored of brides. But you have made many mistakes in your life and must face your consequences."

I was deflated. I lowered my head and shoulders and muttered "I am ready to burn in Hades' fire forever".

Mars looked puzzled. "Be condemned and burn forever?" was his astonished response. "What kind of a savage, cannibal god would do that? Disgusting! I know that kings tell priests and oracles to spout that shit to scare the masses into doing their will. But suffering on earth is enough.

The giant red god bent to one knee as a father might to touch a baby.

The Olympian continued, "But, not you Romulus.

Great Jupiter has sentenced you to live forever to see the consequences of what your partnership with that golden filth has wrought. To see all the ones you love grow old and die. You will remain eternally as you are now; and to have to constantly restart your life and wander. You will never have a real name again…

Although he goes by many aliases the creature's true name is "Asizou". To know it is to have power over him. Never say it aloud or you will summon him. But you need to call him by this name to expel him.

He is one of the greatest evils in the world.

He is the enemy, the adversary. He gives the just the option to do evil. He seduces them to become their worst selves.

But, because the fiend's magic prevented you from hearing my warnings, you can redeem yourself. Jupiter has decreed that you will be Asizou's eternal pursuer and foil. You will find him, wherever he hides and undo his schemes. Every time you defeat him, he will be weakened, and you will become stronger.

He feeds on large and small conspiracies. He strives to have people worship him. Deprive him of these and you will starve him. When you find a way to kill him, you must do it. As you deal the death stroke, say his name.

Destroy all who traffic with him.

He despises women because they are the givers of life. He seeks to corrupt them. He loves the abduction of woman and rape. It is his greatest pleasure. Look for him where women are missing or tortured in mass.

But there is more.

For you to do this I bestow my blessing on you. It is only a blessing for those with nothing to lose. For the three nights of the full moon, you will be transformed into the Wolf of the Mars. You will be an enormous brute. You will be the thing to be afraid of in the dark.

You will have the appearance of a wolf and a bear and when you run it will be on all fours. You will have the strength of Hercules and the speed of Mercury. Your skin will be like that of the Nemean Lion. After every victory, you will grow stronger. The wolf cannot be killed but can feel pain.

If the man is killed or maimed, the wolf will still arise unblemished at the full moon. The man will be resurrected complete with the wolf.

To remind you of all the deaths and destruction the city that bears your name will wrought, as the beast you will need to devour human flesh. You will always crave it. You will have to resist your urges to even to have a semblance of a human life.

Those who you bite or injure, but do not kill will become like you. Never leave anyone you have wounded alive unless you want them to be a companion.

You will never be with Bella again in this lifetime. But she will reincarnate in every generation. She will shine like the Northern Lights and be accompanied by the Muse's finest music. When you find her, you can turn her and be together forever.

However, until your mission is done, you will never be able to sire children again. You will not find her until a time comes when any man has the knowledge of all the ages in his pocket, but mostly chooses to gossip and play.

You will live until Demeter no longer can bestow her bounty on the grandmother earth."

Thunder pealed and the earth shook, and then I was alone in the twilight. I was crying, stunned and had defecated down my legs. I saw Dianna begin her passage across the dark sky.

An enormous hunger and anger overcame me and began running towards Rome. My body was wracked with pain and I could feel the bones expanding under my skin. My mind went blank with pain.

Soon I was running on four legs. I felt a growl erupt from deep inside me.

I was screaming, "Quintus!"

A Tale's End

*"It's weird...you know the end of something great
is coming, but you want to hold on, just for one
more second...just so it can hurt a little more.*
Orson Wells

By this time, twilight was falling.
Van had told me his story and my mind floated away. It was as if I had been standing there observing, my feet planted in leather strapped sandals the sun warm on my shoulders.

I could smell the rich aromas of olive oil and baking breads, hear the echo of children in my head. The swimming of a fetus in my belly; the feel of paved cobble roads and red roofs and pink evening sunsets as seen through stately columns draped in linens that lead out to a vestibule.

The lucid visions inside of me were as if I was watching a movie. Something struck m y core as he spoke. Suddenly I could not breathe. I felt dizzy and ill. A terrible doubt tormented me.

Feeling horribly nervous as I asked him, "Should I call you Romulus? Does this mean you have a wife and children, just where are they?"

He shrugged, "Now I am Van, I shed Romulus like a snakeskin. My children had children and grandchildren. I tried to keep up with them, but their numbers became so great that it became impossible; and twenty-seven hundred years later?

I have found it easier to be consistent if I stay 'in character' for my different incarnations. In the next iteration, I will be someone else."

I pulled away just a little, examining his face as he thoughtfully shut his eyes. I could see the pain and emotions welling up from inside of him. To his credit he breathed out slowly and told me how he ran back to the gates of his city as a terrible creature.

He couldn't find Bella, nor his children and he feared the worst. He ran through the torchlight of the darkened city, craving the bones of his betrayers. His blood boiled within him, in his altered state he was mad, a blood rage.

He rampaged, ripped – slaughtered everyone he encountered until he caught the scent of his beloved wife. "I could smell her blood; her pale body was flayed out upon our marriage bed. She had been split up the front, her legs ripped apart.

The Drachma, my signet coin, had be placed in her hand.

Tears welled up in his eyes and slowly fell on his cheeks; his brown eyes never wavered nor moved as he looked at me. "I burned the palace down and followed the scent trail of my family. My little Helena was captured, but Lucia escaped.

I followed them from a distance until I knew that they were safe with my mother", he said. "I insured that they went as far as the southwest coast and across to Sicily and then to parts unknown."

"People needed answers. They didn't have the words or understanding of how a great king could vanish the way I had. No one wanted my blood on their hands. The loss of a king in those days that had put together such an empire…a city and one that had such power, well…it left my people feeling vulnerable and unprotected.

One of the senators addressed the common assembly declaring that I had appeared to him with a message for all of Rome. They were told that I had miraculously been taken in a whirlwind up to Olympus and that proved that I was true demigod.

I had given Quintus my mantle.

This helped to ease some of their fears. I heard of what he said as it was on the lips of every Roman citizen and slave at the time.

Because I was so well known, I went into hiding. I especially had to hide my wolf each month. As you are now, the lust for blood, meat and revenge was still so fresh for me.

Romans had come to shave their faces and bodies, and to affect short hair. While in my human state, I had grown a beard and let my hair grow out and looked every bit a Greek Merchant.

"I caught up with Quintus and Crassius while they were dining together a little later. Shall we just say, 'I ate them with some Fava beans and nice Chianti'.

Quintus had kept my Helena as a body slave, and I freed her.

From the former slave Drusilla who I had freed the night of meeting Bella, I hired tough ex-legionnaires to protect her. Drusilla recognized me instantly and swore to keep my secret. She herself even escorted Helena to Sicily. I gave Helena as much of my fortune as she could carry and told her to go to her grandmother.

Sometimes criminals are the only ones who have honor", he mused.

From that moment forward I have been looking, searching, and waiting for some very specific things; the men that assassinated me and took my life and my love away, and the demon that had polluted me. But I have primarily been looking for you."

I was a bit shocked, "Van, you said you had been looking for me; specifically, for me?" I asked. "Mary" he replied, "We have always been one heart. Vast time had separated our bodies.

Didn't you almost see and feel the things I just related? Couldn't you almost feel our children kicking and turning in your womb?

You are the re-incarnation of Bella in this generation. I can preternaturally sense who you are in every generation".

I have just missed finding you for almost three thousand years".

I had to sit down in astonishment. But I had to admit, with all that he had shown me and the vivid images I experienced at his tale, it made sense. Then, out of nowhere, I remembered a flight of fancy at a six or seven of a woman in a red dress sitting on a three legged stool and looking into a glowing crack in the earth. I felt dizzy and almost toppled over. I reached for Van, he clutched at me back before I could.

"Dear Mary, let me show you just one more thing" he said. He walked me over to a large oaken wardrobe, inside were all manner of clothes, but in long thin plastic bags were dresses; dresses that I recognized. My hand reached out trembling to touch a red Greek style dress, with a purplish cord meant for wrapping around the waist and breasts.

Van smiled, "That is a copy of the dress you were wearing the night I first met you; would you like to wear again?" He offered. I turned my gaze towards him, our eyes met, and I knew what he said was true. "Yes please… husband". He dressed me in the long flowing red robes and tied the cords around me; he stood back, smiled and then tussled my hair about my shoulders.

He smiled broadly and his eyes lit up from the inside. I turned around and felt the cloth, curtsied and hugged him very tightly.

Then my stomach grumbled loud enough for both of us to hear and all I could think about was rending human flesh; my hunger burned inside like an ache in my bones.

"Yes, we must eat." Van observed. We went to the great aluminum refrigerator and each filled a serving bowl with porterhouse steaks, lamb and pork chops and shared a pork rump roast. He had the nicest dishes; the china was so delicate that they were almost see-through. Van poured an excellent Burgundy into two fine wine glasses, and we ate with our hands.

"How is it that the pork is so especially delicious?" I queried as I chewed at the buttery like meats. "It is for two reasons. The first is that I have a special butcher who puts aside only the best cuts for me. The other is that it tastes closest to 'long pig'.

"Long pig?" I asked, in fascination.

"Yes" he said, "It is what the Maori called the victim of their cannibalistic feasts. It had been the code word among multi-billionaire secret societies who used to give illegal dinner parties featuring it. I am sure they had been influenced by the Cabal.

I have adopted the word as a euphemism. It helps me cope with the fact; to psychologically distance myself.

My butcher keeps a supply; I sometimes buy it around the full moon when pickings are slim". I was amazed that I was not shocked or repulsed by this revelation.

"Do the Maori still do this", I asked and took a long pull of the burgundy, "I doubt it", he replied. "Eating human flesh has long been the ultimate taboo. But now the restaurants in London, Paris and New York that serve entrees made of human meat have almost normalized it."

"I know it sounds horrible", Van sighed. "I don't condone it." He sighed" But, please recall our conversation about not being human any longer. It is a simple matter of survival. These cannibals contribute to our survival by storing long pig with this butcher. He sells it to the restaurants we talked about.

We finished supper, cleaned up after ourselves and then Van took my hand.

Beautiful Dreamers

*Where there is mystery, it is generally
suspected there must also be evil.
~ Lord Byron*

Please Bella...that is Mary...come with me. I have a task to do. We went down the stairs to the basement and I glanced over at Van's machine shop. I saw that he had somehow split one of the demon's horns and was shaping the halves into two scimitars. One was almost completed.

"How did you manage to do that? I thought they were indestructible." I puzzled. Van made a wry face, "Not without a great deal of effort, expense and magic." He replied. "I have put glyphs on some of my carbide and diamond blades and done spell work. It is painstaking but, if I succeed, we will have two weapons that can kill anything even disembodied entities. Maybe even our golden friend.

I have to try".

We went to the back wall and Van muttered some unknown words and made arcane hand and finger gestures and we enter the inner sanctum. I admired the armor suits on the walls and said, "Those are museum quality." They were all different some emblazoned with eagle and lion motifs across the fronts of the breast plates. My eye was out for the skull faced helmet and body armor he wore when he was Romulus. I said. "Did you wear them all?"

Van laughed, "Yes, each in their time.

I am a bit of a hoarder" and he pointed to rows and files of piled covered boxes that went on as far as the eye could see. All of them contain gold and silver coins... platinum bars too except for the ones that contained jewels and weapons liberated over the ages from miscreants.

On our way towards the gated area, we passed a spectacled Viking helm and plate armor. I laughed and said, "What about this one?" He casually offered. "Oh, that was when I was called 'Beowulf'". After that, I started using wolf type names each time I had to change identities.

"No! You weren't", I blurted out; and clapped my hands to my mouth, my eyes wide. He raised and lowered his eyebrows a few times like Groucho Marx. "Were you Groucho too? I joked. "Ya bet cha' life", he laughed.

Van unlocked the barred gate, and we entered the most secure area.

"Hey, Chief! How about undoing these bandages?" A small weak voice cried out. We both looked at the silver cage that contained the imp. "Come on", the sprit said, "You don't need to be a weatherman to know which way the wind blows". We peered into the cage and the imp was lying there looking like a miniature mummy.

"You can talk?" I exclaimed. "Unless there is a ventriloquist in here" the Imp said. We were both flabbergasted. "I'll tell you a secret, we fae are loyal to whoever has possession of us. We are like mercenaries. I and my family were enslaved by that...thing...for hundreds of years".

"But you could be a deceiver", I blurted out. "Hey, look lady; don't judge me by the company I keep. Sorry about stinging you, I was only doing my job." the fae replied.

"Besides, the wards around here are super-duper, and my wings will take months to grow back. Goldilocks...Gold Dome, maybe... can't sense me in here.

You know that, right?" He looked at Van. "I can see the way this thing is going. I need to team up with you. Once you go fae, you can't go away.

"Van," I suggested. Shouldn't we put some papers the bottom of the cage or something". "Jeepers, Lady, I'm not a puppy" the little fae said indignantly. You ain't going to find any raisins at the bottom of the cage. I have a mouth but only for communication. I don't even have a butthole. Take these bandages off and I'll show you."

I live on energy and I don't eat or…excrete. How do you people live with that? Ugh! So messy and earthy!

I am a fire elemental. Not only real fire, strong emotions like passion, anger.

"I know", and now she does too." Van interjected sardonically. "You really are a delicate little flower, aren't you? "

Van thought for a minute and then said, "Let us talk it over and I will come back later and tell you what we decide. Now I need you to be quiet".

"Quiet? Yes sir, quiet you want and its quiet you'll get. I know when to talk and when not to talk. I can be silence itself. Why in my hometown, they call me 'Quiet Ernie', after that movie. "Silent Bob", but that's neither here nor there.

Yeah, 'Ernie'. No crap about 'Bert'. Of course, you couldn't pronounce my real name. What did you think it was … 'Beelzebub'? I went without talking for a whole year once. Just the other day, a friend of mine said 'Man, you can be quiet…'"

Van gave him a stern look, and he looked sullen and became silent. He sat down like a pouting child.

"Mary, I want you to meet some of my former companions". Van said. "I call them my 'Beautiful Dreamers'.

A being can only spend so much time alone. They say, 'alone is not lonely". After hundreds of years, it is," He shrugged his shoulders. "I never could ask them if they wanted my gift. Most were nearly dead when I turned them and could not. Most of them… could never give up their humanity.

There were eight in all, six them are inside another mystical room. Two, took off on their own. Our…priorities …became different.

I can tell you about them later if you wish".

Van picked up a large bowl of water and several washcloths.

Van went to one of the walls and made some more hand signals and mutters some things in an odd language. Then we just walked through the wall into another hidden room.

We were in a pleasant space that could have been a large bedchamber. It was a pastel blue. There was ambient light, but I couldn't find its source. I saw a line of six boxes. The first and the last were old style wooden coffins while the four in the middle were small sandstone boxes. Van seemed to have a thing for lining things up.

I startled and clutched Van's arm when the first coffin moved and squeaking, and guttural noises erupted from the first three boxes. Van hugged me to him and said, "Do not be alarmed, there are nothing dangerous here, only old friends. However, even by our standards, you might find it ...strange".

Van gently lifted the first coffin lid. Inside appeared to be a corpse of a man of about thirty dressed in Colonial American style. He wore a powdered wig and looked like he was in an over-sized bed. He appeared serene. Van produced a wet cloth and lovingly wiped his face.

"Andrew!" Van called. "Andrew! You asked for some more time to decide." I startled as his eyes slowly opened. They were deep blue, but rheumy. Van said casually, "Andrew, this is Mary". He coughed and seemed to be trying to form a word. Van gave him a sip of water. He slowly whispered, "Enchanted, Me Lady."

Van asked him, "Will you accept the meal? You and I and Mary will be family". Andrew sputtered and coughed, "You are too kind, Wolfgar. But I still cannot bear the thought".

"We still have time, Andrew", Van suggested. Shall we visit for a while?" "Too tired, beg your pardon. Madame pleased…to…to…" Andrew said. "Leave the lid open until you go. I miss you… but… no…energy…can't talk… Next….month…please."

Van turned to me and said, "Andrew and I were together from about 1400 until just after the American Revolution. He is an English noble whose brother imprisoned him to rob him of a dukedom. He was a scintillating conversationalist. He cut a dashing figure and was brilliant with a rapier.

We were like brothers. I took him away from terrible torture. We saw the rise of the Reformation, Tutor family, the Round head Revolution and the settling of America. We attended Guy Fawkes execution. We came to this new world together. It doesn't seem so long ago." Van shook his head sadly.

We sided with the Colonial army and pulled them out of a lot of very tight scrapes. It was an ocean of blood. He started having trouble killing Englishmen, whom he still identified with.

He began to feel that it was all too horrible. He also never adjusted to constantly losing the humans he had become attached to. After the War of 1812, he refused to eat.

He is progressively slowing down but there are still decades for him to accept some long pork and be revived. Once a month, I offer it to him again. He has refused thus far."

I looked at Andrew and I could see the torment, but determination in his eyes. He did not seem to have the energy to turn his face to us. I could hear him whisper, "I love you, Wolfgar". I saw tears form in Van's eyes. "I love you Benjamin", he whispered.

"As a lycanthrope continues to refuse to eat, he becomes drier and eventually shrinks into something resembling a large root. He becomes much less mobile. I keep them with me because I don't want them desecrated and I love them all.

They spend their time dreaming.

All these friends are totally self-aware and think clearly. After Andrew I decided to never make any more companions. I could not endure another's tumbling away from me.

Are you ready to meet the others?" I hesitated. I wasn't sure what I would see. It was a little like being at a horror movie and both wanting and dreading the first appearance of the monster.

I knew that this was the fate that awaited me if I could not "adjust". "Van, are you showing me this to pressure me? It is upsetting and more frightening than anything I have seen so far. As thankful to you and as much as I love you, I don't want you to control me or dominate me. I've had too much of that already.

What will you do if I make the same decision?" I asked "Right now, I am pumped up by the power and my need for vengeance, but what if I can't take it after a while? I might not be able to face myself".

Van visibly blanched and I had to steady him as his legs seemed to wobble. He looked stunned, like a boxer who had received a staggering blow.

He looked into my eyes and I could see the pain in his face. "Mary, I know in my heart of hearts that you are my Bella, and we have the same soul. The possibility never even occurred to me.

I swallowed hard, and then asked, "Will you put me in a coffin box one day, and leave me to dream of loving you?"

"I...I...I... have been so excited that I found you, that just naturally assumed that...." Van replied and then sadly shook his head.

He hung his head.

"I would be devastated. I could never dominate you and I am not a manipulator. I was reborn as the antitheses to that type of man. I would not want my life to go on. But I am a soldier and I have a mission. I must oppose the demon and end him.

I took you down here because this is a necessary part of my routine and I also thought you should have the whole truth. Like all these companions, once you get grounded and I am sure you can survive, I will support whatever you want. I need to mentor you, and I want an equal, a wife not a slave or stooge.

Van looked away and reflected for a moment and shook his head, "No, Mary. Our reunion was prophesized by exalted Mars when he gave me my quest. We will be together forever.

Now that I have found you, it means that our quest is coming to an end.

I have much to show you, some of these things will awaken the memories in your DNA that follows your soul. We can awaken Bella in you and all the other incarnations within. There is no need to be frightened and I would never have to place you in one of these boxes; you are different from them from the start."

He replied. "You have no attachments to your family; the yearning in you is stronger than I have ever seen in anyone that I have ever turned. Our reunion was predestined.

And you were the only one who consented to the gift."

I heard a raspy, weak, "Yes...Mary....listen" come from Andrew.

Van shrugged and replied, "I guess we will have to cross that bridge if we come to it".

My heart felt lighter after he said this. "Just which of the stooges would you have me be?" I laughed. "Guess," Van said. "Nyuk, Nyuk, Nyuk, Nyuk". I replied, "Why I'll moider ya" and received a high pitched, "Woo, Woo, Woo, Woo, Woo" in reply. We laughed; but I don't think Andrew got the joke. "Madness", he whispered.

I steeled myself. "O.K., I am ready". I endured like I imagined some brave people face firing squads. Van went to the small, sandstone carved box that was next. "This is called an 'ossuary', he explained. Some cultures collected the bones of their ancestors in them.

He opened the cover and I peeked in from between my fingers. What I saw was very much like a child who was born with Cerebral Palsy. His head swollen and his limbs were shriveled. Van picked him up and gently washed off his face and brow.

Its eyes opened and they were dreamy like newborns. It muttered "Volfbender?". "Mary, this is Charles", Van offered. "He and I were together from about the fouth millennium A.D. to the early eight hundreds." Charles looked at Van and seemed to be trying to focus his eyes. "Volfbender?" he said."

Charles was a monk who was accused of heresy and was being tortured by members of his order. They were burning his feet over coal fire when I broke in the door. He had taught a poor boy how to read. Reading other than by the clergy was considered heresy and they were both condemned to death."

Charles had a sparkling intellect and could discuss ancient philosophies all night long. He was disillusioned by seeing so much evil caused by the church, but he couldn't continue taking lives and still be himself. He is beyond the flesh's ability to revive him"

Van kissed him on the head and said "I love you brother. Sweet dreams". Then he closed the box's lid.

With anticipation, we moved on to the next limestone bone box. "This is Helga, a Viking warrior woman. She was a Geat and had been set upon by Swedes. About fifteen of them had her encircled with their swords and thought to have some sport before they tortured and raped her.

It became less fun for them when her spear obliterated their leader's head.

They rushed her and were choking and carving her when my wolf came upon them. She was within a whisper's breadth of death. After I had nipped and cured Helga's wounds, I enjoyed turning the tables on them.

I impaled them all on their own spears. I planted the blunt end of the spears in the ground and sat them on their spearheads. It took them hours to slip down until the spearheads erupted somewhere in their upper bodies. The art was to try to get the spear to emerge from their mouths.

It was a grueling death, but I reasoned, if they liked penetration so much, they might appreciate this. They howled their gratitude.

Helga and I sat back, relaxed and watched them writhe. We drank their mead and made bawdy jokes. We made wagers on which of them would have the spears erupt from their mouths.

She and I laughed at their wincing, crying and writhing in agony and joked as I ate their leader. She said. "Are you a bear? Are you a wolf? I shall call you Beowulf".

For a moment I felt otherworldly and my mind was taken away. I was in a large hall filled with Vikings sitting at long tables sloppily quaffing mead. The air smelled like wood smoke. The men were all in full armor, their helmets and shields on the table.

Van was clearly there just wearing a wool tunic. He had a long, unkempt beard. At his back hugging his neck, was a gorgeous blond in "Princess Leia" braids.

The men with him were rough and wild. Most had facial scars, and many had broken noses. Some had lost eyes. They made modern bikers look like British finishing schoolboys.

They laughed and pounded on the table to accompany their raucous drinking song. Gruff sing-song voices intoned:

"We rescued the virgins from the beast,

And expected proper thanks!

All we got was to kiss their tits,

But some of us got wanked"

I knew they were in mortal danger, but that they were joyfully anticipating it. I could see the cold light of the moon begin to peek through the venting slits in the roof. I saw Van and Helga disrobe and their eyes became yellow.

I knew something terrible, something murderously otherworldly, silently slinking was coming. Their singing was meant to draw it out.

Then I "was back" to my current experience. Had I just had a psychic experience?

Van opened the next lid. Inside, on a satin pillow was what looked like a three feet long ginger root with twin growths in the bottom and root extensions on either side of its middle. It was tan but looked smooth and moist. The very top looked like it had been carved out to resemble a woman's face. It reminded me of a picture I had seen of a medieval Mandrake root. I leaned in closer to see the details better.

I was shocked when its right eye popped open and a look of fury contorted its face. The eye was blood red, and the look was pure hate. A high-pitched squeal like a bat's cry rang out.

As quick as lightning the right upper body root extension lashed out and thin tendrils encircled my throat and neck. But there was no choking pressure. For the first time since the waning of the moon, I felt my wolf rising. I let out a deep growl and reared up opening my hands to grab and rip.

Before I could bring my hands down on her, Van wrapped his arms around me and gently danced me away. He said, "Ladies! Ladies don't fight over little old me! I am sorry Mary; Helga has hardly moved in over five hundred years.

Unfortunately, this werewolf stuff did not come with an owner's manual. I am still learning. I thought all she could do was rock her body. I could not have anticipated. However, she is a wolf, a Geat and a Viking. She was always very possessive. She is still fiery. As you see, she has no strength and cannot hurt you.

Although that did seem deliberate, one must treat wolves in this state as he would infants who inadvertently grasp your hair or earrings. "

Yes, we were lovers. She was a pugnacious wild woman in every way. I never met anyone so fierce. She was always looking for frost giants to slay. She missed her family, culture and simple way of life.

She loved her religious beliefs; and the Norsemen had strong prohibitions about eating human flesh. I guess that cannibalism was always a temptation when they were iced bound during those awful isolating winters. Therefore, it was strictly forbidden and would incur dire consequences in Valhalla.

Our paranormal adventures just strengthened her faith in the religion of the Norse Gods. She knew there were evil creatures all around. Christianity began replacing the Teutonic religion. After a while she would not eat. It is much too late for the meat for her. After her, I decided not to make any more female companions." Van sighed.

Van wiped off her face and kissed her on the forehead. Her eyes blinked and there was a slight smile on her caricature of a face. "I love you, Helga. Try to be good. You hellcat", he said as he replaced the sandstone lid.

Van continued, "The next two look similar. Nashea was with me about 600 A.D. She was a Nubian. I spent some time in Egypt, following a mass execution of women. There was a cult who was following the golden demon. I ended it.

It was a chaotic time as Rome was no longer dominating the world and the vacuum it left spawned petty tyrants everywhere. Nashea was a huntress who was deadly accurate with a bow. She held off thirty soldiers for two days. Fortunately, it was during the full moon and I got there before they decided to rush her. When they did, I was behind her. She was not injured, but under a death sentence. I turned her.

Van opened the heavy lid to the box, and inside on a satin pillow appeared to be a large ginger root that approximated the shape of a human body. Nashea quivered a little when the lid came off.

"Van took a bowl and wring out a washcloth, "Hello, Nashea, my love. I hope your dreams are pleasant". Two slits appeared in what passed for eyes in the root like woman.

"Because we lived as husband and wife, we experienced a lot of prejudice during our daily life. I was as a merchant in that time. Her family were negro and many of the old ones remember the tyranny and brutality of Roman rule.

They identified me as a 'Roman'. They were always deferential to me, but I could see the hate and resentment in their eyes. They took it out on her.

The rulers of the land were lighter skinned and there was a caste system that favored lighter people over darker. Her family was merciless in their criticism of her. They said she was 'acting Roman', 'not respecting the old ways', and having a 'colonized mind'".

One day, even before the end of her natural lifespan, she simply gave up.

It has always amazed me that she was so brave and defiant against armed men, but that her sisters, cousins and aunts could cause her such torture. Although, the light skinned ones were more entitled and haughtier, the darker ones were much crueler to her." He sighed and shrugged.

As he had done with the others, Van kissed her on the forehead and returned the lid.

We wandered over to the last ossuary. "In this box, Miriam sleeps. We were together in Palestine from the reign of Augustus through the reign of Commodus. She was a Jewess and made a great living cutting and styling Roman women's hair.

She was young and desirable and liked men. They returned the sentiment. Many women were jealous of her. As most people of the time, she loved her religion but found it hard to live it all the time.

A group of orthodox people objected to her accepting Roman coins as payment. The Roman coin, a "Denarius" had a picture of an important Roman on one side and a naked depiction of Hercules on the other.

The religious people believed it was a "graven image" and violated their first and second commandments, a depiction of a false god. Jewish shekels only had pictures from nature or from their temple; perhaps, a menorah or a bird.

They were also concerned because it depicted the most popular Roman and Greek god at the time; a man who had suffered greatly.

One who was fathered by a god, suffered, died a horrible, prolonged death and then raised to godhood by his father.

That was Hercules. The "suffering man-god" has always been appealing to people. It had contributed to the sullying of the Temple in Jerusalem by the intrusion of statues of the Greek deities.

The revolt of the Maccabees that generated the Hanukkah holiday was still fresh in their minds.

I was a merchant in the same town and knew her well. During the full moon, a group of ultra-orthodox people mobbed her house and took her out with the intention of stoning her. They were sewing her into the shroud that was to have immobilized before they buried her to her waist. This was to keep her still and make her easier target.

I fell upon them.

It is strange, but Jews too taste like pork.

They had brought their children with them to see justice dispensed. I am sure that those children were never the same again." He shrugged his shoulders, and I could feel his regret.

He lifted the lid and inside was a large dried out husk that looked like a man shaped ginger root. It was notably drier and dustier than the other.

"My beautiful, Miriam, I hope your dreams are pleasant." There was absolutely no reaction and Van performed his ablution, kissed her on the forehead and said, "I love you, Miriam". Then he replaced the lid.

Having been raised a staunch Christian I got excited, and said, "What did Jesus look like? Did you attend the Sermon on the Mount; the crucifixion!!!?"

Van shrugged, "I saw crucifixions several times a week for hundreds of years. I never heard of Jesus until about a hundred years after his death. I was first told of him by a Greek man.

I first heard his name was Joshua which was the most common Hebrew male name of that time.

I did have business dealings with his uncle, Joseph of Arimathea. He was also a merchant and I visited him at his estate just south of Jerusalem.

It is said that Joseph claimed Jesus' body after his crucifixion. My not being a Jew, he wouldn't have mentioned him to me.

The Jews were religiously zealous and always revolting. The time of their Passover was always the most turbulent. There was no news media during that time and people were crucified weekly.

Either he did not make a big impression at the time, or I was preoccupied with other matters.

I simply didn't know the significance."

Later, I heard of Christians being persecuted in Rome. About three hundred years afterwards Constantine, made Christianity the official religion of Rome. It was strange because he remained a worshiper of the Roman gods until he converted on his death bed."

We approached the last box which was a regular wooden coffin like the first. Van shuddered, "What you are about to see is not a horror. She is quite beautiful. But it frightens and puzzles me more than anything else."

In this bed is Claudia, my first she wolf companion. I had been alone for over three hundred years and I was terribly lonely. She was the slave of a Roman blacksmith and was strong from the work.

She had been sold by her father who was a Plebeian and a ne'er do well. Her master was too fond of wine and when drunk, he'd beat her and burn her with white hot irons. He also used her as amusement while he was with his friends.

One night, some of his friends, in drunken stupors, thought it would be amusing to strangle and rape her just to enjoy her suffering. I heard her screams as I was returning from a hunt.

I pushed all their heads into the blacksmith's molten iron. Now, THAT was amusing. On an impulse, I turned her rather than let her die", Van shrugged.

Then it was only possible to pursue the golden demon in and around Rome. Slaves were often the sacrifices or the gruesome entertainment of the time. Claudia had a passion for freeing slaves and treating everyone as equals.

She accepted her wolf as a great liberator and equalizer. She delighted in freeing slaves, especially women. We always helped them relocate outside of Rome's reach. We did this for two hundred years.

Then came Spartacus. She would talk passionately about a society where all men are free and equal.

We supported Spartacus behind the scenes and destroyed whole legions of Romans. As much as anyone in those ignorant times could be, he started out as an equalitarian and a humanitarian. Hopes for fairness and mercy arose in us. We supported him to the Alps.

Then his men, decided to turn around, pillage and rape Rome and enslave its citizens. We expected that he would disagree and take those few of his followers who wanted freedom home.

In the end, he became a tyrant and a raider. Although she had been a slave and hated it, Claudia was born a Roman. It was then that she lost her faith in mankind and became disillusioned."

I was fascinated by what to expect and Van removed the lid. Inside, as if asleep was a beautiful little woman under a sheet. She had auburn hair and it was pinned up. She was under a sheet and her eyes were slightly open. They seemed to follow us.

"Claudia! Claudia!" Van called. "Can you talk to us? We were met with an expressionless face and silence. "Oh, come now My Sweet, you can talk to me!" But there was only silence. He picked her up and she was loose and flexible in his arms. He shook her and yelled, Claudia!" But he received no response.

She smiled faintly. He placed her back in the coffin tucked the sheet around her, washed her face and kissed her. "I love you, Claudia", he said and replaced the lid.

I was confused. I asked, "Van, she is lovely. She was almost responsive. It is a good sign! Maybe this wasting is not final! Why does it scare you so?"

Van took a deep breath. He looked at me and appeared shaken. "You don't understand, My Sweetest Mary", he uttered. A year ago, she was a rotting root in this ossuary. She was turning to dust. I do not know what changed. It is not supposed to happen. Is it good? Is it evil?" He shrugged and added, "As I said, this werewolf thing didn't come with an owner's manual".

We walked back towards the hidden entrance. We went to say goodbye to Andrew, but he was fast asleep. I could see his eyes under their lids following the dreams that came to him. Van replaced the coffin top.

Van turned to me and said, "Now about Ernie...."

Dark Rider

There's a killer on the road
His brain is squirmin' like a toad
Take a long holiday
Let your children play The Doors
~ Riders on the Storm 1967

We stopped just in front of the exit to the mystical bedroom. "So, what do you think about the fae?" I asked. "Only supernatural beings can see them. I grabbed him for a couple of reasons." Van replied. "The first was just purely philanthropic.

There are four types of fae. They are or less along the lines of the alchemic concept of the four magical elements. 'Ernie' is a fire elemental. They are called 'Salamanders'. There are water fae called 'Undines'… earth fae are 'Gnomes' and air fae are 'Sylphs'. They tend to either enhance or cancel each other. For example, fire fae are canceled by earth and water. They can be enhanced by air and become more powerful. But they don't have to. You understand, right?"

"Sure" I affirmed, "It's kind of common sense. Go on."

"By sight, to other beings they are identical." Van continued. "They vary at about eight to ten inches in height and they are all basically white and have butterfly wings. They vary very subtly in hue by type, some are pure white, some are ivory, some are cream, and some are tan. Or so they say. But once again, it is so minute, only they can tell the difference.

For some reason, perhaps it is because they are allied with opposing earth powers, they can be very intolerant of each other. It is a lot like racial prejudice among humans."

I said, "O.K., it seems dumb to me. Maybe they have other reasons as well"

Van shrugged his shoulders and said, "Perhaps. They certainly have rationalizations. Some say that the others have ugly wings, others don't like the way a particular group speaks. The Gnomes are considered guttural and coarse and at one time were the slaves of the Undines. The Salamanders are considered too aggressive while

Sylphs are considered aloof and too intellectual."

Van said. "Ernie lost his wings and would have been ripped apart by the Gnomes had he hit the ground.

Also, the wizard I told you about taught me that the fae are just treasure troves of magical information and can do some incredible things. Salamanders are said to be able to show you things that are going on far away. Sort of like a crystal ball".

"But he was allied with the demon", I protested. "What if he communicates our location? I am a little afraid to trust him". Van replied, "He is totally contained by the wards and incantations in these chambers and in that cage. Somehow, his wings are vital to his magic. He is also frightened and just saying whatever comes into his head. He does not seem to have much guile. He is likely to give himself away.

He'll have to earn our trust."

"Well, at this point, you know more than I," I offered. "However, he doesn't have his wings and couldn't get far on those tiny legs." I made walking movements with my index and middle fingers on the palm of my other hand and a funny face." We both laughed. "I would only trust him if he showed us loyalty for a very long while. Why not give him a first test?" I suggested

As we walked into the other room Van said, "Good! One comes to mind."

"Boss Man! Boss Lady! It is good to see you back!" Ernie sputtered." My mouth gets a little ahead of my thinking sometimes.

But, what the hey! You can never trust someone who thinks too much; shifty, you know? Plotting, conniving, sneaky, and conspiratorial. Just not trustworthy, I say…"

I held my hand up. "Ernie", I stated firmly, "Do you want to continue to talk. Or do you want to be freed from those bandages?" Ernie very purposely and deliberately closed his mouth.

Van stated "Now, in just a few words, are your back and wings well enough to take the dressings off?" "Well, I am stronger and, my back is not as sore. What is that in your spit, Bud? I have never seen anything like that. But once I saw...

Van held up his hand. "Perhaps we should sew his lips together, my dear. It seems a bit drastic, but…."

"It might be necessary", I finished for him.

"Oh, you guys", Ernie tuned in. "Always kidding! Where are you going to find a needle and thread that small? How ya gonna hold it? Come on, please gets these dressings off me. ".

Van and I looked at each other and laughed. He had his charm and had figured us out. We were growing fond of him.

We walked over to the silver cage, and Van performed the incantations to release the bindings. I reached in and gently took the little man out of the box and onto the table it was sitting on.

Van said, "Before we begin, I want to make a few things clear. You are on probation with us and we will need to see loyalty for several months before you will have your freedom. It would be cruel to keep you bound if you have healed enough to be released. If you are strong enough, once we remove the bandages, I need you to give us an act of good faith. Understood?"

Ernie nodded his head "yes" and Van placed him on his stomach on some towels. There were dark stains on his back which I assumed were blood.

I told Van, "Let me do that, my hands are nimble from sewing". I unwrapped the bandages and saw ugly, encrusted scars around the small round wing buds that were forming. Van looked at them closely and said, "I spent many lifetimes as a physician, and these are healing very quickly. The werewolf saliva did its work. Even your wings have started to come back. I need to put some Betadine Solution on them."

Ernie shook a little and his tiny quivering voice said in a childlike manner, "Is it going to hurt, Boss?" "The usual answer is, 'it will sting a little', but not as much as Iodine which is a tincture of alcohol", Van answered.

Little Ernie gritted his teeth and said, "Do it, Boss Man." He held on to the towels with his hands but didn't say a word and stiffened as the dark solution was applied with a Q tip".

After a few seconds he, jumped up and screamed, "Mother fucker! God damn that hurts! Son of a bitch bastard! Ow! Ow! Ow! Ow!" And he scurried around the end of the table".

Van, said kindly, "Brave soldier! I have seen elite warriors handle it worse." I put my hand down and caressed his little shoulders and face, and he nuzzled up against my hand.

After a short while, Ernie sat down and looked up at us. "Thanks" he said. "I'm not used to kindness or caring. It has been so long. Jeez you guys are big. I never noticed it when I was flying, but looking up at you from here, you are like buildings.

Boss Lady, you have an enormous bat in the cave."

I wiped my nose with a tissue. I looked at him and smiled. "OK, Ernie" I began, "No matter what, you will be free from being physically bound and we won't be cruel to you. You must remember, if you betray us, we turn into twelve-foot-tall were-beasts three days a month. But now Van and I would like you to do a little something for us. One hand washes the other..."

"Talk about bad cop worse cop", Ernie laughed. "No, honestly, no one has ever treated me as good as you two have.

Van said, "I have some doll house furniture and clothing from the Victorian age that will fit you simply fine. We will find them, and we will make this cage comfortable for you. How many fae have rooms fitted with priceless antiques?

Now we would you to use your 'crystal ball magic' to show us our next threat. If you please..."

I owe you for saving my life. I already like you. Chemistry, you know. I will do what you ask. No sweat. Either way once we are done, I'll have a favor to ask you".

Ernie sat on the floor, made a strained face, and began to glow. He became brighter and then became a cold blue flame. It quickly became translucent. Soon a hazy image began to take shape within the flame.

There was a tall gaunt bald figure in a black priest's frock and collar in what appeared to be a library. He was ghastly pale. He was seated at an elaborate, desk of what seemed to be ancient. He was intently peering into a black faced mirror.

On a marble coaster at his left-hand side was a crystal goblet filled with what seemed to be a rich red wine. Behind him were large glass walls with what looked like hermetically sealed doors. To the rear of these, were high shelves lined with books and covered police case evidence style boxes.

"That is a research library that contains ancient manuscripts and artifacts." Van observed. "They are usually in museums that have archaeological artifacts that must be climate controlled. Otherwise, they would age rapidly or simply disintegrate. I have visited the ones in Egypt and Israel but this one is the largest I have seen so far."

Suddenly, the scene became intensely clear like going from standard picture to digital TV. The man was terrifyingly familiar. He had a Roman nose, a crown of Caesar hair style that made a semicircle around his bald spot and the hint of a salt and pepper goatee. He was staring into the black faced mirror intently.

With a pronounced flash we seemed to be standing unseen in the room with him. We could see in all directions and get closer or further away at will. I knew that this was merely an illusion because at the same time, I was aware of being in Van's secret room.

We could discern that it was larger than a city block and the glass enclosed rooms were too many to count. On his desk was a name plate that said, "Cardinal Ramos".

A European style phone rang. The Cardinal moved to pick it up. His movements were fluid but at the same time seemed segmented. I was reminded of a robot and a lizard at the same time. The impression was that he was being animated by an outside force.

"This is Cardinal Ramos." He pronounced it "Ray-Moose". "Yes, yes. His voice was also uncannily familiar but had a hollow tone like some old car phone speakers. "The fee is acceptable if you can solve our problem. The cost of the silver bullets likewise is acceptable. I understand that you will need hundreds of them because you all have fully automatic weapons.

Yes, stop the wolf at all costs. Eliminating it will get you a bonus. Remember, however, the primary objective is to protect the participants at the conference in the Koker Building.

He turned his eyes upward and pursed his lips in a look of disgust. Yes, yes if you can stick you M-16 up his ass and pull the trigger that would be…er… 'Swell'; so hyperbolic; such colorful Americanisms. Yes, I understand there is no such thing as an 'ex-Marine', "Colonel". Of course, 'Sempter Fi'.

As long as you protect our benefactors."

The Cardinal hung up the phone and announced out loud to no one, "Pretentious ass!" Then he let out a grim laugh. He moved in that odd, slithering, robotic way back to the desk. I noticed that he didn't appear to be breathing.

He took a long deep draft from the goblet. There was a rich red mustache of liquid on his upper lip. It was thicker than any wine could be. He sighed in content. Then I realized he was drinking blood.

He returned to the black faced mirror. All of a sudden, it was like we were face to face. I smelled rot and decay. The smell was like roadkill on a lightly travelled country road.

"Ernie, cut contact immediately", Van shouted. At once, Ernie was sitting there looking concerned. He said, "Boss, he was scrying for you!"

"I just realized, he was thinner and wore his hair differently, but he looked like you Van", I exclaimed. "And he pronounced his name like the ancient Etruscan for "Remus". Van responded. "Perhaps he is a decedent. I would think that my genes would have watered down after twenty-seven hundred years.

But that is not what bothered me the most".

"What is that My Love", I asked.

"He appeared to be Stigoi Vii; a vampire. "Van offered." I have tracked one before with a companion who is not in the room next door. It was in Romania in the fifteenth century. They are only native to the Balkans and Eastern European countries. There are very few of them. Unlike the folklore, they cannot produce more of their own but must be animated by a demon. They are crafty beyond belief. My 'made man' left me to continue hunting him.

That wolf and I remain in touch. He still is searching after six centuries."

Van said emphatically, "I am sure those were the Vatican Archives." I shuddered.

"Let's break this mood", Van said. "It is time to make Ernie more comfortable."

We went into the storeroom and found a group of old Colonial and Victorian doll houses. They were a little girl's dream! I took some time picking an appropriately sized rug, bed, chairs, end tables and drapes and we made up Ernie's crate as a small Victorian bedroom.

I totally enjoyed it. We also gave him a small wardrobe of Victorian and Edwardian male doll clothes. He looked like a dapper little gentleman. He even sported a tiny derby." Looked at us and quipped. "Cheerio Guvnor! Care for a spot of tea?"

"Boss Man and Boss Lady, I have never actually owned things before. I don't know what to say." Ernie effused. "But I have to impose on you for one last thing. I need one of those high-definition TV's, with cable. I need to watch movies and shows with violence and sex… 'Casa Erotica' would be great."

Van and I looked at each other and laughed explosively. "Casa Erotica, yet", Van guffawed.

"Aw, you guys! Stop it! What dirty minds! It's not entertainment perverse or otherwise. I am a fire elemental. The drama of those shows gives off passion. It is what I ingest. Capiche? Ouch, sorry Boss Man I forgot you are an Italian.

Err, one last thing."

Go ahead Ernie "I said. The tiny elemental squeaked. "Could you visit me? I'm a little lonely and frightened. That vampire guy was scary up the ying-yang. And the guys next door are…. a little…. a lot…extremely…eerie."

We both nodded our heads. Van replied. "Sure, at the very least we have to check those wounds daily. Be assured that nothing can get into these rooms. The wolves next door cannot get up... But if they could, they would defend you with their lives.

I'll set you up with that tv a little later ".

I added, "You are a little cutie. Don't worry, we'll be here."

Ernie nodded his head and sighed resolutely. He reminded me of a child who is afraid of the dark. He is a brave little heart, or whatever organ he has similar to it.

Van showed me the hand signs and whispered the incantation to me. I practiced but could not open the way to the storeroom. He corrected my finger positions and some of my pronunciation. "It seems more complicated than it is", Van instructed. "It's more a matter of repetition and intent." I tried it again and then we walked right into the magical storeroom.

"So, Dr. Gentlesse", I said. "Are you going to show it to me? I have wanted to see it for a long time. Will you let me touch it?"

Van let out a soft laugh and looked down. "But, Baby, you've already seen it." He rejoined. "I am proud of it, but it is getting a little old. It is still in good shape and it is getting a little flaccid. I don't want to wear it out. I polish it every so often."

"Oh, come on Van!" I laughed. "Please, let me see Romulus' black armor!"

Van directed us down a corridor adjacent to the west wall. We walked for perhaps five minutes and came to a notch built into in the grey stone walls. Van turned on a light and there was the armor itself!

It was much like I had seen it in my visions. It was like medieval articulated armor, but not as sophisticated. It had an anatomically correct man's torso displayed on the breast plate, deltoid like pauldrons and segmented arms and legs. The helm was like those of the plain trooper helmets, but it sported a jet-black comb. Its face plate looked like it functioned like a visor shaped like a sliver grinning skull.

My only surprise was, I had envisioned it as shiny; it was flat black. This made it more practical, I reasoned. Behind it was a round shield with an eagle sitting on a skull emblazoned on it. I could also see a Greek style Kopis sword with its heavy black blade sloping downwards.

For a moment, my mind whirled and I dreamed myself on a bloody battlefield at sunrise. Body parts were everywhere, and men were horribly mangled and moaning in agony. Many were calling for their mothers or to the gods.

Smoke arose from things that had been set on fire. On the direction opposite the rising sun was a bright glare that hurt my eyes. Emerging was the figure or silhouette of a warrior. I could only see his bottom half. As he got closer, I could see that shield, but his head was just a brilliant light. Did he have no head? As he was within a few feet of me, I could see that, under his helmet was a leering skull.

Death had come for me!

I had had another psychic vision!

That sense of otherworldliness stayed with me and I ran my hands over various dents and dings in the steel suit. "This is where a Veii arrow caught you. I touched one of the pauldrons, and this dent was caused by an Iocian Ax! And this was from a Valarian sword! I somehow remember."

"Bella had the "second sight" and used to examine the suit and ask me about new 'close calls'." Van reported. "You are accessing your memories from then." Van ran to me, picked me up in his arms and swung me around. We made our way to the bathroom to shower preparing for bed.

We moved up the stairs him leading me along the marble floors back to our bedroom, I unpinned my hair and went into the shower to turn on the taps. The room flooded with steam and the strong odor of almonds.

A vision crossed my eyes of a large stone room with a bath, sumptuous red drapes, and the carved heads of goddesses at enclaves in the room.

I clutched the doorway swooning. I was seeing through another's eyes, a shimmering pool steam rising from its watery movement. A nude man walked past me, a smile upon his face entering the hot water.

It was Van, the echoing sound of his voice, "Davena" he said to me in Latin. His eyes looked up at me as I entered the hot waters of the tub. As I stepped down, I felt the swirling of a child within my belly.

I knew the word, he repeated it smiling at me, the room spun, and I heard the word echo in my heart, "Davena-Beloved".

Memories flooded my mind, battlefields, armor, fear, love, parties, triumphs, babies, burning love, fingers entwined, his hair, our bed, the depth of his eyes, the scar on his thigh from his childhood, making love, kissing in the crowded palace, joy, pride, passion a soul's home.

I fell forward into the shower smacking my head against the tile bottles of soaps and perfumes falling with me. The word had broken loose parts of my memory, my memories with Romulus.

He must have heard the thud as I fell. When I awakened, he had me cradled in his arms smoothing my wet hair out of my face and eyes. The shower still running, he called "Bella, wake up".

My eyes fluttered open, "It's you…Romulus, my love, where have you been? It seems I was asleep for so long. I remember things, like dreams that are vivid…my love". I breathed out in a whisper and held him hard to me. "You are with me now Bella, everything will be alright" he said in Latin as he hugged me back harder.

I held his face with my hands and looked into his brown eyes, a stirring in my loins and a need that had not been quenched. I kissed his eyes and cheeks. "Maritus" I sighed as I kissed his throat. I pulled at his shirt. "Husband" I murmured into his ear, pulling at his wet clothes. I pulled his shirt off and over his head as he slid his boxers off.

Van was ready for me; he was shaking slightly with intensity of love and devotion in his eyes. He kissed me hard on the mouth and stood me up in the shower his hands found my breasts. I explored his muscular back and buttocks, my fingers digging into his firm thighs.

We kissed under the spray of the hot shower, tears mingling with relief and joy. Van turned off the shower, picked me up and carried me wet to the large bed.

Van reached over and retrieved some strawberry scented oil and sensually rubbed it on my body. His hands explored and toyed.

I straddled him as he sat on his knees, kissing his soft mouth; I leaned back on the bed pulling him on top of me. He looked down into my eyes. His eyes were sparkling as they had been the first time, I had met him, a wry smile crossed his lips, and he began to dance inside of me.

Our lovemaking was magical. We clutched and grinded like the wild animals that dwelled inside of us. The bed slammed in beat to our passion.

We screamed and moaned our frenzy and savageness.

We simultaneously exploded in ecstasy.

I kissed him and held his face as he lingered. I smiled up at him and he held me close.

I slipped into peaceful oblivion.

I awakened about three in the morning wheezing. I reached my hand over to touch Van, but I could not move it. There was an oppressive weight on my chest. My mind raced. Was I having an asthma attack, a heart attack? I tried to call out to Van and then began to feel a terrifying muffling of my breathing. My heart began to race. And adrenaline rushed into my system.

My wolf was enraged, and I violently bucked my hips up push with my arms at the same time. As my wolf instincts kicked in, I got the smell of what might be an old woman's talc and saw a shadow figure was pushed violently off the right side of the bed.

I sat right up and saw the deep black shadow dissipating into a cloud. It bolted right back on top of me. Misty fingers wrapped around my throat and the figure straddled my waist. The pressure on my stomach and chest were incredible. It felt like thousands of pounds. The misty figure's fingers throttling my throat were anything but ephemeral.

My wolf became enraged.

Gradually the misty figure began to solidify into a transparent small woman in what appeared to be a coarse white nun's habit. She had a leathery face and a bulbous nose. The hood of the woman had blue stripes around it. Then I recognized the crone who had committed suicide when we foiled the attempted sacrifice of my sister. I managed to push and kick her off me one more time.

In an eye blink, the crone was back on top of me and exerting crushing pressure on my body strangling me. It felt more like drowning than choking, more like an inundation than suffocation. The wraith had no actual earthly mass, and I could not grasp it.

My she-wolf strength was useless against it. I began to feel myself beginning to black out.

At that moment, the door exploded open and Van appeared with a golden saber in his hands.

The crone turned to him and screamed. It was a like a shrill, piercing siren that shocked me and pushed me into a dream like state. Van swung the weapon like it was a baseball bat with a grunt and it bisected the specter at her midsection.

The sword made a purring sound and cleaved the figure in half. As the blade sundered it diagonally at the waist the ghost made a grunting "OOOOFFFF". The hag froze for a second, and then her top half slid down and the bed in front of her legs. Black smoke and fire and then soot replaced the two halves of the specter. Soon it all just vanished into nothing.

Van rushed to me and hugged me in his arms. We hugged for a long minute and when we separated, I saw that the ghost left a deep, red impression and indentations on my stomach and chest.

"Saving me is getting to be a full-time job", I said to Van. He replied, "That was a succubus. Few beings could have thrown her off even once. You would have destroyed anything solid. They usually drain you slowly and over several months, but that bitch was trying to make fast meal out of you. It would have killed a normal human very quickly".

"But Van, "I exclaimed, "I thought we were protected by spells and wards and a time delay in this house? How…."

"We are." Van replied," She must have ridden in on one of us after we destroyed the church. She meant business. She probably planned to take us as we slept. Of course, we would have resurrected the night of the full moon. But she couldn't have known that."

"Do you think it is related to the vampire?" I asked.

"Maybe". Van speculated. "I am still not sure what to make of him". More likely she was a vengeful spirit. Or sent by our golden friend, but even that is a slim probability. We would have been hard pressed to destroy it in either of our forms. I am very gratified that the sword destroyed it. My suspicions were right.

These demon horn weapons can kill supernatural entities. This and he pointed to the saber on the floor, "is the first edged weapons I will fashion from one horn. You will have a similar saber, and I will make smaller knives that we can always carry concealed. I will craft one of each of us and for Ernie out of the slivers. I believe that they can also cut through anything.

I can carve sigils and runes on them to give them special abilities. But I must consult with my wizard friend".

Van had made a work of art in the sword. It was about four feet long; bronze and had a neat, distinct temper line and blood groove. He had shaved off some of the top edge and it came to a wicked point. The guards curved upwards. He had made the handle out of ray skin and cord wrapping it Japanese katana style. It was polished to perfection.

We hugged each other tight and I offered, "The idea of mercenaries armed with silver bullets scares me." Van scoffed, "That silver bullet nonsense is just folk lore. Silver is a soft metal and even bonded with some harder metal; it will be less effective than lead or steel bullets. Believe me, others have tried it before.

Still, it could kill the Strigoi. Mercs are tough and deadly. However, they usually depend on the element of surprise. They will not be a problem for either of us. And they are expecting one wolf and we are two. We have the strategic advantage"

"I am glad you came in when you did. Did the wards on the house alert you?" I questioned.

"No, I was with Ernie, putting in his television. He warned me you were in danger. He also advised me to take the demon sword" Van responded.

"He is coming in handy, our little man", I replied.

"In this case, definitely", Van answered. "But even though I like him too, we must take time before we trust him completely, unless we learn something additional.

Anything else would be naive".

I nodded my agreement. "Now, if you can go back to sleep. If not, let us get on with this day", Van continued. Because today we are 'off to see the wizard'".

Off to See the Wizard

Any sufficiently advanced technology is indistinguishable from magic. Arthur C. Clark

Considering the excitement of the night before, we got an early start that morning. We had a leisurely breakfast of a few eggs each and raw thick ham steaks and about a pound of bacon. We sat for a while and lingered over gourmet Vietnamese coffee. The condensed milk made the luxurious brew; the best I had ever had.

Van began, "You know that you are not going to be able to go back to Mt. Summit. People believed that you died in that slaughter at Creedmoor Hospital. The police are blaming a pair of rouge bears. I am off "on leave", so I can go back. I will have to go back sometime soon and take care of some unfinished business. It is psychology business, not wolf business".

"I assumed that much", I replied. "I suppose that I will have to change my appearance and get new I.D.s. I could cut my hair and dye it. I'll have to get a pair of big sunglasses. They are stylish now anyway".

"That is a good idea, in a few weeks your new physiology will cause you to gain so much muscle and lose so much fat, you will look quite different anyway. Oops! I forgot that I was talking to a woman! I am not saying that you are fat, but rather that you will look like a competitive bodybuilder. Your face will be leaner, your posture will be the best it can be, and your gait will be like a dancer's".

"You better mince those words, Dr. Gentlesse," I laughed. "The new clothing that you gave me is also very different from my usual style."

"I also have wigs for you, and I think you should use a spray on tanning product just for a while." Van continued. "Oh, I also got you these". Van handed me a pair of Ray Ban oversized, round "Jackie O" style sunglasses and a large wide brimmed floppy hat.

"How about identity documents?" I inquired.

"We are going to see a man today who has mentored me since the first century B.C... I call him, 'The Wizard", because he is incredibly adept at so many things such as this. He has new identification for you. I also call him that because he is an actual staff wielding, magic conjuring 'wizard'."

Images of Gandalf, Merlin and every other movie wizard danced through my mind. I imagined a stereotypical old man in a rimmed conical hat with stars and half-moons emblazoned on it. I saw long white beards and ankle length robes. For some reason, the image came vividly to my mind of stately Ian McKellen standing on a stone bridge, slamming down his staff and shouting, "You shall not pass" to a titanic black entity with a fiery maw.

We prepared and I wore a blond wig and had the floppy hat and sunglasses with me. I wore blue jeans that I never would have worn prior to meeting Van. They left little to the imagination. I chose a silk blouse and bolero jacket. Van wore a pair of double pleated khaki pants, a button down light blue oxford shirt and a brown tweed sports coat.

Under his coat he wore a double holster belt with matching Colt Gold Cup 1911 pistols. "In this business, you never know. I have a 'concealed carry' license.' he explained. He put on a pair of horn-rimmed glasses with plain glass lenses and Ivy League cap. He was transformed into the perfect academician. However, his massive shoulders and scared hands betrayed him.

For the first time, I entered Van's garage. It was large enough for six cars and there were four automobiles and two motorcycles housed there.

I didn't know much about motorcycles or cars, but I could see the "Harley Davidson" emblems on the bikes. All the cars were late models, but not flashy or highly expensive. We made our way past a Kia Optima, a Toyota pickup, a Volkswagen and entered a Chevy Volt. "It would be incongruous for a college professor to be driving a Bentley. We don't make that kind of money. No need to draw attention." he explained.

Van opened the passenger side door and I got in. He then got behind the wheel and adjusted the rearview mirror. "Do you know how to use a pistol", he inquired. "Yes, my father took all of us girls out and we used to target shoot with his .38 Caliber revolver. I have shot some rabbits and coyotes." I responded.

"Good, you are a good shot and a predator! There is a Smith and Wesson .38 with a four-inch barrel and some speed loaders in the glove box", he reported. "We probably won't need it, but just in case, it's there." I nodded.

Van used the remote and opened the automatic garage doors. We backed out on to a well-kept dirt road. I could hear the wood chips crunching under the tires. I was amazed to see that what appeared to be a large rectangular space open in a rich grove of popular trees. Inside of it, I could clearly see the garage's contents. Van used the remote again and the garage door closed. All that was visible were the trees.

"It's kind of like the Bat Cave, but with a modest car and magic. It is also included in that five-minute time lag spell and it is virtually undetectable and inaccessible." Van chuckled.

We made our way around a sharp curve in the dirt road and saw a four-lane highway. "Out here, there isn't much traffic." Van stated. We easily slipped onto the highway and headed east.

"Are we going to a temple or arcane mansion?" I asked expectantly. "No, actually, we are going to State University in Gainsburg", Van chuckled. I was taken aback. "We are going to the physics department and conferring with the Theoretical Physics Department Head. His name is Giorgos Fotopoulos. He and I are similar in a lot of ways. Please allow me to tell you a little about him and our association."

"George started out as 'Daedalus' and became an ancient Greek mythical figure" Van began. "While he was held captive by King Minos of Crete, he designed and built the famous labyrinth which concealed the Minotaur.

The most famous story about him was that he crafted wings of bird feathers and wax and he and his son Icarus escaped. They were actual early forms of hang gliders. According to myth, Icarus flew too close to the sun and the wax melted and he plummeted to the ground. Like many modern hang gliders sometimes do, he was caught in an updraft and Daedalus never saw him again. He probably froze in the upper atmosphere.

Daedalus continued to Sicily and found protection under King Coculas. There he built a temple to Apollo and then moved to Athens. He cultivated an incredible thirst for knowledge and insatiable curiosity. There he lived as a philosopher, teacher to tradesmen and inventor until his death.

It is said that he became arrogant and excessively proud in his later years. He eliminated his closest rivals. He even contributed to the death of a nephew who designed the Parthenon.

As punishment, the Olympians resurrected him and cursed him to walk the earth until he became weary of life and was sated with curiosity. Ha! That was almost five thousand years ago. He is still going strong and has been a scholar and scientist ever since. However, although they are greatly weakened, he is still on the Olympians' radar and they are alert to his name.

I met him while I was with Claudia at the beginning of the second Millennium B.C. He had developed an impressive understanding of the academic knowledge, science and the mystical arts of the time. He recognized my wolf right away and we became fast friends. Having lived and thrived for over two thousand years by that time, he took me under his wing and gave me guidance about how to transform as the generations turned from one identity to another.

Daedalus was the person who created the magical catacombs under my house. He convinced me to start gathering wealth and set me on a course of learning."

"But Van" I interjected, "You somehow made it to America before the Common Era?" Van chuckled, "The cavern isn't really physically located under my house. It is in a parallel plane of existence and has entrances to the various homes I own around the world. I'll tell you more about that later.

George has a similar structure. They are connected and we can be together in moments. He is a loner, but we visit.

"How did he create it", I asked. Van thought for a moment and then responded, "Let me back track a little bit. For five hundred years, Daedalus studied magic in Egypt. He learned how to command, and control elemental forces and they did the actual physical work. It is the same way the famous King Solomon built the First Temple in Jerusalem. I could not tell you the exact mechanics of it. He himself created the entrance and exit spells.

"We have remained close over these years. He is unbelievably adept at creating documents and hacking computer files to insert us into official records. He used to take the identities of infants who died close to birth, establish academic credentials and state licenses.

But that has become common practice and I am not sure how he does it now. He'll give you a few different identities and the documents to support them. They will also legitimately be validated in an all the necessary government agencies".

"And what do you give him in return", I asked?

Van laughed. "Well, a virtually immortal scientist and magician can always find uses for a twelve-foot-tall werewolf. But I have also lived a long time and have accumulated some wisdom. George is incredibly good with things and concepts, but not so good with people. I have a lot of people skills. Besides, it is wonderful to be comrades with someone who has lived through much of the history that I have."

About forty-five minutes later, we entered the grounds of State University. The campus was very modern, and all the buildings were contemporary. There were high rise dorms. We entered the area where old Victorian houses were converted into Sorority and Fraternity Row. We found a parking garage in that area and bought a ticket for all day parking. We exited the car, went down the elevator and began to ambulate towards the Physics Building.

We walked along the sidewalk and I admired the old Victorian houses of fraternity row. On one of the lawns, four hefty fraternity boys wearing their hawk logo football jerseys were tossing a Frisbee around in the front yard in the local Delta house. They looked like football linemen.

The Frisbee came close to me and the boys ran up to collect it. I bent over to retrieve the little disk and I felt are hard smack on my bottom accompanied by a loud, "Oh Yeah! Nice Ass".

Without conscious thought, I swung around and slapped the boy closest to me. He dropped like a felled bull.

The other three boys ran up to us and started shouting. "You hit the Fish-man!", "Hey, can't you take a complement, bitch". Let's pulverize them." They reeked of beer.

Before I knew it, Van was between us and had dropped two more with a left and then right palmer slap. The fourth boy tried to run, but Van caught him by the scruff of his neck and threw him to the ground.

"Gentlemen", Van began, "I think that the college would not approve of drunken rowdiness by its football players at one o'clock in the afternoon. Further, you assaulted my wife and you better wish that she does not choose to file charges. At the very least, you would be kicked off the football team and lose your scholarships."

I smelled a pungent odor like old sweat socks and gym clothes. I realized that these frat boys were getting a testosterone rush. Their faces contorted in hate and became white with rage. I could see that they were preparing to become aggressive again.

The boy closest to Van cocked his fist. Van slipped smoothly to the opposite side from the fist, grabbed the boy's other thumb and pulled back, spinning the football player forwards head over heels and onto his back.

One of the boys said, "Pay back's a bitch man. For twenty bucks, you can find anybody's house online."

I observed, "Isn't the Frat House made of wood?" Van added, "And old wood burns quickly. Perhaps at three o'clock in the morning when everyone is too drunk to get out safely.

If they attack, kick them in the knees, My Dear. They will never run again."

He made a dismissive fluttering movement with his left hand. "So, go play, or we will cripple you all. Fly away little birds. Fly, fly. fly…fly, fly, fly" The boys flushed and rushed off and back into the frat house.

It was a short walk to the Physics Building. It was four stories of grey stone and tinted glass. The electronic door opened. We walked into the lobby past the students reading on the benches and entered the elevator. Van pushed the button for the fourth floor. I felt that sinking feeling as the elevator travelled upwards.

We got out and walked to the left and found the door with a bronze sign saying "Giorgos Fotopoulos, Ph.D., Department Head". Van knocked at the door.

The door opened and there stood a short, balding, pear-shaped man with a broad face, gaped tooth smile, and a short white beard. He had broad features, like the actor Ernest Borgnine. He could be described as "pleasantly plump".

He wore the standard yellow oxford shirt and double pleated khaki pants of an academician. Both had chalk on them. His belly dropped over his belt line. He was effusive, rushed to us and welcomed us both with a warm, expansive hug. "How are ya!" he effused.

Van and George said each other's names at the same time and laughed. "George meet Mary", Van said. George took both my hands in his and said, "Pleased to meet 'cha. I have looked forward to meeting you since Van called and told me you were together!"

"Daedalus?" I asked incredulously. George, put his index finger on his lips, looked nervously around and said, "Shush! Sh,Sh,Sh, don't say the D-word". He looked at me sternly and I got a vivid image of two men jumping off a mountain wearing hang gliders. He was young then, and quite handsome.

"I have coffee, tea, Coca Cola, bottled water, fruit drinks", George offered. We declined. "Cookies, cake, baklava, donuts, pretzels?" Again, we declined.

"George, Van has told me about you. You have been around a long time. May I ask you how you can be a hardnosed scientist and a wizard at the same time?" George gave me a little laugh and said, "That's not an easy answer. Theoretical Physics is hardly 'hard science'… Some nuts, potato chips, pistachios? No, huh… I mostly sit around and daydream and then justify my daydreams with mathematics.

I prefer the term 'sorcerer'. The world is much more mysterious than people think. You could say nothing is magic and everything is magic; nothing is science, and everything is science. It comes down to how you choose to explain reality.

It is all in the narrative. People believe what experts tell them. They focus on certain things and cannot see others.

Physicists describe a mechanical universe. People think the world is like a clock. Things happen routinely, on schedule, calculable. Tick tock, tick tock. This makes it feel safe, predictable, comforting. It also allows them to not have to take responsibility for anything. It is God's will or its fate? It is what it is. Blah, blah.

Some, chocolates, jellybeans, Twizlers? No?

Modern science establishes theories and rules and then sets up experiments to show how certain phenomena can be reproduced. It has conventions about what is appropriate to study and what is not. For example, in the 1890s, there were mathematical formulations that 'proved' heavier than air flight is impossible. So heavier than air flight wasn't considered a valid field of study.

Some ice cream, frozen yogurt, sorbet? No?

The Wright brothers didn't believe them.

Those same Victorian scientists thought that they had already made every important scientific breakthrough.

What people forget is that science can be viewed as today's explanations replacing yesterday's explanations. Theories are just interpretations, stories if you wish, about how things work. However, there are more exact stories that can be told.

Scientists often will not give up the theories they formulated despite evidence to the contrary. That is how they make their livings and fame. They have enormous egos and make their money by advocating pet theories as the 'truth'. Often, theories only change when their founder dies.

Frequently, technology is years ahead of science. Things work and we just suspect how or make up a story about it.

For example, no one has ever been able to explain electricity. The idea of it being streaming electrons is just a teaching modal. Physicists make it sound like a bunch of little marbles rolling through a tube.

However, electrons contain no physical matter. Recent thought is that they are just the probability of a negative charge being in a particular place at a particular time. Further, they can be in two places at one time.

I like theoretical physics because it explores at the lines between the natural and supernatural worlds. When you get down to the subatomic level, matter seems to break down and we see that the world consists of one percent matter and ninety nine percent electric, light and other forces. That "ninety nine percent world" is the province of quantum physics AND metaphysics.

Every solid thing is connected by a force that is called the 'Zero Point Field'. It is a web of mysterious activity that fills in the space between solid objects. I call it "the source".

Also, the human brain is much more complicated than we could have ever imagined. We only consciously use about seven percent of it.

We have still not been able to find the location of human consciousness. Some scientists suggest that conscious is like a radio signal from outside of us. Additionally, there is more and more evidence that consciousness survives death. For example, there are devices that measure electrical activity and record voices at haunted sites, as well as photographic evidence.

There is strong evidence that what we consider 'reality' interacts with what humans pay attention to and expect to happen. It is called "the observer effect". Things seem to exist as a wave of possibilities until someone focuses on them. Then they collapse into one alternative that we call reality.

But all the other possibilities spin off into their own separate realities.

In some ways what we consider real is a simulation, a façade like a video game. It is like having cable tv with infinite channels. While we are watching one channel, the others are still running and available. We just don't notice them.

We are always limited by our five senses. There is ample evidence that humans can perceive `things are beyond our five senses. For example, how different does reality appear if we look through glasses that reveal ultraviolet or infra- red parts of the visual spectrum? There are huge gaps, and the mind fills in things to make sense.

What is in these 'holes' is the elements of magic. Their connection in the Zero Point Field is "sorcery."

I learned in ancient Egypt that there were incredible phenomena that could be recreated with certain materials, under specific circumstances and at discrete times. That is not any different than the experiments in science or the manufacturing processes.

Magical rituals can be quite reliable but certainly include unnecessary elements out of sheer happenstance. For example, if a magical spell requires a bat's heart, what component is the necessary ingredient? The valves, the arteries, which chamber? Why do the procedures have to be done in a specific order? Are some steps unnecessary?

As a physicist, I both contribute to human knowledge and I make my magic stronger. I also have access to super-computers and the world's knowledge at my fingertips. What fun!

Van laughed and said. "That was just off the top of his head. You should hear him lecture! It is positively mesmerizing!"

But you are here for more everyday help…" George continued. He handed me a large manila envelope and began discussing runic symbols that Van could inscribe of the weapons made from the demon's horn. He later showed me a hand position with the fingers of both hands intertwined with all of them turned into the palms. He said, silence your mind, stay very still and repeat, "makasish lecura absalik". No thinking!

I did as instructed and I notice that the outline of my hands and body became, indistinct and foggy.

"This is the Ninja procedure for creating invisibility", George revealed. "You are blurry now, but with practice you will become completely invisible. Practice daily and you will develop a greater sensitivity and ability to control elemental forces. When you can be completely unseen, and I will show you more."

We visited for several hours. The two old friends reminisced and joked. I was thoroughly charmed by them.

George opined that our fae ally would be loyal and suggested that we could collect a team of fae who could accompany us and help in difficult situations. "For example," He stated "A water fae and an earth fae have been known to be able to instantly produce a mud wall for protection, and a fire fae and air fae can project a stream of fire almost as hot as the sun to incinerate enemies. The trick will be getting them to get along".

George got a twinkle in his eye. He said ", I have a friend who I think can help you." He excused himself and returned from one of the back rooms with a fae perched like a parrot upon his right shoulder. "This is 'Harrison'".

The small creature resembled Ernie in every way. He was thinner but seemed to have identical wings and coloring. Harrison bowed crisply and said in a precise manner, "I am incredibly pleased to make your acquaintances. George has explained to me your situation.

I am a Sylph and your Salamander and I should be quite compatible. I will keep him company and will help facilitate his healing".

George smiled broadly. "Harrison and I have been friends and allies for a long time. He is what is called a 'servitor', which suggests a servant, but he is more of a close friend. He is a staunch enemy of evil and would like to volunteer to help you".

Harrison offered, "Quite right. We fae have been ravished by evil entities like your demon and it is my honor to help defeat him.

I hope that all fae can unite one day and work for the betterment of all."

"But how will we get him home? He is too big to conceal in our clothing", I asked.

"Have no fear, my lady", Harrison offered. "Humans simply will not see things that go against their belief systems. I can perch on one of your shoulders and no one will even notice me."

I said, "Will not see? Don't you mean, "Cannot?" Harrison laughed, "It amounts to the same thing."

"Please, Mary" George said, "Look inside the envelope." I opened it and found driver's licenses, birth certificates, Social Security cards, a credit cards, baccalaureate degrees and master's degrees and a State license to practice various occupations under different names" "But how…." I asked.

He chuckled and said, "magical fingers" and his hands began to glow and emit light blue sparks." Just kidding. I did it with a computer and an exquisite laser printer with access to all of universities and official governmental records worldwide. All of it is legal, proper and documented. You have a credit history with an excellent score."

We said our goodbyes and George insisted we take a bag of Baklava that he had made that morning.

On our way back to the parking garage, Harrison sat on my shoulder and we did not get so much as a glance.

On the Way Home

*Let friendship be the instrument for being
a better nation and a better home.
Anonymous*

We made our way back out of the Physics Building. The little fae was perched on my shoulder but he had no discernible weight.

Although we encountered dozens of people in the building and on the street, no one gave us a second glance. One girl asked us for directions and seemed no wiser. I was enjoying the strangeness of the situation.

We walked right past the Delta House and the only incident was the noticeable slamming of a door as we passed. I could smell frat boys cowering behind their closed doors. I fought my impulse to go in and pull them out by their hair. Van said, "Leave the little piggies alone". I giggled and wondered if he somehow knew about my dream.

We found our way to the parking garage and made continued up to the fourth floor.

We entered the Chevy Volt and Harrison floated just below Van's sight in the rearview mirror. Van glided the little automobile around and down the structure and we made our way to the main road leading out of Gainsborough.

"This car is a wise choice", Harrison said. "Fossils fuels are running out and their exhaust is poisoning the planet. It is so quiet".

"Yes", Van answered. "It is exactly the kind of car one would expect a college professor and psychologist to drive. Keeping up a consistent appearance is one of the absolute necessities in our situation."

"If you'd like to, we would love to hear a little bit about you", I inquired. "How long have you known George?"

Harrison laughed, "Oh he and I go back forever; almost literally. Several thousand years ago I felt a strong drawing. George was casting an enchantment to prevent a tropical storm from destroying a small Mediterranean Island.

I was fascinated by all the Sylphs he could gather and his compassion for the islanders. He got us together to move the upper atmosphere steering wind currents and away from land. George and I enjoyed each other's intellects and had many interests in common. I have hung about since".

"Won't you miss him", I asked.

"Oh, most assuredly," Harrison answered. "But, in the world of enchantment, we are never really separate. George likes to talk about 'the Zero Point Field' which is a kind of electric matrix between all aspects of the universe. Tapping into this field is essential for any kind of what is called "magic".

Physicists propose that it attaches anything to everything else. It allows for bilocation; being in two or more places at once. Whatever the explanation, we are always in communication and can be together at will."

Van added, "our magical catacombs are connected, and a short walk will allow us to visit anytime."

We began to leave Gainsburg and were noticing the density of the houses thinning out. The apartment houses of the city trickled down to the single-family homes of the suburbs.

"Why did you agree to come with us?" Van asked.

Harrison reflected for a moment and then responded. "For several reasons, I suppose. The different worlds are coming together. Humans are clever and are developing ways of detecting the other denizens of this planet. They have invented technologies for seeing into the world of spirits and both science and popular culture are beginning to acknowledge that there are invisible inhabitants in their environments.

Once they generally accept this, they will fear us and then seek to find a way to control, hurt and kill us. When they do, they will exploit and control us. It has been their way since they began of their domination of this planet.

Most fae do not believe that this will ever happen. However, the popularity of the ghost hunting shows, the evidence that they are collecting that can be seen and heard is causing more and more interest.

There is more scientific study of the actual dying experience where scientists are experiencing paranormal events. Further, they are recognizing that some of the spirits are not friendly and are even malicious. They are beginning to uncover demons and other predators in the dark.

I suppose that it is just natural to want means of protecting themselves from danger. Some companies manufacturing ghost detecting equipment are now developing what I call 'ghost vacuums.' That is devices that take electricity away from paranormal entities rather than apply surges to them. Soon they will have means to literally hurt preternatural entities, and the supernaturals will retaliate. I foresee the coming of the first normal verses paranormal war.

Before this can happen, I think that fostering understanding between all the dwellers of this earth is necessary.

The way to begin this is to work on my own race to bring us together. We fae have come a long way since the Undines enslaved the Gnomes, but there is still incredible misunderstanding and even hatred between us. George and I have talked about teams of fae that can work together like military or industrial units for the benefit of all earth's inhabitants.

Sylphs and Salamanders have a natural affinity because our natures complement each other. Undines and Gnomes likewise have complementary natures but hate each other because of the period of

Gnome slavery. The Gnomes are looked down upon by the other fae and have become hostile to the rest of us. If we can develop a team of all four kinds of fae, and at least among ourselves we will have an example of cooperation.

I want to partner with your Salamander and begin to work towards these aims. We will get along and then, once we work well together, we can recruit an Undine and a Gnome."

"How do you know that you and Ernie will get along?" I asked.

"As I said, our natures are compatible, and Sylphs and Salamanders always are friendly. I can help him focus his healing powers to regenerate his wings. Because you saved him, he will be loyal to you, and you will have two new allies in your war against this arch demon." Harrison replied.

Van asked, "Ernie has the ability to scry, is there some similar thing you can do."

"Yes," the floating fae answered. "All Sylphs have the power of precognition. It is perfectly compatible with scrying. Ernie can show you what is going on now at a distance, while I know with increasing amounts of certainty what will happen in the future."

"With a certain amount of certainty?" I reflected.

"What I mean", Harrison elaborated, "is that the further out I look, the less accurate I can foresee specific outcomes. It boils down to probabilities and intervening events. It is a little like weather forecasting.

A week out and I can tell you that an event is forming. A few days out and I can tell you direction and most likely outcomes. Within a few hours, I can tell you exactly what is happening and where intervention would be the most effective.

Combine that with Ernie's ability to tell you exact events occurring at that specific time and you have a powerful predictive combination."

I noticed that we were passing farmlands and the forested area in which we live.

"I also know the ways of the air, and with Ernie's knowledge of the forces of fire, we understand half of the magical universe. I have lived for thousands of years with a sorcerer, so I have picked up a thing or two."

"By combining our abilities; right now we could project a large funnel of flame towards a target. We could also generate lightning strikes quite precisely. We can project a small thin intense flame like an acetylene torch. Sylphs and Salamanders have been doing this for eons. We could experiment with other phenomena such as these.

In emergencies, I have seen a group of Sylphs, Salamanders and Gnomes form flowing lava; also, instant stone walls. Sylphs and Undines can great tornados and if a Salamander is involved the storm could have lightning. Undines and Gnomes can cause mud that would slow an army. Undines alone can cause flash floods. All of these are formidable weapons on the side of good."

Van eased the small car off the highway and we slowly circled around the angular dirt road to a clearing surrounded by trees on all sides. Van stopped and pushed the garage remote. A large section of the trees seemed to fold upwards leaving a garage door shaped opening. The bulb on the garage door opener illuminated the contents of the garage. We eased into the garage and Van closed it behind us. Harrison perched on my shoulder. We seemed to have an affinity for each other.

We exited the car, walked past the vehicles and Van reached up and took a set of keys off a large peg board. "These are the keys to the Volkswagen", Van said. "It is yours now. The registration and insurance papers in your name are in the envelop George gave you."

We made our way into the kitchen and proceeded to the cellar stairs. "Your machine shop is admirable", Harrison said. "You could manufacture just about anything down here".

Van nodded. "That's the point. Sometimes I need to create things that are not easy to come by. I have made everything from edged weapons to flamethrowers to silencers for pistols, rifles and hand grenades. I have even made screws and bolts that went missing from IKEA furniture,

Harrison saw the demon horn weapons Van was creating. "That is a brilliant idea!" He exclaimed. "Such weapons are supposed to be able to kill anything supernatural and cut through everything".

"They seem to" Van replied. "Recently, we had to dispatch a succubus that had planned to make a quick meal of us".

"That is impressive", the fae continued. "It looks like you are making an additional saber and two smaller knives. Have you thought about making the knives as folders with thumb opening studs?"

"Humm," Van mussed. "That's a good idea. Fixed blades would be stronger, but folders would be easier to carry. Hmm, I can back engineer the locking mechanism from one of my 'Cold Steel' folders and they would be almost as strong as fixed blades. I could also add pocket clips and thumb studs to aid in rapid acquisition."

"I am sure that Ernie and I together could generate power that would be helpful, and we could assist your engraving sigils onto the blades to make them even more powerful", Harrison reflected.

We walked to the back wall and Van said, "Let us introduce you to Ernie."

A Meeting of the Minds

A real cousin (or friend) is someone who walks in when the rest of the world walks out Proverb

We entered the magical catacombs and began to walk towards the secret room.

I was always impressed by the enormity of this place. I was getting used to it, and I found the sets of armor on the walls and the neat corridors of boxes somehow comforting.

Harrison remarked, "George does good work. We have a similar structure, and it expands as it needs to because George has been around about twice as long as you have. He is also every bit the hoarder." Van offered, "He designed this to automatically enlarge when space is needed and to connect with any house that I build".

"Yes, George impressed upon me the need to accumulate riches because wealth gives one freedom and options." Van continued. "I know George has stores of gold, precious metals and gems as well. He also accumulates magical objects and conceals things that are too dangerous to be in the world at large".

I asked, "What are some of the magical items that George has?"

"He has Heracles' club. It is too large and heavy for one man to lift, but, if thrust into the ground it can create earthquakes." Harrison replied. "Also, Artemis' quiver and arrows. The quiver never runs out and the arrows can hit any object no matter how far away and through any barrier. He has an Egyptian priest's staff that can become a hooded cobra with the right spell. Orpheus' mirror that allows one to enter the afterlife and bring a shade back. But we have never tried that. A Chinese puzzle box that can unleash actual fire breathing dragons.; Many of Merlin's talismans. Some books by Nostradamus that he believes are not for public consumption. We could spend half the night naming them off."

"But, if you don't mind my saying, I sense that you have some enchanted relics here too". The fae responded.

"I know I have 'wolf belts' that some German warriors used to transform themselves." Van answered. "I used them once or twice when I needed the wolf between the full moons. I thought they should not be out there so that just anyone could find them. But other than that, I am not aware of any.

Especially at the beginning of my 'career' as a werewolf, I tended to plunder indiscriminately from my adversaries. I took anything that could have value so that I could barter for things I needed".

"I sense several enchanted items", Harrison response. "If you will permit me…."

"Please", Van replied.

The fae floated off my shoulder and glided to a closed box, moved the top and rummaged around for a moment. It seemed more like he was floating rather than flying. He emerged with a round obsidian and ivory object and placed it in my open hands. He then returned to his place on my right shoulder.

I looked at the object and was a broach about one inch in diameter that had the exquisitely rendered profile of a woman sculpted on it.

It looked practically new. "It is beautiful", I said. "What is it"?

Harrison responded, "It is the 'Bulwark of Theresa'". When activated, it prevents the wearer from being touched by harmful objects. The Wizard Harab created it for his love Theresa of Carthage to protect her from a family purge. The royals at the time were eliminating anyone who could have a claim to their throne. Ironically, she was poisoned.

In retaliation, Harab insured their defeat by Rome."

Van said, "Thank you, Harrison. Permit me". He pinned the broach just above my left breast. Harrison floated down and touched it. "Hasuma, behla, ahmamart!" A sparkle of violet light erupted from the broach and dozens of streaming lights seemed to form an oval four feet out around my body. Then they disappeared. "This will only protect you in your human form". Harrison said. "Your wolf is pretty much indestructible, anyway".

"I sense there are more, I will search them out over time", Harrison offered.

We came to the secure area and were greeted by Ernie. He was dressed in a grey frock coat and pants and his signature black bowler. "Boss Man, Boss Lady and…. Hello, Cuz! Well, I'll be gol-danged! I would ask 'What are you in for', but I see you are a guest. Business or pleasure?"

"Quite correct, Ernie. "I am Harrison." replied Sylph. "I am a guest who is a mutual friend of Van's closest comrade. I am here to help you and these fine people".

"As of this moment, you are our guest as well", I said to Ernie. "Harrison will help you heal and keep you company. We are one family now".

Ernie's jaw dropped and he looked up at us with big eyes. He took of the derby and held it in front of his lap. He looked up at us with big eyes. "Do you mean it? Are we all going to be together! I never dreamed I could have anyone like and trust me again. It has been so long." He sobbed.

Harrison floated off my shoulder and put his arm around Ernie. "There, there, buck up Cousin. You are not alone any longer. I will be living with you and we'll get your wings back in tip top shape". He said. Ernie sighed, his body relaxed, and he seemed comforted.

I said, "Ernie, we are all too personally familiar with other people determining our fates. Daedalus and Harrison vouch for you, and that is good enough for us. We will work together against our common enemy and protect each other as family do. We are all stronger if we stand together".

"As far as I am concerned, you two can have the run of the house." Van added. "How are your back and wings progressing?"

"I am still a little sore, and the areas where my wings were itch a little. But I am stronger and have more energy', Ernie reported.

"Let's have a look", Van said. The fire fae took off his coat and shirt and I put down some towels down for him to lie down on. He laid on his stomach and Van and Harrison took a close look. "It looks like the scabs are drying up and that accounts for the itchiness. Your wings are growing back slowly. The bulb on the right side is bigger while the left is actually taking the shape if a small wing."

Harrison added, "I will conduct some healing energy your way and I think we can at least double the rate of your healing."

Van applied some antibiotic cream to Ernie's back and then covered them with bandages. Ernie put on his shirt and coat.

"They are going to need a bigger place to live. This cage is too small, and it is a place for enemies not for friends." I stated. "You are right", Van responded. "We could move one of the larger Victorian doll houses in here. Why don't we all go and choose one together?"

Harrison alighted on my right shoulder. Because Ernie needed full wings to balance himself, Van removed the large 1911 Colt pistol on his right side and placed it on the table. He gently placed Ernie in that holster. The fae boosted himself up by his underarms and stood up on his toes.

Together we walked into the catacombs. We searched for a few moments among the neatly piled and covered relics and came to the area were the doll houses were stored. There were two Colonial era doll houses and three Victorian ones. There was also a large box filled with doll clothes.

"What do you think?" Van asked. "It would appear that only the largest of the Victorian houses would be big enough for us to be comfortable in", Harrison suggested. "I don't want to be any trouble." Ernie offered. "Don't let that even be a consideration", I replied. "You are our family now and we want you to be comfortable. We want you to have the best."

The largest of the Victorian doll houses was an enormous Tudor style home with a large turret in the front, two stories and a porch that went three quarters of the way around it. It was grey with white trim and had belonged to the daughter of a Nineteenth Century railroad tycoon.

It was a painstakingly crafted exact replica of his actual home. Further, it was completely furnished as it was at the peak of that man's power and prosperity. Van had saved the family from a horrific murder plot by the father's rivals. He had had a lifetime relationship with the woman who had owned it and she gave it to him after she grew old.

The doll house was designed to be unhinged lengthwise and had sturdy clamps to hold, it together. We separated the halves, and I was impressed by the craftsmanship and detail. It was incredible!

The tycoon had the same builders and furniture makers who crafted the actual house duplicate it in exact detail. There were two floors with an elegant staircase leading up to the second floor. The bottom floor had a formal Victorian parlor, large kitchen, a study, a library and room for a miniature pool table.

The family had three bedrooms and two guest rooms on the second floor: a servants' apartment in the rear with a functional dumbwaiter. The doors had miniature-stained glass windows. The foyer had a tiny coat rack with umbrella stand built into the base. Inside it were tiny functional umbrellas. The kitchen had coal stoves of the period that were functional but never used for obvious reasons.

It had been the made during the age of the great American robber barons. Overall, it was an exercise in extravagance by a man who had too much money. But it had been his to spend.

We open the chest of doll clothes and Ernie and Harrison picked garments they liked that would fit. I was concerned about having to alter the clothing to accommodate Harrison's wings, but he showed me how he could fold them flat against his back. We loaded the clothing into the parlor room and latched the halves together.

"Let's carry it into the backroom", Van suggested. "How are we going to lift it?" I responded. "It must weigh four hundred pounds!" "You are right; it would be too much for two human beings, but…" As the insight hit me, I said "Of course, of course…We are not human!"

We each picked up one end. I was amazed that it seemed to have no weight at all. We easily maneuvered through the neat corridors of piles and placed it on the floor in the gated room.

Ernie and Harrison entered and chose their bedrooms. They put their clothing in the tiny closets on miniature clothes hangers.

When they came back out, each was dressed as the perfect Victorian gentlemen. They sported dark frock coats and high-waisted pants of the period. Ernie had on his derby. Van laughed, "You two could be Holmes and Watson". "But who is who?" Harrison laughingly retorted."

Van said, "At the risk of being rude, Mary and I must excuse ourselves. We must eat or else things will get uncomfortable for us." Van retrieved his pistol.

"We'll leave you to get aquatinted", I added.

I took Van's hand, and we began to walk out of the gated room. We could hear Harrison and Ernie talking. There was a sting of high-pitched whistles, clicks, grunts and ticks. I guess that this was their actual language. As we got further away from our tiny friends, we could not hear actual details. But I noticed that Ernie's speech patterns sound like short staccato bursts. Harrisons were more of a smooth legato.

We made our way into the cellar and up the stairs. We entered the kitchen and went to the refrigerator. I pulled out the exquisite translucent china plates and silverware. Van retrieved a large serving bowl and filled it with the select cuts of meat that he always acquired.

I sat down and Van filled our crystal goblets with rich aromatic Chianti. I swirled the wine around the goblet, watching the alcohol cling to the sides, and cocked my head watching Van through the wine.

I wanted to tell him how I knew him but didn't know him at the same time and how this made me feel.

We had a pork roast and several buttery veal chops each. I noticed that my eating was less voracious. I managed to take smaller bites and took more time to chew and swallow. I mentioned this to Van.

"You are adjusting well. Prior to this, we ate when you were just too hungry. It is better for us to eat on a schedule. It controls the ravenousness and makes us more civil." Van replied.

"We had a productive day", Van continued.

"After a sumptuous shower and a fantastic bout of sex, let us go to sleep. What's up for tomorrow?" I asked.

"I think we have some training to do. I want to get those knives done and then show you how to use them." Van replied.

Disguises

"If you are not prepared to use force to defend civilization, then be prepared to accept barbarism." Thomas Sowell

I awoke from pleasant dreams in my massive bed feeling like a bride aboard a boat, cresting white caps of down comforters and bright white linens. Early dawn just breaking through the curtains. I felt complete and satisfied, my body soft and pliant after making love with Van, remembering his soft touches.

I moved my hand across the sheets searching for his body. He was probably in his workshop working on the knives.

I spent a few moments luxuriating under the covers feeling the lingering warmth and smell of his body on my skin and on his pillow. The bed had a pillow top on the mattress that made me feel like I was floating free in outer space.

The king size pillows cradled my head as I nestled into them. The sheet and comforter exerted a delightful weight on my body and warmed me from head to toe. I felt comfortable, warm and calm for the first time in a very long time.

Some of the dreams were so vivid that I was certain they were memories as my incarnation as Bella. I recalled a long table, with a long lace runner, silver cups and dishes, filled with food and lingering family dinners with my husband and children.

There were an attractive, thin middle-aged woman and a large, jovial white-haired man at the table, salutations and happy cheer at the King's victories.

I saw myself dressing babies and toddlers, running my fingers through the curls of my sons, kissing the soft cheeks of daughters and running a large household with many servants. There were the usual dreams of moving through houses finding objects; dreams populated with people I didn't know. Most of these dreams slipped away as I became more awake.

I got out of bed and stretched. I put my nightgown in the hamper padded to the master bathroom and began my morning regimen. As I was opening the shower door, I caught a glimpse of myself in the mirror. I had always been thin but had a feminine smoothness and softness around the edges.

I was surprised at the change in my face and body. I was aware of being able to see my high cheek bones and the line of my jaw was more pronounced. My shoulders were noticeably broader, and I could see the muscles playing under my skin.

I could see that my formerly rounded lower belly was now a flat "V". My oblique muscles were lightly outlined, and I could see the faintest beginnings of the tracing of a "six pack". My thighs showed faint diamond shapes where the three thigh muscles came together just over the knee. My arms were noticeably thicker. My body resembled those of the female gymnasts I knew in high school.

I recognized that the she-wolf inside of me was transforming my body.

I opened the etched shower doors and felt my feet on the cool marble tile. I was immediately aware of the smell of sweetness and almonds. Once again, the parallel linear shower streams felt like the most delicious of massages as they cascaded over my body. I once more smelled the subtle salty smell of scrumptious minerals in the water. The almond and aloe soap's texture and aromas were almost overwhelming.

I shampooed my dense, wavy black hair and the lather felt like a crown and veil of clouds; I watched as the aromatic suds flowed down my belly and thighs and down the drain making small circles as they funneled away.

But then I became aware of an invading scent that I could localize at the top of the shower stall. It smelled like the pungent earth mixed with other indiscernible odors. It was slowly moving. I reached up and found a tiny brown ant in my hand. All the alienating sensations emanated from it.

Then I was struck with the insight. There was nothing especially unique about the contents of the bath. It was that my human faculties were so heightened by my developing wolf senses.

I finished rinsing off my hair and body and stepped out of the shower stall. I dried myself with the royal blue Turkish bath towel; and then it occurred to me.

My luxurious wavy black hair had been my signature feature since high school. If I was going to be able to move undetected through the world of my old familiar life, I needed to change it. I wondered how I would look as a blonde or a bright redhead and if Van would approve.

Changing it would be my rite of passage into a new life.

I dried off and put my hair up. I found the can of spray on tan that Van had purchased and gently applied it to my face and body. Van would spray it on my back later. I put on my kimono and slippers and went into the kitchen.

I could see the light peeking out from under the basement door and I called down to him. Van shouted up to me that he would clean his hands and be up the stairs in a moment. So, I went about setting the table and frying some bacon and eggs. I set up the Geneva Coffee Maker and rummaged through the hoard of meat in the well-stocked refrigerator to find two polish style sausages. I placed them on a round large serving plate.

Soon Van joined me in the kitchen. He was wearing a pair of grey workman's coveralls he looked sort of bulky; I cocked my head as I looked at him. His muscular frame was evident under the thick cloth. "I have my 'doctor clothes' under these", he said with a grin. "I have to go to the hospital and finish up some details of the study".

We kissed, remembering our previous night of bliss, and gave each other a lingering hug. I smelled Van's strong, aggressive masculine scent. I sighed and turned away to scramble the eggs, while Van prepared the Vietnamese coffee.

We sat at the round kitchen table and began to dish out the meat and eggs. Van poured the coffee.

We sat at the round kitchen table and I began to dish out the meat and eggs. Van poured the coffee. We sat down and neither of us could keep from smiling.

"Did you sleep well, Darling?" Van asked. "Incredibly" I responded, I told him of my dreams of family. "That sounds like our life in Rome alright", he affirmed. "The older couple sound like my mother Rhea Silva and her husband, Vincus Arius. Some of the dream fragments were probably from other incarnations."

I watched as his eyes moved subtly upwards and to the right. I knew he was having strong visual memories.

I wanted to know what they were like, what it felt like back then. I wanted to remember all of it; but I could see that the memories also came with emotions that could be a heavy burden.

We ate our scrambled eggs, raw bacon and raw kielbasa slowly. Every bite was a small gourmets' feast. I savored the texture, the smell and the rich taste of the food. I was able to discriminate the different animals in the meat. I could tell by the smell and taste exactly what each animal had eaten.

I could taste the fear as they were slaughtered; I found that exhilarating. These sensations somehow added to my enjoyment. Then we talked over the meal and lingered over our rich Vietnamese style coffee.

"What is on the agenda today?" I asked Van. "As I said, I must go back to Creedmoor and begin winding down my work there. I will scope out the official story behind the slaughter and what is left of Sterling's project". Van reached into the pocket of his coveralls and produced two medium sized folding knives. He handed one to me.

The folder was about four and a half inches closed and appeared to have an ivory handle. There was a half inch long and wide square appendage on the back of the blade. It was about a quarter inch thick and weighed only a few ounces. It had a clip that could attach to a pocket or waist band. The workmanship was exquisite.

Van asked me to pass it back to him. He stated, "This square is both a thumb opening stud and can catch your pocket if you clip it inside."

He held a knife in the palm of his right hand and put his bended thumb under the thumb opener. He straightened his thumb and a roughly four-inch blade swung out of the handle. There was a slight "snick" as the blade snapped completely open.

The knife's blade had ended in a forty-five-degree angle. It appeared to be Damascus steel. It was about one eighth of an inch thick and I could see the temper line along the bottom side up to the tip. The top edge was shaved about a sixteenth of an inch on either side.

Van turned the blade over and showed me a small piece of what appeared to be steel inside the frame of the knife locking the blade closed. He pushed it with his thumb then closed the blade back inside the handles.

He then snapped the blade open with one hand and closed it deftly with the same hand. He handed the knife to me.

Van began, "Harrison, Ernie and I made these from the demon's horns last night. They were crafting swords for themselves but have retired for the day.

We have used Viking and Enochian sigils to make them appear as everyday steel knives. The sigils make them never leave your hand in combat and can render them invisible to others when they are in our hands or our pockets. They can penetrate anything.

I will begin teaching you some self-defense and knife fighting skills this evening. I will store them safely until I show you a few things later."

"I am sorry I have to be away for a while, but I must do the professional thing. I have to start closing down shop." He said. "Do you have any plans?"

"Yes", I replied as I swallowed my coffee. "I am going to find a hairdresser in a small town, and have my hair cut and dyed. I will also see what the public knows about Creedmoor."

"Great!" Van replied. "There are several laptops in the office, and they don't require a password. I have been using the big Dell on my roll top desk. You can pick a different one and take it with you. They are all connected to the house's wireless network.

You will also find several "burner" cell phones in the top right hand draw of my desk. Feel free to use any of them. They are fully paid up and charged."

"You have the credit cards that George made up for you. Use them to get some clothing and accessories that you like. Cost is no object.

But remember, I am supposed to only have the income of a college professor, so try not to be ultra-extravagant. Try to choose a vastly different style then you had had. Something that is uncharacteristic for you. It is a disguise. Given our circumstances you would probably be wise to have this."

Van handed me a small, unloaded revolver in a blue plastic box that had "Colt Firearms", printed on it. It was a stainless-steel Colt Detective Special with a two-and-a-half-inch barrel. He said that they were no longer in production but that this one had never been fired. It carried six rounds of .38 special ammunition in its cylinder and had a relatively large, rubberized grip. The grips had circular discs emblazoned with rampaging stallions on both sides.

The front sight had been replaced by a translucent fiber optic "electric orange" sight and bright phosphorescent looking yellow dots we painted in the rear on either side of its sighting groove.

"I chose this because your father's gun was a Colt Police Positive. They are identical D frame revolvers except for the barrel lengths.

They will be loaded with Liberty Arms +P plus hollow points. These hit almost as hard as rifle fire. Here are some speed loaders and they are loaded with the same load."

He handed me three round cylinders the size of the revolver's cylinder. They had knobs on the reverse side, and each had six rounds of silver tipped ammunition fitted into the front. My father had taught me to eject spent rounds from the revolver and fit loaded ones from speed loaders into the pistols cylinder.

Then, the knobs we twisted, and the speed loader fell off. Such education is one of the advantages of growing up in the South.

We cleaned up after ourselves and put the dishes in the dishwasher.

After a few more minutes of pleasant chat, Van looked at his Citizen's Eco Drive Moon Tracking wristwatch and said, "It is getting late and I have to go. I should be back in about four hours." We kissed and he walked out into the garage.

I saw him take his coveralls off and he had his standard work uniform: an oxford button down shirt, double pleated khakis and a Jerry Garcia tie; he looked so very handsome. Perhaps as an act of rebellion, or as a fashion statement, he wore a pair of burgundy Shepler's cowboy boots. These made him stand about six feet two inches.

I heard the garage door open and the Chevy Volt hum on. A few seconds later, I heard the garage door close.

I went back into the bedroom and hung up my kimono. I put on my underwear and opened the armoire. I chose another pair of Levi's jeans, a red V-necked shirt and high heeled boots. These enhanced my height to about five feet ten inches tall. That affect would help to conceal my identity. I then walked into Van's office.

I opened the double sliding doors and found that it was surprisingly decorated in a pre-World War II style. I first noticed the ceiling fan with its globe light, an intense green frosted glass with floral markings. Directly across from me was a wall of mahogany bookcases with a rolling wooden ladder that allowed access to the upper shelves.

Books! I giggled on the inside, there were so many volumes, gold and silver bound copies everything from Poe to Plato, Byron to Pythagoras. Some looked old and hand made with sewn bindings in languages I could not read.

My father had only allowed us to read the Bible.

The right part of the room had a large bay window that looked out over the lake; I noticed the billowing clouds; how dark they were as they seemed to creep upon the lake surface. I felt a foreboding in my bones. I noticed that I could clearly see my reflection in the panes of glass.

There were a pair of burgundy high-backed leather chairs and next to each were pedestal tables. Along the window was a long table and its top had four different unboxed brands of laptops. There was an Apple, a Compaq, Hewlett Packard and one of the lesser-known brands.

On the left side of the room was a roll top desk with its tambour rolled up. There was nothing in the open slots in its rear, but on the desktop were two Dell computers. The larger one was older and showed signs of use. The smaller one was plugged in but appeared new. I sat on the oak swivel desk chair and opened the newer computer.

I pressed the "on button" and was greeted by the Dell logo. Soon, I was on the Windows desktop. I got onto the internet and searched for hairdressers in a neighboring zip code. I selected one about thirty miles north of Mt. Summit. I had never been there before.

I opened the top drawer of the desk and found at the top of a pile a Samsung Galaxy with a yellow sticky note saying, "I recommend this one". The draw was filled with unboxed non--contract phones. I picked it up, called and made an appointment for an hour and a half later. I turned the computer off and slipped the cell phone into my pocket. I wound my way around the room admiring the books again, and then slid the doors shut.

Since I had plenty of time before my appointment, I felt little pressure. I sat on one of the overstuffed chairs and decided to practice the skill George had shared with me. I folded my hands as he suggested and repeated the mantra" "Makasish lecura absalik", but my mind meandered away to other things.

I could not focus, and I was becoming frustrated. Then I either actually heard or imagined George's voice in my head. "You must clear your thoughts. Silence your internal dialogue: don't talk to yourself. Force your mind to think only "makasish" as you inhale. And then "lecura absalik" as you exhale.

When you find your mind wandering, gently bring it back to the mantra. Controlling your wandering mind is the central practice." It did not seem strange or alarming when I heard this.

I practiced for about ten more minutes. For a brief time, my mind was empty except for the words I was repeating. I kept my hands folded and opened my eyes for a moment. Where my reflection had been, was a vague translucent outline of my body, but the chair was clearly visible. I could see the indentation my body made in the chair's seat. I got up with a start, and then I could clearly see myself reflected in the mirror.

A spontaneous titter erupted from my lips. "Wow! This is powerful stuff", I thought to myself. And my communication from George was another psychic experience! The world was so much more astounding than I had been taught! I promised myself I would continue practicing it daily.

I put a light cotton blazer over my shirt, reached into my jewelry box and the "Bulwark of Theresa" amulet to my left lapel.

Immediately, a deep violet light emitted from it and formed a cage around my body. Then it faded away. I put on my floppy hat and Jackie O Ray-Bans.

I made sure I had all my new documents and wallet containing four hundred dollars in twenties in my hobo style purse. I took the pistol and speed loaders Van gave me and locked them in the glove compartment of the Volkswagen. I placed a small transparent vinyl folder with the car's registration and insurance information in there as well.

After pulling out of the garage, I drove along the winding country roads, the leaves were beginning to turn from bright lush greens to coppers, scarlets and flashes of gold. There was hardly any traffic on the roads, and I easily found the boutique parked and went in.

The hairdresser was a plump woman with long fingernails; I barely noticed when she said her name was Barb. I could smell something inside of her but did not know what it was; it was a growth of some sort. The smell confused me at first; her heart was pumping harder than normal.

"Honey…what are we doing with your hair today" her voice echoed, and I snapped out of my internal reverie. "Um…a cut please and a new color I think!" I said with a distracted tone. "How would you like it done?" She asked. "Um…a sort of bob, or like how Marilyn Monroe's style and I want it blonde, platinum blonde please." I murmured looking at myself in the large mirror; "You sure Honey?

You got a nice thatch of hair right here, maybe just a trim?" She asked. "No…cut it off, dye it and style it like Marilyn" I said with a halfhearted smile. I was confused by the acetone odors in the beauty salon, but the smell coming off her confused me even more.

I was lucky that I had just eaten a large meal, but it was not a hunger I felt as she moved around me. Barb tried to make pleasant conversation with me, but it was hard to focus on what she was saying. I was only catching bits and pieces of what she said as she moved furiously around me, large chunks of my black hair falling to the floor.

That smell, what was that smell? She had a different hormonal dynamic. Then I heard it as she led me to the sinks to wash the dye out of my hair and treat it, my head was level to her belly. It was another heart beating within her. I felt a deep longing. I swallowed hard and pushed the thoughts out of my mind.

She put pins in my hair and sat me under the dryer. I watched the room, women coming and going, making small talk with each other about men, children, families, and then my heart started to hurt, and my stomach began to ache.

I listened to the women and some of the talk turned to the strange events at Creedmoor Hospital and the destruction of the New Earth Church. From bits and pieces, I gathered the new sheriff had appeared in a local news photo with two large black bears reportedly turned rogue and killed by his party of deputies.

Apparently, the bears' den had been found and there were gnawed human bones in it. It was said that they had tooth infections that had driven them into frenzy. It was a mystery how the pair had managed to get so far inside the complex of buildings.

The fire at the church was still under investigation. They suspected a gas leak.

Barb fluffed my new tresses that were blonde, and it made me cackle out loud at the look of myself. I thought of the famous Marilyn Monroe picture with her skirt blowing up from the movie, "The Seven Year Itch".

The instant tanning spray gave me a slightly darker look, but it brought my blue eyes out and made them sparkle; or it could have been the tears in my eyes. Thinking about the life in her belly, I paid her and gave her a generous tip. I wanted to go home. I reached up and ran my fingers through my now much shorter tresses, and headed down the street, looking at the shop windows trying to remember that I was the wife of a king.

I found a small boutique with a large selection of clothes. I tried to find a style that was unlike anything I had ever worn before. I decided to change my style to 'Rockabilly' and a selection of throwback clothes, tight jeans, and sweaters, sumptuous heels, and sunglasses, period dresses from the 1940's. That would be a distinct change from my country mouse, schoolgirl look.

I thought Van would get a kick out of my new style. I felt guilty about how much I spent. For some reason I was more emotional than I had been other days. I thought to ask Van about what this meant; the sense of foreboding, the longing I questioned what all of this meant and what I would feel if it would ever go away.

I managed to gather all my shopping into two large tote bags. I was surprised how light they were. They should have been weighty, but there was no straining or uncomfortable pinching or numbing of my hands. I walked down the tree lined sidewalk towards where I had parked my Volkswagen. The air was crisp.

I was enjoying this quaint old American Main Street. The old, 1880s style brick false front buildings, lamp posts, the statue of the war hero in the town square, the clock on the Town Administration Building, the weathered and mottled concrete sidewalks.

The smells of the autumn leaves were both sweet and acrid. Their crunching under my feet made dull little roars. I could hear each leaf that hit the ground as a distinct plop.

A cracking sound about six inches away from the top right of my head made me flinch. Then I glimpsed an acorn that would have dropped on my head deflected as if it were swatted by an invisible hand. Then I realized that the amulet had protected me from its impact!

I laughed to myself. This new world I occupy is just filled with wonders!

I got to the car and clicked the fob to open the trunk. It popped open and I bent to put my packages inside. I had always enjoyed the smell of a new car. However, the acuteness of my heightened senses hit me like an ocean wave, and I recoiled slightly. I thought, "There definitely are pros and cons to my 'new' body".

I entered the driver's seat, buckled my seat belt and adjusted the mirror. I looked at my new Citizen's Lady's Eco Drive Champagne

Dial watch and saw that it was approaching 2 P.M. Van would be home soon. That thought filled me with joy.

The V.W. growled to life and I eased out on to Main Street. Within a few minutes I was coasting towards home. I became aware that I didn't notice the usual incessant internal dialogue harassing me. My mind was buzzing with undiluted sensations.

The world felt like it was reaching out to me. The trees were a collage of green, copper, blaze and gold patches. The clouds were three-dimensional cotton ball sculptures floating on a calm pool of blue. Above them were white feathers spreading across the sky. The separated lines on the road were a rolling ribbon of yellow and black. The hum of the road was a pleasant musical droning. The car seemed to be self-propelled.

Before I knew it, I reached the hidden entrance to our driveway. My thinking snapped back in and I carefully curved around the entrance to the cul-de sac. I pressed the remote. The familiar garage door sized opening appeared in the grove of trees and I slid the VW into its slot in the garage.

I opened the trunk and gather up my trophies. I had no trouble hefting them and unlocking the garage door. I was astonished that I did not have to put them down in order to do that. I just curled up my right arm, like we had done with dumbbells in high school gym class and hoisted one of the large shopping bags and the key.

It was 2:35 P.M. I expected Van about 3:00.

I carried my treasures into our bedroom and put the shopping bags on our bed. I laid them out on the bed and picked a white, late 1950s to 1960s style white low-cut pleated dress and white opera gloves. I put on nylon stockings and chose a pair of white stiletto heels and got ready to meet Van when he got home.

A little after three o'clock P.M., I heard the garage door opener. I heard the Chevy Volt engine hum off. I heard the door slam, and rear doorknob rattle. A moment later, Van's athletic form was silhouetted in front of the garage door light.

I stepped out from behind the door to the kitchen and did my best Marilyn impression. I sang, "Happy Birthday to yoooou. Happy Bithday to yooou. Happy Birthday ...Mr. Pes-i-dent! Happy Birthday to you!" I dramatically pointed right hand at Van and dipped my knees putting my left hand between them. "Happy birthday to yoooou".

Van guffawed. He dramatically looked to the left and right, put his right index finger to his lips, and said, "Hush Marilyn, Mary might come home at any minute!" We rushed to each other and Van picked me up and twirled me around.

"On my great Minerva, I just love it! "Van exclaimed. "You look as beautiful and it is so different from your previous appearance!"

"I'm not so sure you will like it when the credit card statement comes due! It might make a dent in your net worth" I said in a subdued manner.

Van laughed and said. "What is the amount greater than a trillion? I have heard it is a quadrillion! Yes, that is it! A quadrillion! "His eyes rolled upwards as if he were searching for something in his mind." He continued, "Next come a pentillion, then a sextillion, then an octillion and quadrillion."

"Excuse my wordiness. Professors do that sometimes. Well, often; O.K. always"

"You have seen the stores of platinum gold, silver and gems in our catacombs. If we were to release them it would make the world's monetary systems collapse. That is not counting trillions in currencies in Swiss and Cayman bank accounts. Or the incredible amounts of real estate holdings.

Sweetheart, George estimates that we have more wealth than the rest of the world combined. It is an inestimable, ludicrous amount. It is mine…and yours".

I laughed with glee and relief.

When we become free of this curse, we will use our fortune to end many of man's miseries.

"Of course, to maintain our cover…our" He continued jocularly, looked both ways in an exaggerated way, put his index finger up to his lips and continued "…Dum…Dum… Da, 'secret identities' we must appear to be…maybe…upper middle class… Live the lifestyles of whatever professions we take".

Show me the rest of your purchases and then we will eat.

The Way of the Hand and Blade

"For those who fought for it, freedom has a flavor the protected will never know.
Saying of the United States Marine Corps

"I do not fear the man who has practiced 10,000 kicks once. I fear the man who has practiced one kick 10,000 times." Bruce Lee

After supper, Van and I changed into t shirts and loose blue jeans and retired to our home gymnasium. He carried a small navy-blue gym bag and opened the polished wooden door for me as we entered. With its bamboo wood floor and wall that was a mirror; it looked like a dance studio.

There were some blue exercise mats on the floor and incredibly heavily weighted Olympic barbell sets with weight benches in one half of the room. I saw a large medicine ball and some enormous kettle bells and a chinning bar. The other half was empty except for a boxing timing bag, a heavy bag, and a hard foam human head and torso on a pedestal.

I felt pretty confident. I had been a high school cheerleader and dancer and I have an aptitude for learning complex sets of movements.

"Why aren't we wearing those karate pajamas? What kind of belt do you have?" I asked. Van smiled kindly and said," They are called 'gi's'. They were the traditional Japanese peasant clothing and were adopted about a hundred years ago when the Samurai killing arts became sports.

The belt system was a means for assessing skill was invented then as well. For most of my history, staying alive was my only 'belt'. It is more realistic to train in clothes we wear everyday".

"O.K.", I said. "But does this fighting system have a name?" Van replied, "No, I just incorporated the best things I learned over the years. Most of the fighting skills of the world are based on the ancient Greek hand to hand combat called, 'Pankration'. Alexander took it to India where it was spread to the Shaolin Temple and then to Japan. Everything else is based on it, even gladiatorial fighting". He shrugged.

"I guess that what we are going to do is similar to some modern fighting systems: Filipino Escrima; Japanese TantoJutsu; and Aki-Jujutsu.

I could see that he was in his professor mode…again.

Van took two rubber knives out of his bag and handed one and a towel to me. The "knives" looked more like elongated rubber paddles. He also took out the two knives he had black smithed.

"The fighting skills I will teach you can generalize from the knife to the empty hand. The strikes, body positions, and other movements are exactly the same for all handheld weapons and your own empty hands. The kicks will be the same as will the limb trapping movements and any throws and grappling.

He handed me one of the demon horn folding knives. "These are identical but pick one and keep with it. It will mystically bind you and the blade. Clip it into you right front pocket or in your waistband. Others will not be able to see it.

The first movement is learning to draw the blade, open it and get into a 'ready position'."

Van held the folder in his right hand put his bent thumb under the little square on the blade then flipped his thumb straight. The blade flicked open. I could see its razor edge gleam. He then deftly turned the knife over, and with the meat of his thumb closed the lock on knife's side and pushed the top of the blade. With a push from his forefinger and then his thumb pad he closed the knife

"The sigils will keep the blade from cutting either of us."

I imitated the movement and was surprised that I could not budge it by straightening my thumb. "I think it is stuck" I said. Van gave me a short gentle snicker and said, "Everyone says that at first.

You have to get the feel of it. Most people get too tense and hold too tightly. You are probably pushing into the blade rather than straight up on the thumb stud", he said. "Try it again. Do not get frustrated, it is just a matter of practice."

I tried it again and I managed to get the blade to peek out of the handle. By my fourth try, I was snapping the blade out quickly.

Van clipped the knife into his right jeans pocket. He pulled it out and it snapped open on the way. "The trick to this is to drag it on a forty-five-degree angle out of your pocket". I tried it and had no problem drawing the knife with its blade open".

I said, "You rat! Why didn't you show me that first?" Van shrugged and again chuckled and said, "Yes, I am. But you need to know both ways. Sometimes the blade does not open when you draw it out of your pocket.

I will let you practice that on your own and closing the blade with one hand. I tried it a few times and, although I was relatively slow and felt clumsy, the blade unhinged and folded back into the handle every time. I started getting the knack for it.

"Once the blade is open, you put your right side forward. The knife is in your right hand and held down by your right thigh. Your left palm is placed over your heart. This keeps it from being slashed and ads a layer over your heart if you are stabbed.

"The aim is to destroy an opponent's ability to attack you. When we are surprised or attacked, every human's deep brain causes us to automatically crouch and put our hands up. Since our enemy's arms are up, our first agenda is to take them away. Once his arms are cut, blood loss and shock cause them to drop uselessly.

This is generally true for humanoids as well.

Most often, weapons or bare hand attacks begin with a strike with a right hand towards the left side or center of your head, a stab, punch or a grab for example. We counter this with a forty-five-degree slash intercepting the inside of his hand or forearm. Since we have two hands, we then push out with our left palm and press the inner edge of his damaged hand down or grab it."

He demonstrated these movements for a while on the dense foam punching bag like a human head and torso on a pedestal called a "Bob" bag. Van had attached foam covered sticks pointing towards us to simulate arms.

We practiced this with the rubber knives on "Bob" and I picked it up easily.

"The next movement is to slash out at a forty-five-degree angle to his left upper body to block an attack from that side. Then we practice striking to the right and then to the left to block and cut both arms. Then back again from the left to the right."

With my wolf-born athleticism, I picked it up easily. "You have to be fast, but, since we are wolves, we are naturally so. Don't concern yourself about speed. Just practice the movements. Repetition alone will develop smoothness and smoothness creates speed."

"What if he grabs my hand?" I asked. "Usually knife attacks are so quick that he cannot," Van answered. "He will usually miss and that presents us with his open palm. As we withdraw our blade, we turn it upside down and cut his palm". He demonstrated how to do this.

"If he manages to grab our hand, we gouge his eyes or palm strike his face with our free hand. Old "Bob" got smacked right in the kisser. "And if he does some kind of judo move and tries to do an arm lock, we simply reach over with our other hand, take the knife, and cut or stab."

We practice these moves. I was learning them so quickly and it was invigorating!

"The next two strikes are the same as the first two but are aimed at the carotid arteries on the sides of the neck. First is to the left and then to the right side. The only difference is that the slash is pushed forcibly through the flesh as we withdraw.

Then the final movements are straight stabs to the eyes, the throat, the heart, the stomach or the groin; up or down the body."

Van continued. We do this in a series one right after another. He demonstrated and we practiced these movements.

"Often, a simple blitz stabbing attack is the most effective thing to do. "He demonstrated about ten straight strikes at a speed that was just a blur. "It is primitive, simple and brutally effective. This is the way shiv attacks are done in prisons. This was a favorite trick of Roman Legionnaires and is highly regarded by the U.S. Navy Seals.

You must get his hands out of the way first. You can do this by cutting them as I showed you. It works well if you then grab his hair and pull him into the stab. From the front, grab his forelock or grasp the back of the neck. Or from behind, grab the back hair or wrap your left arm around his throat and attack one of the kidneys."

I have seen many decapitated by this method. "We will keep this simple for today. Tomorrow we will work on blocks and attacks to the lower quadrants of the body.

There are two more things I want to show you." Van continued.

"If your enemy surprises you, lean back a little and do as 'push kick with your sole to his knee or any part of his leg. This will hurt him, push him back and let you draw your knife." Van instructed. He bent backwards, kicked out with his front foot. "You have to thrust your hips out and sort of push as you are kicking".

Van kneeled holding a thick pad in front of him and I practiced this movement. At first, I just rocked him a little. By my tenth kick, I knocked him back and hard on to his behind. I rushed to him bent over and said, "Oh Van! I am so sorry! I didn't mean to kick you over! Did I hurt you?"

"You didn't even hurt my pride". Van laughed and we stood up together. "Well, I see your wolf is coming along well. That is exactly what we want. Knocking me over is a complement to my teaching. You've got the power and technique."

"The final thing is what to do if you are grabbed from behind. Go behind me and put your arms around my body. Van said.

I got behind him and pinched both butt cheeks. He yelped and danced forward chuckling a little. "What!

It's just so cute", I suggested, trying to look innocent. I looked slightly upwards, pouted and waggled my shoulders and hips.

"O.K.", he chortled. I can see where this is going".

"Let me show you this one last thing, and then we'll…." he gave me 'Groucho eyebrows' again. "Now, unless you want to end for today, please grab me from behind in a bear hug."

I replied, "You are a hard task master. No let's finish up". I got behind him and couldn't get my arms around his huge chest. He stated, "If this happened, take out the knife and stab and deeply cut along your attacker's forearm all the way up along his bicep and shoulder."

He took one of the rubber knives and put the point on the top of my forearm and traced it up to my shoulder.'

If your hands are pinned hold the knife in a 'reverse grip', the blade facing downward from your palm and stab his groin and legs. There is a vein just above the public area that will cause him to bleed out.

But don't take any chances, either way. Turn around and slash his neck and continue to stab him until he is dead". He showed me this. And then I practiced on him.

"But what if I cut it off?" I teased. "Then you will not be having much fun tonight", he laughingly replied. "Besides, it would just grow back next time the wolf is upon me. Let us hit the shower… together.

I have one last thing I want to show you about a more pleasant kind of penetration."

We gathered our things into the gym bag, and I tucked my folding knife into my right front jeans pocket. He held the door for me as we left the room and I squirmed as it was his turn to pinch both of my butt cheeks. We giggled and I said, "Oh, yeah! We gonna have some fun to night! "

Van let out with a passable version of the old Little Richard standard; "We gonna have some fun tonight! We gonna have some fun tonight. EEEEEE! Everything alright! Have some fun…some fun tonight. Hooo-weeee!"

And we danced into our bedroom.

The Gathering Storm

"If trouble comes when you least expect it then maybe the thing to do is to always expect it."
– Cormac McCarthy, The Road

"Democracy is two wolves and a lamb voting on what to have for lunch. Liberty is a well armed lamb contesting the vote." – Benjamin Franklin

The next two weeks passed joyfully and thus too quickly. Van and I were inseparable, and he spent only a little time closing down the research project he had been hired to assess.

It was concluded that the results obtained by the lobotomy project were more the "product of Dr. Sterling's dynamic personality than the actual surgeries themselves". It was recommended that they not be replicated further.

Donations were being collected by the good people of Mt. Summit for the new "Hayward Sterling Commemorative Wing" of Creedmoor Hospital. One of Van's shell corporations funded a statue of Sterling with his arms outstretched, standing in front of a larger Jesus who had his hands on the Doctor's shoulders. Sterling's smile was more of a smirk; Jesus looked sternly at him. The inscription will be: "Suffer the little children."

I enjoyed the idea of Sterling eternally having Jesus pressing his fingertips into his rotting shoulders; constantly reminding him of his perversions.

The cover stories of rogue bears attacking the surgical amphitheater and the "gas explosion" in the church stuck. I was surprised because they stretched credibility.

"Like UFOs travelling across three states in twenty minutes are explained away by the Northern Lights, swamp gas, or the morning star. People accept the improbable because they need to believe that the authorities have things under control." Van offered with a chuckle.

"Of course, since the beginning of time, the Cabal had used such fictions to deceive the public."

I was amazed, "Are there really flying saucers controlled by aliens? You know, little green men?" Van thought a minute and said, "Most of the lights in the sky are fae; except for the ones that are controlled by extraterrestrials. They are usually little grey men and praying mantis like beings that are fond of probing orifices." He made an upwards trill like a slide whistle, laughed and poked his forefinger upwards into thin air. He added playfully, "I suspect that some are extraterrestrial fae."

I giggled and gently pushed him for his teasing.

My sister Sarah had recovered from her physical injuries. She didn't remember anything about that horrible night. She was grieving the loss of our family who had died in "a house fire" and me. She was told I passed during a surgical operation.

She was being adopted by my aunt, my mother's sister and her husband. They were taking her to live with them and their children in Connecticut. I was relieved that she was going to be with loving relatives who are more 'mainstream' religiously; and that she was getting her own fresh start. It made my heart a little lighter knowing she was going to be safe.

I thought of my family's massacre and my heart went cold. Anyone connected to the Cabal must die.

George showed up frequently. He was like a close relative who lived next door. He always brought some homemade baked goods.

Ernie and Harrison were our constant companions, especially down in the 'dungeons' as I liked to call them. As Ernie's wings were still healing, Harrison floated him along on a sort of platform created by an updraft. They developed many variations of shaping and honing their combined powers.

Each had a wide understanding of his area of the magical universe. I learned a lot about alternate views of reality. Their predictive capabilities showed us that the Hindaberg Group, an enigmatic group of billionaires and world leaders, were meeting at the Koker Building on the sixteenth of October; the first night of the full moon.

It was almost too easy. I could see the rage and desire in Van's eye. I had no idea how deep his hatred ran towards the Cabal, or what they had really done to him in the past. The idea that they wanted to hurt my beloved stabbed at my gut. The idea frightened me. I wondered if they knew about me

I continued to practice my invisibility meditation and I could remain unseen for periods of time. I somehow knew the next phase was just interlacing my fingers inside the palm and remaining invisible. We continued our close quarter combat lessons, and I was learning quickly.

We enjoyed long lingering meals and made love several times a day. We simply lay together often and had wonderful conversations. We shared our every fear and concern he would listen and watch me talk, I could feel his eyes watching my mouth, his deep brown eyes looking into my blue pools.

One day as we were lying in our bed after particularly gymnastic love making, I revealed, "Van, I am very discouraged because we can never have children. I have always wanted to be a mother". Tears began to well up in my eyes.

Van looked at me with loving eyes and put his right arm under my head. He compassionately asked, "May I tell you a few things?" I took the Kleenex he handed me and dabbed my eyes.

"It distresses me too. After the demon is eliminated, we will no longer carry this curse. George and I believe we will live out the rest of our natural lives. I suspect that this will include the ability to have children. I know that it is in the future but let us choose hope. My finally finding you means that the end is near"

I looked at his face and could sense that more than anything he wanted this to be true. I worried that the many years he had lived had made him despair for humanity and that he had soured on the world.

I replied, "I guess in many ways that we are like a regular couple starting out. We have things to do before we are ready to bring children into the world. The gift of children is never guaranteed". That thought made me feel a little relieved. Van nodded kindly.

Then he added, "You are also Bella and during that lifetime, we had children. How many people worldwide have a rich shock of black hair such as yours and Bella's? How many have 'Roman noses' like mine?"

I thought for a minute, "Most of the Southern Europeans, I would imagine." "Hundreds of thousands of them descended from us. We have thousands of children worldwide! We are making the world safer for them!" Van exclaimed.

He added, "We are the mother and father of Rome; perhaps the greatest influence on Western civilization."

It made me feel better thinking of all our descendants in Italy and across the globe. Perhaps it wasn't what he said, but rather that he listened and understood my fear. My wolf man was fierce, but he was gentle too; at least he was with me.

I intertwined my fingers through his and said, "I have to ask you about some things that are happening to me." Van replied, "Ask me anything, my Darling." I have been experiencing vivid scenes from Roman history, and I have been hearing George's voice in my head. Is that part of this changing thing? Am I losing my mind? What..."

"Of course, you are not losing your mind. I am not entirely sure why it is happening, my love", Van suggested. "But, because these visions started when you activated the spirit of Bella within you, it is probably a carryover from then. Some of them are probably your soul's memories.

"As I said, Bella had what was called 'second sight'. She foresaw the conspirators attack on our family and had warned Vincus to get our family away. She then stayed behind to delay those raiders to give the rest of the family a good head start."

I saw him tense and clench his fists as he spoke. In my mind I felt physically weak and had a sudden flash of large armed men approaching me and being dragged towards my marriage bed as quickly as it came the vision faded.

"The incorporation of the wolf brings out latent talents." I pondered this for a moment.

"Humm, I always have been intuitive", I replied. "But my parents forced me to suppress it because it wasn't 'of God'." Van thought for a moment, "You probably would have had these occurrences anyway. But you would have understood them in a Christian context; the Holy Ghost, perhaps?"

One evening, we had just finished cleaning up after a sumptuous dinner when Harrison glided into the room and informed us that George was in our gated room and needed to speak with us. We accompanied the air spirit down the stairs and passed the corridors of treasures.

We welcomed George who was sitting by the doll house talking to Ernie. He gave us his infectious, gap toothed smile and enthusiastically hugged us both. "What's going on, George?" Van asked.

George seemed uncharacteristically serious and urgent, "I have received some vital information that you need to know right now! I hurried through the chambers connecting our homes. The meeting at the Koker Building on October sixteenth is a ruse. The actual meeting of the Hintaberg Group is in another location on the same night.

They have planned an ambush for you by a group of mercenaries. But the real trap is by a dangerous new player who will be in the building. They are sacrificing the soldiers of fortune so that you enter the building overconfident expecting to find only soft rich men.

"Go on" I said.

"When you blinded the Demon and while he is recovering, his primary henchman took over. You have heard of Shabbetai Zevi, the false Jewish messiah of the mid-sixteen hundred? No?

He was a charismatic rabbi who many Jews of the day believed to be the messiah. The Ottoman Empire feared a Jewish uprising, so he was disgraced and forced to become a Muslim. When he died, your demon reanimated him.

He has become a Kabbalist necromancer and has mastered the summoning of demons using the reversed seventy-two names of God. I call him the "Hara Shem Tov."

"I don't follow you", I said. Harrison and Ernie echoed this concern.

"What the hey!" Ernie uttered.

Van offered "Part of the mystical Kabbalah is the technology of the 'seventy-two names of God. It is grounded in Jewish numerology.

It is based on Exodus 14:19-21. This verse is graphed out so that by grouping the letters in columns of three, the names of seventy-two angels or positive attributes of divinity are unleashed. This is why it is called the '72 names of God'.

Saying these names in reverse conjures seventy-two corresponding demons or malicious forces. It is said that King Solomon compelled these demonic names to construct the first great Hebrew Temple."

Ernie replied, "but what about this Harry guy? "Harrison interjected, "I believe he said, 'Hara'. That sounds Japanese or possibly Irish." George elaborated, "It is a Hebrew word that means 'bad' or 'evil'. Prepare for another lecture." He chuckled, self despairingly. "I must take you to a sidebar to explain it."

"About a hundred years after Zevi, a rabbi named Israel Ben Eliezer founded the Hasidic movement in Judaism. He used the power of the 72 names to heal the sick and perform miracles. He invoked the angels for the good of people.

The Hassidic teaching tales are filled with magical things he is said to have done. He was called the "Baal Shem Tov" Baal' is 'holy', 'Shem' is 'the Name' of God, and 'Tov' means 'master'. In English, the Master of the Good Name." He looked at Van.

"This is the first time I am hearing about this villain. O.K., Van said. "But you are such a hard act to follow! "He shrugged and continued. 'Hara' means 'bad' or 'evil' in Hebrew. The 'Hara Shem Tov' must be the master of the evil name. He is the invoker of demons.

George agreed. "He is an archfiend himself. He is raising the demons and Strigoi Veii. He enlivened 'Cardinal Ramos' who I suspect is either your brother or son, 'Remus'."

Van's gasped and his body stiffened. He turned away and I could see he was tightly gripping the table that we had laid the golden cage on. His face flushed and I could hear cracking and crunching sounds from the table.

"So, we are in a familiar dilemma." I questioned "Do we go after the billionaire patrons or do we go after the evil sorcerer?"

George offered, "Both can't be done in the same night. That is always the Cabal's failsafe."

Van turned to the dapper little fae gentlemen. "What do you think?"

Harrison proposed, "Which group poses the greatest risk to mankind". Ernie agreed, "Always take out the greatest threat first."

"Humm", Van offered. The billionaires fund the operations, but the magus is the power behind the throne."

George suggested, "I believe that the Romans coined the phrase, 'cut off the head of the snake'. I think the malicious magician is the worst threat. He spends most of his time in hidden otherworldly places. You can always get to the money men in this realm.".

Van and I gave each other mischievous smiles. I concluded, "We get the sorcerer and deprive an important asset to the demon." Van added, "Also it may give us another chance at the fiend.

We kill the mercenaries because they know too much, and because they are psychopathic sons of bitches."

George offered, "I think that is the best decision. I have some things that will help you." He leaned down and handed me a backpack that was sized for my wolf body. It had a scabbard attached, "You can carry your demon sword in this and gather up anything of value."

"I have something additional for Van, but I need to do something before I can hoist it." He mumbled some things under his breath and his hands glowed blue and then the color ran up his arms. We watched as his hands and arms began to steadily grow. His hands became as large as catcher's mitts and his arms tapered towards his shoulders. He reminded me of the cartoon character "Popeye".

With those gargantuan hands he hefted another titanic backpack. He opened it and produced a cudgel that was six feet long and about ten inches in diameter. It was roughhewn and had knots in the undeterminable wood. It had a handle on one end and a large, heavy bulb with imbedded fangs on the other.

"The Club of Hercules," he announced proudly. "I gift it to you. Your cousin would be proud to have you wield it. You will find it invaluable to your mission. Between that and your demon sword, nothing can stand against you.

I will hide it under your raised deck, because you can't lift it unless you are in your wolf body." He tucked it back into the knapsack but about a foot of it protruded out of the cover. I will go now, and the knapsacks will be there when you need them next week.

He turned to me and added. "You have done well developing invisibility. It could prove indispensable against these enemies. I will continue to guide you telepathically."

George pointed with his head to the table where a white pastry box. "I brought you some Basbousa."

We thanked George and chatted with the fae for a while. They agreed to track our foes with their predictive powers. We said our goodnights and I had an excited yet fearful feeling as we headed back into our living room. I could feel his angst rise, a tension created by him as I followed.

Van said, "First Nations people call the full moon in October, the 'Hunter's Moon'". He gave me a lupine smile. "And mercenaries are the dogs of war".

Hunter's Moon

*It is forbidden to kill therefore murderers are punished, unless
they do it in great numbers and to the sound of trumpets.*
Voltaire, War
Cry havoc and let slip the dogs of war!
Shakespeare, Julius Caesar

We spent the next week preparing for our assault of the Koker Building. We used a wench to load the giant backpack holding Hercules' war club into the back of his Toyota 4X4 truck.

Van completed the demon horn saber he had been smithing for me. It was almost identical to his but had a top guard that curved forward and the bottom curved backwards. It seemed to "sing" different tones when I swung it at various angles. I liked the way it felt in my hand.

We kept them under the bed. There were scabbards built into the packs for the swords. At the size we would be, they would be more like large bowie knives. We estimated that this would be all we needed.

Our natural attributes and Van's knowledge of sorcery would be our primary armaments. The remainder of the space inside the rucksacks would be saved for objects we might "liberate" from our enemies.

We would put the pack with the swords and war club in the truck bed. We decided to drive to a wooded area a few miles from the target building. The truck would enter the woods where we could hide it with a camouflage net; after the transformation we'd terminate the mercenaries and then breach the building.

Van got some topographical maps and architectural blueprints for the building. We poured over them planning our strategy. We went out on his Harleys and scouted out the area. I felt like I was cheating because mine had an automatic transmission. I had never learned how to ride.

We found recent activity disturbing the ground, broken brush, and tire tracks were obvious. Having been an expert tactician in many wars, it came as second nature for him to pick out the only place where an ambush was probable. I marveled at how he could read the landscape from the maps or from our scouting; determine where men would go, hide, and attack from.

He found a cache of fully automatic M-16s, rocket propelled grenades, and metal ammunition boxes. He smiled when he uncovered that these were filled with silver bullets. "These will be like water pistols to us", he scoffed.

They intended to lure him into clearing behind a copse of thick trees and then cut him off and form a "kill box".

However, they were only expecting Van and not both of us.

I reasoned that turnabout is fair play. We continued to strategize. Van would enter their kill box and engage them. Once they are focused on him, I would attack from their rear. It was simple and would be brutally effective.

We were much more concerned about the dark magician skulking in the building. We had no way to prepare for him.

I found myself anticipating the battle like I looked forward to Christmas morning when I was a child. I felt a thrill at facing these hired killers and my mouth watered in anticipation. I was even enthusiastic about facing the necromancer and pitting my strength against his magic.

On October 15, my body began to respond to the waxing moon. Van apprised me that the change would be unlike my first; it would not be gradual or painful. I would experience a "quickening" throughout the day and then, when the moon rises, I will burst into my she-wolf. I found myself quivering with pleasure at the thought of moon rise at 7:25 P.M.

As the day wore on, I noticed an aggressiveness and irritability creeping over me. Although my senses were getting more acute over the entire month, the world seemed to be intruding on me. I couldn't go near the kitchen sink because the smell of the cleaners grated on me to the point that I wanted to smack them across the room.

My vision became almost like a zoom lens and I could focus on almost microscopic detail. About three in the afternoon, I saw a jackrabbit in the woods and had to stifle the urge to chase it. I could see that Van was similarly affected, but he was better practiced in coping with it.

At 6:00 P.M., we got into the truck and Van eased the 4X4 onto the highway. Before he accelerated, we gave each other knowing smiles. "We used to smile like this before we got into mischief in Rome, didn't we", I asked. "Yes", he answered, "we would sneak away from the guards and sometimes play tricks on my mother and Vincus or make love in semipublic places."

Van accelerated in the opposite direction from Gainsburg. "We'll be on the outskirts of Upton in a half hour. I'll drive the truck into the woods, and we will hide it." I felt a tinge of delighted anticipation in my stomach.

A cool rush of air cascaded though the side windows and I could detect the subtle lowering of the temperatures as the sun began to set. I could see the rose and pinks of the billowing clouds beginning to swathe the sun. Golden streams of light stretched out to hug the earth. I could discriminate the scents of different cars and their individual occupants that had preceded us. The monotone of the highway's melody was somehow comforting.

The landscape became thick woodlands and I saw a sign that said, "Upton 5 miles." We came to an opening in the trees and Van eased the Toyota off road and concealed it in a small cluster of young birches. Moving like one person, we covered it with a camouflage net and attached loose branches to it. We disrobed and hugged under a blanket as we awaited grandmother moon.

This would be the second full moon I had turned, I swallowed hard full of anticipation.

The moon peaked over the distant mountains and slowly turned from a semicircle into a globe. At the point where it cleared the horizon and darkness could be seen between it and the earth. I felt a hot current rushing up my spine. A swelling and expansion became a sensation of soaring upwards.

I cried "Hell yeah! Mama's home!". I had a giddy, euphoric sensation. I found myself staring at my grisly colossus, who looked at me humorously. His rolling voice murmured, "You enjoyed that a little too much". I laughed and quietly replied, "Your whispering sounds like the Mormon Tabernacle Choir". He chortled and then a muzzle formed on his face. I imitated him.

I tied a piece of canvas I had turned in to a halter top around my bare chest. We shouldered our behemoth backpacks.

We caught the scent of twenty men of various races, metal, oil and gunpowder about a mile north. Although the fighters whispered, we could distinguish every word as if we were just in front of us. Half were about fifteen yards in front of the others. Without a thought we were drawn in that direction and I felt like I was ice skating.

Then there was the exhilaration of the hunt. We slipped through the thicket, every sense at peaked readiness. We left no trace, not even the cracking of a leaf. Only long after our passing, the keenest night birds piped their warnings. It took mere seconds to cross a half mile just before the bottleneck.

At this distance from a clearing in the woods, I held back and watched Van slow his mass down to an agonizingly slow walk. I could hear the static and clicking of radio transmitters and hurried whispers.

"Condition orange! I repeat Condition Orange. Puppy in the crate. Repeat, Puppy in the crate". I could see five men in olive drab M-65 field jackets and boonie hats step out from the outermost part of the clearing and raise their M-16s to the ready position.

As I watched, Van seemed to be lured through the bottleneck as he rushed the visible men. Once he was in the center, he was attacked by ten men to his front and ten to his left pouring automatic weapon fire into him. The gunfire looked like lines of white flame impacting his gigantic frame.

The gunmen closed in and Van managed to crush one with a downward blow. The man's head was mashed into a forty-five-degree angle. On the upsweep, his sharp claws gutted another, and he and Van were washed in a fountain of blood.

Van reared up and roared and then clutched his hands to his chest and fell heavily on to his face. There was a boom and the ground shook when he dropped. A great steel net dropped, and he was surrounded.

A lean man with close cropped grey hair stepped forward and crowed, "Werewolf my ass. Ha! Ha! He was all reputation! I told that mackerel snapper that I would stick my M-16 up his ass and pull the trigger!" He was greeted by belly laughs and high fives by his men.

The team barked "Hoorah, Colonel!" and pumped their arms in the air enthusiastically. "Superior weapons! Superior tactics! Superior attitude! We didn't even have to use the grenades and RPGs. Let's get some pictures of this big old boy!"

One of the mercs asked, "Why isn't he returning to his human form?" The colonel replied, "How should I know? This ain't no movie Jar Head!"

A photographer quickly set up his camera tripod. Eight men began to climb on top of Van and eight started to kneel in front of him. The same merc cautioned, "Wait a minute, this doesn't seem right!"

He was shouted down and degraded by the group. The colonel stated gruffly, "Talbot, get in or out of the picture!" Then he puffed up his chest, pulled in his stomach, lit a cigar and began to put his right foot on Van's head.

From under them, a thunderous voice rumbled, "Say Cheese!" Van burst upwards, shredding the heavy steel net and throwing soldiers forty feet into the air. Half of them died from the impact of the fall. The others lay in agony from broken limbs.

Fourteen hundred pounds of were beast dropped heavily crushing six soldiers who had been kneeling in front of him. Van then punched his right fist through the torso of a black brigand. He rose on his feet and came down on the backs of two who were fleeting and squashed them like cockroaches. What remained were crimson smudges that were unidentifiable.

Their startled leader backed away, turned and pushed the photographer towards Van. The four mercs who survived limped to the bottle neck. Talbot dragged behind them.

I was waiting in a batch of bushes. Just before I revealed myself, I yelled in deep voice, "Who's that walking through these woods!" The mercenaries froze and I revealed myself. In a falsetto voice I cried, "Must be Little Red Riding Hood"

They pulled their side arms. I knocked the head off one and then with a backhand crushed the other's head and shoulders. I grabbed the arms of the two remaining. I had one in each hand and slammed them together. They merged into one grotesque figure: two faces, four arms and four legs. They tasted like veal and blood sausages.

Talbot froze, but he was no coward. He pulled out a large bowie knife and charged me. Part of me wanted to let him go. However, this would leave an eyewitness to this event. I rushed toward him and trampled him. It was like his being hit by a car.

When I lifted my head, Van was sitting on their leader whose muffed pleas were coming from beneath him. He was casually gnawing some meat off the photographer's thigh. I walked over. He offered me the other leg and said, "I do prefer the dark meat, breast or drumstick, my dear?

Will you lend me a hand?"

Van held the colonel down on his stomach while I ripped his pants down to his ankles. The merc screamed, cursed and pleaded. Van wrapped one of his massive hands around his head to muffle any cries. He put his head close to his hand and said, "You are a disgrace to the uniform".

I then took one of the M-16s and forced it into the officer's rectum and upwards. I couldn't stifle the urge to say, "Spit isn't lube!" The front sight ripped and tore him as it progressed up his torso.

As it reached the middle of his chest, his hemorrhaging blood made it almost too slippery to grasp. Blood, teeth and gore erupted from his mouth as the barrel poked out. What appeared to be part of his stomach dribbled from the rifle's sight.

He twitched and writhed, and I knew it would take him a while to die. "We treated you to your favorite thing. Now you are an ex-Marine. Too bad our hands are too big to pull the trigger." Van mused. "I trust that the cardinal will get the message."

Van patted the agonized colonel on the head and said, "Now, don't go anywhere."

We spend a few minutes gathering up and concealing several of the rifles, pistols, rocket propelled grenades, and all boxes of ammunition. "We will use the silver bullets to hunt the Strigoi", Van affirmed. About thirty yards away from us stood the Koker building. The entire top floor was lit up like New Year's Eve.

"It looks like the party has already started.", I offered. "That just means we will be fashionably late", Van replied. We strapped into our backpacks and cat footed our way along the side to the front of the building.

The Hare Shem Tov

"Science and religion are not at odds.
Science is simply too young to understand"
Dan Brown Angels and Demons

"If my devils are to leave me, I am afraid my angels will
take flight as well." Duino Elegies (German Duineser
Elegien) Rainer Maria Rilke from 1912 to 1922.

The Koker building was a multistoried edifice of dark tinted windows surrounded by an obscenely huge parking lot. I thought of all the woodlands that had been obliterated to supply "ample parking."

A flight of half-disk shaped stairs rose to the front entrance which was had double glass doors before a small waiting area containing modern sofas and a guard desk. A security officer sat behind it busily perusing computer monitors displaying the views of security cameras. Beyond that was a short corridor leading to a locked steel door. Embossed above the door were the words "Koker Enterprises".

Standing on either side of the doors were security guards in tan uniforms. They had five pointed police caps on their heads. These sentinels were not the usual obese or over the hill rent a cop. They had broad shoulders and flat abdomens. Each displayed a large Glock 10 mm pistol in a holster at his hip and sported a thick bullet proof vest. I could see the coiled wires running from inside their collars connecting to radio receivers behind their right ears.

Van motioned me to stay where I was and seemed to evaporate into the darkness. A second or two later, I could see him on the opposite side of the building. He held up three fingers, closed his fist, and then held up one, two, and then…three. At this we surged forward.

Van grabbed the first watchman by the throat pulled him backwards crushing his gullet. I grabbed the other one's skull in my jaws, pulled him out of sight and bit his head off. I chewed and savored the sweet taste of long pork and gore.

I licked the backs of my massive hands, smiled a sparkle in my yellowish green eyes and looked to Van. He mouthed, "As we planned" and I intertwined my fingers into my palms and repeated the mantra for invisibility.

As I sat repeating the conjure, my thoughts slowed, and all internal chatter came to a close. My mind came to pinpoint focus. Everything faded away; all that existed was, "Makasish lecura absalik". "Inside" and "outside" had no meaning.

As we had strategized, once I became veiled, Van rushed the big glass double door. At the abrupt shattering, the clanging of sheets of glass, I opened my eyes, kept my fingers intertwined into the backs of my hand and stood up.

The clarity and purity of my sensations was pristine. The world existed of familiar but ineffable shapes, colors, textures and smells. I crept to where the double doors had been.

The formerly immaculate waiting room appeared as if it was covered by shards of ice and diamond dust. The guard's desk was turned over and a pair of uniformed legs and cheap black brogues twitched from beneath it. A pool of burgundy was rapidly spreading throughout the room.

The steel plate door hung gingerly from its top hinge. Van's behemoth back was disappearing down a tall broad corridor. I could see the ray skin hilt of the demon sword and the last foot of the war club peeking out from the knapsack. I hurried and stayed undetectable a few feet behind him.

There were sounds of a party far above us; men and women laughing, the tinkling of glass and dance music. Inestimable grip strength silently defeated the locks to the stair wells. Huge, clawed feet made no sound mounting ten flights of stairs. The sounds of the gathering became ever louder.

The door to the tenth floor vibrated to the bass of the Eurrymthics "Sweet Dreams are Made From These". Van's behemoth fist encircled the doorknob, and I could hear the crunching of metal and the tinkling of small bits of the lock as it ruptured.

I was amused that Van's signals indicating that I should work my way around the perimeter to the same place than I stood. Van placed his body in front of the opening door to keep light from warning the occupants of our arrival. Then he twisted into the room deftly closing the door behind him.

I copied his entrance exactly.

The room was pitch and the sound of the music was deafening. Then a glimmer appeared in the furthest corner of what was a ballroom. It revealed a gross parody of a large human silhouette. The dense outline could be clearly seen, but no distinguishing features; except for large eyes and a mouth that flickered like an orange flame. These were bright enough to dimly illuminate the room.

From its light we could see that the room was empty except for the garish figure of the demon. It gestured towards Van with a short staff and an overwhelming gale began to assail his body.

Van tilted his body into the tempest. With his fur blowing backwards and his lips fluttering outward began slowly progressing towards the shadow man.

He raised his colossal left hand to shield his eyes from the insistent wind. The veins in his head and neck stood out from his effort. Van reached back and drew his saber. I hugged the left wall put my side into the wind and made my way forward.

Abruptly, the figure seemed to be writing in the air from right to left. Translucent Hebrew letters formed, and he cackled the name, "Baal".

What had been letters was a large, winged dragon and rushed Van. Van mirrored his movements, quickly drew letters in the air and shouted; "Vehu"! A crimson avian man materialized and leaped on to the lizard's neck.

One of the bird-man's great arms wrapped around the beast's neck while the other pulled back on its top jaw. The lizard hissed and thrashed its scaled tail into him. With a crack that blotted out the raucous music, they imploded into a collapsing globe of light.

The black magician looked startled at this and took a step back. Van inched ever closer.

The necromancer then gestured and shouted, "Agares!" and a Cyclops rushed from where the letters had been. Van responded with, "Yeli!", and a beautiful blue hound sprang forward and grabbed the monster by the throat.

The ogre kicked the dog's ribs and it yelped. The canine leaped up and wrapped his jaws around the giant's head. They struggled in midair and then collapsed into an ever-shrinking ember.

Then there was a sound like a balloon popping.

Van and I struggled forward towards the shadow man. The evil magician seemed to wince and appeared frightened.

With his attention on Van, I was closing in on the necromancer. Once again, the evil shadow drew in the air and shrieked, "Eligor"! From the glyphs sprang a slithering serpent with gaping jaws and flicking tongue. Van signed and yelled "Heri!" and a resplendent golden eagle rushed to meet the lizard.

Talons slashed and coils squeezed.

This time the two eldritch beasts struggled and wrestled with each other. They screamed and thrashed on the floor and the eagle repeatedly lifted the snake and dashed it to the ground. The serpent tried to strike eagle's head, but the giant bird kept bobbing it out of the way.

The eagle pinned the serpent's head down with one of its claws. But the reptile started to coil around it. Van crept forward and I got within striking distance of the fiend.

I raised my saber and slashed down on the demon's outstretched arm. The sword hummed a high note. It met only slight resistance and the staff and arm thudded heavily to the ground.

A hissing smoke gushed from the stump. The smell of sulfur filled the room. The gale abruptly ceased. The fiend screamed and I jumped forward and wrapped my arms around him.

With the tempest stopped, Van leaped and cleaved the snake's head in two. The eagle shrieked in triumph lifted the snake up towards the ceiling. Both folded into a shrinking ball of light and finally winked out.

Van sprang in front of the devil with his saber pointing at its throat and said, "Shabbetai Zevi!" With the pronouncement of his true name, the black figure slowly congealed into a small, frail bearded man wearing dark clothing and a skull cap. He slipped from my grasp and collapsed on to the floor.

At my feet was a small, skeletal man with a hawk like nose and deep brown eyes. He lay on his side with his right hand on his chest and his left hand extended. He coughed and said, "Please…please…enough". His voice was high-pitched, and his tone rose as he spoke. Van and I were wary of deceit, but we could see that his life was slipping away.

"I never asked for any of this…" he continued. "I was a respected and beloved rebbe. I loved the Torah, Talmud, Midrash, Kabbalah … I loved to read and teach …I was very learned…but then they started calling me, 'Mashiach-messiah,'… …my mind was sick…and then the energy illness was upon me…

I didn't need to sleep for weeks…my thoughts came too fast for me to follow them…I believed it…" He shook his head sadly from side to side. "And the masses followed me…when the illness devoured me…I spoke so grandly…1666 was supposed to be the year of the apocalypse and we went to Istanbul.

I expected to be loved, to bring the nations to Hashem" …He slowly shook his head again.

"Then rough hands pulled me before the Ottoman Sultan…" He sobbed. "My grand feeling broke… I was so scared…ashamed… repentant…my mood plummeted… I was forced to convert to Islam…and the Sultan made me his doorman.

It became apostasy for Jews to even say my name…I prayed for death and welcomed it when it came.

Because no one had ever said Kaddish for me, I was not one of God's true dead ..." he gasped. "Then the master came and took me out of my grave."

I found my eyes filling with tears. "He never wanted this Van; he is a poor sick soul". I pleaded.

I saw Van shake away his snout. He kneeled before the dying man, clasped his hands in prayer and began reciting Kadish: "Yisgadal v'yiskadash sh'mei rabbaw. Amein;B'allmaw dee v'raw chir'useiv'yamlic malchusei,b'chayeichon, uv'yomeichon,uv'chayei d'chol beis yisroel,ba'agawlaw u'vizman kawriv, v'imru: Amein. Y'hei sh'mei rabbaw m'vawrach l'allam u'l'allmei allmayaw Y'hei sh'mei rabbaw ...

At this point, the building trembled and the floor split spilling Van and I to opposite sides of the ball room. The room was filled with the scent of Frankincense. A great golden arm reached out of the chasm found Zevi and began pulling him towards the chasm.

A rich, melodic baritone rang out, "You have grown strong, Old Dog, but you haven't finished with him yet!"

I could see Van re-sheath his sword and draw out Hercules' club. He yelled, "Jump out the window and run" and raised it over his head.

I hesitated but crashed through the glass pane. I found myself falling headfirst down ten stories. The ground seemed to rush up meet me. I managed to fold the back of my arms, tuck in my head and rolled forwards to my feet.

I hit the ground running.

Milli-seconds later, I was back in the woods but turned when I heard a booming crash from where I had been. The entire structure collapsed in upon itself like a controlled demolition and within seconds it was reduced to a debris field.

An immense dust cloud arose wh xere the building had been. My heart sank as I thought of my beloved buried under all that rubble. Then, I was engulfed by the spreading cloud of grey powder.

Coughing and spitting out dust, I shook off the grime and rushed to the flattened building. I became alarmed when I noticed the vast chunks of concrete and steel girders piled on top of each other.

I imagined the crushing weight on my mate; the lack of oxygen and dust filling his lungs; his disorientation in the blackness. I began franticly lifting and tossing the ton sized slabs. After a few minutes I heard shuffling and scraping just below the surface.

With a few minutes, several of the giant pieces slid away in a circle from portion of the messy debris field. I could see that someone was tunneling up from the wreckage. I stepped back and a grey dusted giant erupted from a heap.

Van pulled himself up and then pushed clear. He spent several minutes wheezing and sputtering; coughing up dust saturated sputum. When he had gotten his breath, he reached into the pit and pulled up his backpack and the war club. He shook himself as a dog might shed water and was rid of the heaviest of the grey coating.

He looked at me and smiled, "I guess indestructible means indestructible." He reached into his backpack and showed me the rod with which Zevi created the gale. "We better leave before the first responders come."

We hugged and walked together into the woods. "What happened in there", I asked. "I hit the golden demon's arm with the club. His arm broke and he withdrew back into his rat hole. But it brought the whole building down. I don't know what happened to Zevi," He replied.

"I hope we freed him" I offered, "He had so much suffering and abuse in his life." Van mused, "Yes, he really would not be held responsible by today's standards. He was 'non corpus mentis'. But the Seventeen Century was unforgiving."

I reflected, "And then to have to serve over a thousand years doing the will of a demon…" I shuddered. Van said sadly. "I did not get to complete the prayer. We can only hope".

We stopped by the site of the ambush. The colonel had stopped struggling and writhing but was still softly moaning and twitching. He lay in a pool of his own blood and gore.

I patted his head and said, "Dismissed Marine".

Van liberated a pair of matched ParaOrdance P-15 LDA pistols from him. We collected all the M-16s, magazines RPGs and army green ammunition boxes filled with silver bullets. We put them in our rucksacks.

Some we would use others we took to keep them out of the wrong hands.

In the distance, we could hear sirens and the growling of the first responder's vehicles as they arrived at the fallen building.

We made our way back to the concealed Toyota truck and removed the netting. We placed our backpacks into the bed; and waited until dawn. As the sun's round ball broke the horizon, I felt a shrinking, winding down sensation.

I looked at the now naked Van who had buckets of water and towels and we cleaned ourselves off. We would finish the job when we got back. We donned the sweat clothes we had left in the cab. A sense of weariness overcame me, and I napped leaning against the door as we made our short way to home.

The Waning Moon

No good deed goes unpunished
English axiom

Sometimes the cards we are dealt are not always fair.
However, you must keep smiling & moving on Tom Jackson

We spent the final days of the full moon mopping up the remaining cult members from the sheriffs and police departments. Certain county and town officials and their families also had to be purged. Many of them had not yet had a chance to become murderers but were already casting around for new demons to serve.

Over the next several weeks we took care of the remaining details.

We insured that their young children were taken in by uninvolved relatives. I found it emotionally painful to cull the newer cult members and those that only had offered logistical support, but they knew too much, and we had to clean the slate.

The unusual number of disappearances and "accidents" brought Mt. Summit to the attention of the national media and the state authorities. Corrupt state officials spun the facts as best they could, but we knew our time in the area had come to an end.

"I will take you to my favorite hide-a-way", Van told me. "I must be gone overnight to arrange things. We will leave tomorrow."

I hugged Van and said, "I hate to be without you for even a single night". Van smiled sadly and said, "I as well. It has been an eternity since we have been together. We need to move quickly, and to divide up the work.

I must go and see to our housing and it will be best if you pack those things you want to take. Do not worry we can buy whatever else we need. Put them in the 'dungeons' because they will remain the same no matter which of my houses we go to." I nodded my agreement.

I filled up two of duffle bags with the clothing I wanted to take with me. At Van's suggestion, I wore the "Bulwark of Theresa" and kept my saber next to the bed. I also kept the enchanted knife clipped to my pocket and my now loaded revolver close by.

I had everything packed and just inside the entrance to the catacombs by early evening. I was surprised at how easily I hefted the bags filled with shoes, handbags and clothing. I took comfort that my 'dungeons' would be a constant and my little fae gentlemen would always be my companions. We could also visit George whenever we wanted to. I went into our bedroom and turned on the tv.

Ah, Netflix!

I had been working all day and felt grimy. I took off my clothes and went into the bathroom. As I entered the shower stall, I didn't recognize the woman in the mirror. There was a sassy blonde looking back at me. She looked like the female bodybuilders I had seen; broad shoulders tapering down to a slim waist. Thick muscular legs and diamond shaped calves; six distinct squares on her stomach.

My breasts were only slightly smaller, but I carried them higher on my chest, rounded biceps and a horseshoe shapes on the back of my arms. I thought of statues I had seen of Amazon women. I made them look like little girls!

I cackled, slid the shower door and basked in the sweet smelling, slippery water, fragrant soaps and shampoo. I toweled off and dried my blonde bob. I found myself letting out a relaxed sigh. I opened the bathroom door and went to the bureau to get my night gown. I slipped it on.

I was about to pick up my soiled clothing when I heard the basement door opening and smelled an odd rancid odor. I scanned for Van's masculine scent and, not finding it, my inner alarms went off.

Instantly, I felt a half out of body, other worldly sensation. My knees went weak and I had to sit on the bed. I was having a psychic vision.

I seemed to be in the beautiful dreamer's bedroom. I felt myself slipping into sleep. But I wasn't dreaming; I was soul travelling. I was just a ball of consciousness exploring inner worlds, strange vistas surreal and indescribable.

Suddenly, I was unable to move as if I were immersed in quicksand. I saw a large black form skittering over the horizon. I had the impression of being a moth caught in a spider's web. There were eyes and a mouth that were flickering orange flames dashing towards me; the Hara Shem Tov!

My wolf became enraged. I grabbed the Colt Detective Special and slid out the bedroom door into the kitchen. I cautiously glanced around the corner. Just by the open basement door I was met by a horror like I never imagined.

Not twenty feet in front of me stood what I can only describe as an abomination.

Before me was a short woman with auburn fright wig hair dancing to an electric current. She was floating about six inches above the ground. Her skin was cadaverous grey. Her bulbous eyes were bulging out of her head like a popeyed goldfish and her lips were grimacing unspoken words. Her arms began to writhe and coil as if they were boneless tentacles. Her tongue suddenly flicked out and thrashed like a worm on a fishhook.

Under the grotesqueness, I could recognize Van's first companion, Claudia.

With grim deliberation, I raised the revolver, lined up the blaze orange front sight, and fired off three precise shots. All hit her in the upper central chest I could see clear holes where they hit. Each impact caused her to clumsily stagger back. The smell of cordite filled the room. However, they self-sealed as soon as they formed.

The basement door jerked completely open and I could see Ernie and Harrison streaking to me. They each perched on one of my shoulders. Ernie cried, "We've got you back, Boss Lady".

Harrison said, "You are not alone Mary". Each stood in ready, En Garde positions pointing their swords at the creature. Their four-inch blades looked menacing.

With a prolonged scream like a woman being murdered, at blurring speed the ghoul slid forward as if on ice-skates. She was on me in an eye blink and clutched my arms. My revolver was knocked from my hand. Her head split open into a cavernous mouth of fangs. I could see several rows of shark like teeth leading down a gaping maw.

I hooked my hands behind her neck and repeatedly kneed her in the stomach and groin. She grunted and was rocked backwards. When her grip loosened, I hit her with a right uppercut followed with a left straight punch. They made smacking noises upon impact and she yelped and groaned. She spit out several triangular teeth.

Ernie and Harrison swarmed around slashing and stabbing with their swords.

She again staggered back drunkenly, and I could see that the numerous places where the fae had punctured her were non-bleeding gashes.

Cascades of dust streamed from the wounds. I knew I had to get to my saber or knife to have a chance against her. I turned and dashed towards the crumpled pile of clothes I had left on the bedroom floor.

Ernie and Harrison hovered at the bedroom entrance and formed a thin, white hot stream of fire that gushed into that hellish maw. She paused and seemed to swallow it like seltzer water.

I was almost to my rumpled jeans where the knife was clipped into the hip pocket. I felt a strong squeezing and pull on my legs. My head and chest were slammed into the floor; the wind knocked out of me. I was dragged backwards.

I risked looking over my shoulder and saw that the terror had my legs coiled in her snake like arms and was pulling me backwards. Above her head, I could see the blur of the fae's swirling aerial assault. Ernie was an absolute whirlwind.

We scuffled and grappled for long seconds. I thrashed and pulled forward. Then Earnie streaked in and cut off one of her ears. She loosened her hold on my right leg to try to swat away her winged attackers.

I took this opening to kick her several times in the face and chin. She was jolted slightly upwards with each strike. She loosened her grip enough for me to slip free and reach my folding knife.

The blade self-opened from the pocket with a snick. Its hiss sounded like a mocking laugh. The blade pushed itself forward and seemed that it starved to rend death. Claudia and I leaped to our feet. She reached for me with her right arm.

As Van and I had I practiced, I slashed across my body, the knife blade bit deep into her forearm. The force sunk the blade an inch into the limb. I then pulled it down widening the wound to six inches long. I then quickly swiped outside to the right, slashing and immobilizing her other arm.

Her arms dropped uselessly to her sides.

I clutched her forelock with my left hand to steady her head, and repeatedly stabbed her neck and throat as rapidly as I could. Soon her body dropped, and I was holding her head by the hair in my left hand. There was no blood, just a cascade of dust.

A pile of ash covered my feet. In disgust, I threw the head onto her rumpled body.

Ernie and Harrison flew to me and landed on my left palm. With shouts of joy and relief, they 'high fived' me. "We did it!" Ernie enthused. "Huzzah!" Harrison jubilantly shouted. I looked at the now motionless and human appearing Claudia and said, "Ding, dong the fucking witch is dead!"

Ernie laughed and Harrison reddened in embarrassment.

The two elementals transferred to my shoulders and we watched as Claudia quickly shrunk and morphed into what resembled a dried-out ginger root. The top of the root which had been her head slid back into position.

I wrapped her up in a towel and carried her down to Ernie and Harrison's room and locked her in the golden cage. Ernie welded the door to the frame. We then entered the dreamer's bedroom and placed the cage into the coffin set aside for her.

Ernie, Harrison and I slept in my bedroom together that night. I placed the "Bulwark of Theresa" on the teak headboard and we passed the rest of the night protected and undisturbed.

At first, I found myself awakening with a start and looking around about every hour. But as the night went on, I slipped into a restful sleep.

Epilogue

Entering the Borough of Brooklyn Fugheddaboutit

I am happy everywhere except in places where I see glitz and rich farts. I am happiest in Brooklyn, where the concentration of rich farts is minimal. Nassim Nicholas Tale

I think I want to move forward. I want to \ move to Brooklyn and find a business Italian guy to take care of me. Nicole Polizzi

Van returned at 8 O'clock A.M. and I had our favorite breakfast of scrambled eggs a pound of raw bacon and ham steaks waiting. He rushed over and we hugged a prolonged embrace.

Ernie and Harrison sat at on the table as we ate and talked. Van was shocked by the attack of the previous night. "I was really blindsided. I had a creepy feeling about Claudia's revival. I never knew that the sleeping wolves were soul travelling.

I will have to investigate that further. We will have to set up some safeguards so that it won't happen again. I will discuss it with George and do some out of body investigating myself.

But this shows us that you all can take care of yourselves. How does it feel Mi Cuore to no longer be the fair maiden in distress?" Van offered. "Zevi is back enthralled to the golden demon. I know it was not his fault, but we were too tender minded."

Van shook his head in regret. "He was just so pathetic. They used to say, 'sympathy kills.' It would have been kinder to everyone if we had ended Zevi quickly and prayed later.

I won't make that mistake again."

Harrison offered, "The demon slipped right past Ernie and me". Ernie added, "I got a psychic vibe that Boss Lady was in danger and we reacted." I said, "And you purported yourselves like lions! You are both my heroes".

I kissed each of them on the head.

Now it was Ernie's turn to blush and Harrison's to laugh.

As we lingered over our coffee I said, "Once we are done here, I'll load these into the dishwasher. Where are we going?" Van smiled and said, "That would be telling. I want you to be surprised.

It's a city in the northeast. I think you are going to love it". I speculated, "Why the mystery?" Van giggled and said, "You'll have to see it to believe it."

I replied, "Humm, I've heard that one before and that turned out well. O.K., I'll play your game."

We shut all doors, lowered the blinds and went down the basement stairs. "I have some good people caretaking the house while we are gone", Van offered. We entered the mystical entrance to the catacombs, and each picked up one of my duffle bags. We walked down a side corridor and it seemed to unfold as we continued walking. I noted what appeared to be bricked in archways at several points along the way.

"I never saw this corridor before", I said. Van laughed, "Or, did it not exist until you noticed it?"

Van put his hand through one of these thresholds and we stepped into a finished basement. It was longer but narrower than our previous basement. There was a similar machine shop, survival supplies and gun safe. I noticed a small set of concrete steps that led up to the ceiling. "What is the purpose of that?" I asked. Van responded, "Oh, that used to be a coal shute."

We went up the freshly painted basement steps and opened a plain wooden door. I could see that the building was laid out so that all the rooms were in a straight line.

"My great, great grandfather", Van made quotation mark signs with his index and middle fingers, "bought this building in the middle Eighteen Eighties. It was designed as what they called 'railroad' apartments, all the rooms in a row like box cars. Four apartments were built one on top of the other."

We walked through a thick glass door with a wooden frame into what I could see he had converted into a home gym. There were heavily loaded Olympic barbells, weight benches and a large rack to support the weights.

I could see a large window with a wrought iron bar grating to a small brick paved pathway, bordered by a concrete fence and leading up to a small flight of stairs. A city street was just outside, but above my sight. "There is an entrance to the backyard in the next room. The room closest to the street is the martial arts studio, "Van revealed. "Please come with me".

We went back out the door and into a thin corridor enclosed by a paneled wooden wall. We went through a door onto an enclosed flight of stairs and found ourselves on the second floor.

"I am very proud of this floor", Van said. "Except for absolutely necessary modernization, it is as authentic to the era as possible. Our living quarters are on the next two floors: all ultra-modern. We'll leave our bags here.

After I show you around, let's go out and explore the neighborhood.

We were in a hallway, with mahogany stairs and rails. From the high ceiling dangled a Tiffany acorn chandelier. The parquet floors led to fancy lattice double doors framing stained glass windows. There were mahogany double sliding doors on the left and a flight of elaborately carved stairs to the right.

We turned around and entered the first-floor apartment.

We walked into a short hallway leading into a large kitchen. On the right wall was a period kitchen sink and to the left was a window looking out across all the neighborhood backyards. Looking out the window, I could see the backs of similar four and five storied buildings.

On the right wall was an old square, white wooden table with four chairs. Across from it was a functioning coal stove. On the facing wall stood an old 1890s ice box and a bay window looking out onto a small flagstone lined backyard. This was tastefully decorated with dwarf popular trees, stone lined flower beds and a marble table and bench set.

We walked back up the hall and turned left into a small room with high backed wing chairs and pedestal end tables. On the floor was a Persian rug. It had a faint scent of pipe tobacco. "I use it as a 'sitting room'. In the nineteenth century it was usually the children's bedroom." Van reported.

We went to our right through a small mahogany paneled hallway. "Victorian mothers used to put their cribs and basinets in this space." Van said.

We stepped into the largest room so far. It was wallpapered with a tight floral pattern. The floor was wood parquet. There were two identical Persian area rugs. On the wall closest to us was an old-style bed with a lace bedspread. On the left side was a smooth paneled fireplace with an iron fireplace screen.

A painting of a mustachioed Van in a frock coat and holding a derby was above the mantle. "You bear a strong resemblance to your great, great grandfather" I quipped. "Indeed" Van laughed, "We could be twins". "Oh", I rejoined, "Do twins run in your family?"

On the left were the sliding doors we had seen from the hall. The room opened into a hexagonal space and straight ahead was a large bay window with a window seat. A Victorian Davenport was on the left wall and two winged backed chairs on the opposite side.

Peering out the window, I saw a recessed area directly below that was framed by ochre stone stairs on either side. I looked out on to the pleasant, tree lined streets and as far as I could see were similar buildings. Parked cars were lined the streets and children played catch with a pink rubber ball on the lightly trafficked street. People were walking hurriedly along the concrete sidewalks.

"Those are Brown Stones! I exclaimed. "Are we in New York City?" Van chortled and said, "You are so smart! Right genus, but what species?"

"Are you up for a walk?" Van inquired. "Oh yeah! I am so excited; the Big Apple; Metropolis!" I effused.

We walked hand in hand through the stained-glass front door into a wood paneled enclave. On the right wall was a built-in mailbox, with the name "Janus Wolfgang" embossed on it. We walked down the flight of steps and turned left up the street.

The ambient light seemed grayer than in the south. I detected a distinct odor of car exhaust. People were walking quickly but smiled and said "hello".

There we many young mothers with their children and some were pushing baby carriages. The street was all brown stones with wrought iron fences. Many of the houses were painted bright colors.

We came to the corner of the street and I noticed that the cross signs said, "President Street" and "6th. Avenue". Van pointed to the left and said, "Union Street" and then to the right and said, "Carol Street".

We walked up President Street, past brown stones that were all slightly different. We came to an area with taller, classy, white buildings; most with door men. "This used to be called the 'Gold Coast' Van said.

Across the street was a long line of black wrought iron fences and high hedges on a tree lined street. We walked up "Prospect Park West" and in front of us were a large traffic circle and a structure that resembled the Arch De Triumph in Paris. "This is the Grand Army Plaza' and that is 'Soldiers and Sailors Arch'", Van reported. "I was here when Glover Cleveland dedicated it."

As we walked further, we came to a large building with stone lions decorating the entrance. The sign said: "Brooklyn Public Library, Park Slope Branch". I put my hands to my mouth and said, "Oh my God! Brooklyn?!"

Van laughed, "There was a time when New York City was the most populated city in the world and Brooklyn alone was the third most populous.

Where better to hide than in a crowd?"

We walked a little further. Van said, "Just up the street a bit are the botanical gardens and a museum. There is also a zoo. I retreat here often.

I watched this area become a bedroom community for Manhattan in the late Eighteen Hundreds and then home to an immigrant community of Italians and Irishmen. The people of the time were so much like the villagers who raised me; genuine and open.

I used to go to the Italian club on Union Street. I was a physician and delivered many babies in these buildings. "Back then, we made 'house calls.' The flu outbreak of 1918…it was…just awful. So many of those wonderful people died gagging and gulping for air," I could see him remembering and sadly shaking his head.

I watched the Brooklyn Atlantics play in Washington Park on 5th Avenue and 3rd. Street. They later became the Brooklyn Dodgers.

Since the Nineteen Nineties, wealthier people have brought up the homes in this area. It is now one of the top ten desired areas in the United States.

Not everyone in Brooklyn 'Sitz on da coirb eatin' doirty woirms'.

It is called "family friendly" but if the truth were told it always was. There is incredible dining and shopping on the avenues. Close enough to Manhattan to take advantage of Broadway and all of New York's cultural advantages.

Did you hear? Young women have been mysteriously disappearing in Manhattan lately. And bad things happen nightly in Prospect Park.

Van slipped a small wooden box from his pocket. He opened it and bright golden knotted ring was inside.

Tears filled my eyes as our years together in Rome flooded my memory. Our twin sons wrestling on the floor as toddler's; our daughters wearing their first dresses; babies suckling at my breast. Shopping in open air markets. Dark nights where every star shown as just for us. Holidays with feasts with family and rich Roman bread dipped in olive oil. The great pageants and quiet moments with my family.

Van took my hand, and I could see tears in his eyes too. "Meis uxor" he said, as he slipped the ring on the third finger of my left hand. I hugged him and said "mirate te amo". We hugged and remained that way for a while. We knew his search was finally over.

Shall we go home and prepare for a night on the town, Mrs. Wolfgang?" I took his hand, and we made our way up tree lined Union Street. Although it was midafternoon, I saw the half-moon peeking out from over the tall buildings.

I thought, "Diana is smiling down upon us". I snuggled up to Van as he continued to play tour guide. This was going to be good …very good.

We walked up the street, and I found myself softly singing the old Frank Sinatra standard.

"Those little town blues
Are fading away
I want to be a part of it,
New York, New York …"

Are You Not Amused?

Are You Not Amused?

www.ingramcontent.com/pod-product-compliance
Ingram Content Group UK Ltd.
Pitfield, Milton Keynes, MK11 3LW, UK
UKHW022228230426
12048UKWH00016BA/1136